ANDALUSIAN LEGACY

An Argentina Saga

WILLIAM JACK STEPHENS

To Pat,

W. Jack Stephens

Sterling Adventure Group, LLC

BE THE STORY

The most enjoyable part of my life is sharing my stories. Everything I write about has elements of things I've actually experienced, places I've seen, and people I've known. Sometimes it's the grittier side of life, and sometimes it's all about the beauty. It could all be real. If this sounds like what you enjoy reading, we need to connect.

Stay In Touch - Occasionally I like to discount some of my books, or even give one away for Free. I send a message to everyone on my **Mailing List** when the discounts are about to happen. I also let people know about New Releases.

You can sign up to the mailing list here: **Mailing List Sign Up**

Or at my website: www.williamjackstephens.com

Can people change? Change into something fundamentally other than what they are now? Or perhaps, we never really change at all, but are born into a world that shields our true self with layer upon layer of cultural veils from the world around us.

Maybe the real journey is the path of peeling those layers slowly away through the years to reveal the glowing orb at the core of us. Our true self. Who we were born to be.

BLOODSPORT

Juan Carlos was born into a life layered with hunger and violence. The man he might become, lived in a future that was far beyond his visible horizon, and a very long and arduous journey. His journey to find the core of himself would take a lifetime, and he was going to take many lives along the way.

For the moment though, all the boy could think about was the wrenching pain in his vacant little stomach. He spent the night sleeping under a stack of apple crates in the alley behind the old Franciscan Mission building, out of the wind and constant drizzle. The friars fed the orphan boys living on the streets sometimes, but they weren't often kind either, and the feeding was more akin to bloodsport for the friars. It was a risk he took when he hadn't eaten in a few days.

Wearing tattered rags and shoeless, covered in the dirt and dust that gathered where he slept, he was hardly recognizable as a human child. His dark hair hadn't been cut for several years, but it hung barely at shoulder length in matted clumps because it didn't grow well when he barely ate enough to survive. His young bones demanded what little nutrients he could find.

He put his knees down on the moldy cobblestoned street, bent over to the ground and turned his face up to the orange morning sky, and let the dew from the rusty gutter pipe drip into his mouth. The coppery taste made his stomach twist even more, and a throbbing ache grew in the back of his head. If the friars didn't offer food today, he would have to steal something. He couldn't afford to get any weaker, or the stronger boys living in the barrio would look at him like easy prey.

He peered around the corner out into the open plaza in front of the mission. Nothing moved except the pigeons squabbling over a few wind blown seeds in the cracks between the stones. Then he heard the metal latch on the huge oak door squeak, and it groaned its way open. A round little friar with a bald spot on his head waddled out.

He wore a faded brown robe that looked more like a yurt draped over his short, wide body, and secured with a length of rope all the way around. His only distinguishing feature was the large wooden cross that hung from his neck on a beaded chain and lay atop his large belly, facing more skyward than forward.

He was holding a large tablecloth at both ends, and it bowed in the middle with the weight of their dinner scraps. The friars were all fat and well fed, and they didn't leave much meat on the bones, but this day at least, they were going to put the leftovers out for the orphans.

The Franciscans had first arrived in the new world not long after Christopher Columbus made his historic voyage. Sent by the Spanish government in the early 1500s to establish settlements and begin the conversion and control of the native Mayans, they lived in relative exile from the higher order and their lives and methods devolved over time. When verbal instruction in Christianity and the Spanish language failed, they resorted to physical punishment; and when that led to violent uprisings, they fell back to more passive methods. They opened schools and orphanages to indoctrinate the young and convert new generations from their earliest years.

The fat friar walked down the marble steps, and with a great heave, he threw the leftovers of gnawed bones and a few hard breadcrumbs and apple cores out onto the street. And out they came. Young, filthy, half-naked boys, running into the plaza from parts unknown like scavengers.

The strongest and fastest seized the big pieces first, then stood their ground. The youngest and smallest came in pleading for just a bite. Then one who was past the point of craze-driven hunger lunged into the pile. They kicked him, and smashed his little grabbing fingers with their calloused heels.

Juan Carlos was one of the middle-aged boys. Not big enough to claim the first prize, but well grown enough to challenge for a meal when he was really hungry. And today he was hungry. He pushed his way past the crowd of small and frail boys until he faced the four biggest who stood back to back in a guard around the scraps.

Then he started to slowly circle, looking for his chance until he saw it. A big juicy drumstick with fully half the meat left on the bone, lying in the center of the pile. He dove forward through the legs of the biggest guard and grabbed the drumstick, then instantly felt the bigger boy's weight fall on his back and pin him to the damp cobblestone.

A few other friars had wandered outside onto the steps, hoping to see a little blood today, and they were about to get their wish. The bigger boy kept Juan Carlos down with his weight, and punched him in the small of the back with his right fist, while stuffing a handful of food into his mouth with the left. Juan Carlos rolled underneath him, never letting go of the drumstick, and kicked and flailed until the bigger boy jumped to his feet.

Then the two squared off, staring into each other's eyes like starving dogs, and both clinging to a scrap of food with one hand. The other three big boys grabbed as much of the food as they could hold in their tattered shirts and raced off, and the little ones leaped for the bits left on the street.

This was not a fight for food anymore, there was hardly anything left on the ground. It was a fight for pecking order; a place at the next banquct. Juan Carlos was tired of having to beg for a rotting leftover. His instinct to survive had surpassed any trepidation of facing a dangerous enemy.

HE WAS LYING face down on the street when it was over. His vision was blurred from the sweat and blood seeping into his eyes from the cut just below his dark black hairline. He could only hear muted sounds as his brain struggled to regain full consciousness. When he lifted his head from the cold cobblestone, he thought for an instant that he had been badly beaten.

He couldn't remember any part of the last few minutes. Then through blurry eyes he saw the bigger boy, staggering slowly away. The boy glanced back, and the pain and fear was etched across his bloody face. He was walking away from this one, but he never wanted to face the wraith that was Juan Carlos again.

Juan Carlos pushed himself up to his knees, and then an enormous hand reached down and gripped him around his frail arm and lifted him to his feet as if he were weightless. His natural instinct to fight back kicked in again, and he tried to turn and face his attacker, but he was held fast as if by a mechanical vise. He rotated his head and looked into the eyes of the tallest and most imposing man he had ever seen.

One thing for certain, he wasn't a local Bolivian nor a Franciscan friar. He stood over six feet tall, with neatly combed hair so black and shiny it glinted a blue cast in the morning sun. His eyes were dark, and his skin was like salt-cured brown olives and glistened with a faint sweat from the humid air. He wore a white silk shirt with long sleeves, which was particularly uncommon in this district of La Paz, and polished black leather boots beneath his blood red pants. He had the appearance of a genuine Spanish noble.

Juan Carlos had never seen a man of stature before, and the sight made him go limp in his grasp and his mouth fell slightly open. After the first second or two of direct eye contact, he turned his eyes to the ground, and his shoulders and back fell into a fully submissive slump. He was completely at the mercy of this well dressed monster of a man.

"You are a very brave boy. You fought like a lion until the end," he said. Then he released his hold, and reached down and gently lifted Juan Carlos' chin up, and held his gaze. "You may look me in the eyes, young lion. Now come with me, and you will never be hungry again."

The Spaniard turned and strode down the alley alongside the mission, never looking back to see if the boy was following, but knew well that he would. These were the "Castas". The children born to mixed heritage in Bolivia during the time of the First World War.

Most were a mixture of some European immigrant or refugee from Spain or Portugal, who fathered a child with a local girl of distant Mayan descent. Many were cast aside into the streets, or placed into the hands of the Franciscans to raise. But in the end, they all had to raise themselves in the backstreets and alleys of the outlying barrios of La Paz.

Juan Carlos had no memory of his mother or father. He remembered sleeping in a cold dark room on a thin mat woven from palm leaves, and made to work in the courtyard of a Franciscan orphanage until he decided he was better off fending for himself. He was around seven years old when he used the towering branches of an apple tree to climb over the wall and fall to freedom on the other side. He was ready to accept his fate on his own terms.

That was three or four years ago he reckoned. He didn't have a good sense of time. One day always seemed like the one before. He mostly counted the passing of time by the varying levels of pain in his stomach. Each day without food taking on its own unique signature of discomfort.

He had never found any reason to trust a single living soul, and he didn't yet trust this Spaniard, but the words kept ringing in his head, *"You will never be hungry again."* So he followed.

The Spaniard walked for a long time, twisting back and forth through the streets and barrios with houses painted in bright yellows and greens, and the occasional blue. He walked through open markets and plazas, and down narrow steep stone stairways, until he came to a building that had three floors. It was made of brown brick and covered in limestone cement plaster that was chipped and peeling near the foundation from the constant moisture that came up from the Bolivian rains.

There was a small cafe on the bottom floor that faced the main street, and a doorway from the alley with stairs that went to the upper floors. As they turned off the main street and down the alley, little Juan Carlos' head was pulled to the right by the aroma of meat and vegetables steaming in the kitchen of the cafe. The fresh smell of cleanly cooked food grabbed every ounce of his attention. Then he turned his head back around to see the tall Spaniard stopping in front of him at the doorway in the alley.

"My name is Ramon Banu Lasso de la Vega. You will call me Don Ramon," he said as they reached the door. "I will show you where you are going to sleep, and you can wash yourself in the fountain in the courtyard. Then we will have a meal in the cafe, and I will tell you about your new life." (*You will never be hungry again*) still rang in the boy's ears.

He took him up the stairs to the second floor of the building and led him into a room that faced the main street, looking out over the top of the cafe. The smell of fresh food was even stronger here, drifting upward and into the open window. There were four small wooden beds with mattresses stuffed with straw, one in each corner of the room.

"You will share this room with three other boys, but since you are the first, you can choose your bed. When the others arrive, you will tell them where to sleep," the Spaniard said. "You will always be my first, and I will take care of you like you were my own son."

"I have a real bed?" Juan Carlos asked.

"Yes, a real bed, in a real bedroom, out of the rain and cold," Ramon answered. He reached down and gently laid his giant hand over the back of Juan Carlos' neck and thin shoulders, and smiled.

"I will take the one by the front window," he said, thinking of the wonderful smell coming up from below all day long.

Ramon Banu Lasso de la Vega took him down to the enclosed courtyard of the building. It was an open square, and the interior balcony from the second floor ran around three sides, forming a covered gallery below.

The gallery was draped with crawling bougainvillea that covered it in magenta flowers in the summer. It belied the corrosive exterior of the building, and looked like a private garden. In the center was a stone fountain with a round basin on the ground, and a statue in the center that looked like a baby angel with a pot on his shoulder, and water bubbled out into the basin below.

"Take off your clothes and wash yourself in the fountain. I can't take you into the cafe smelling like a little pig. I will bring you some clean clothes to wear."

Juan Carlos was suspicious. He had heard the friars telling young orphans to remove their clothes before too, and nothing good ever came of it. Sometimes they were flogged with thick leather straps until they bled, and sometimes worse things happened. But he was starving, and the lure of eating real food, in a real cafe, sounded like something he couldn't even imagine in his most glorious dream. So he did as he was told.

The Spaniard came back in a few minutes with a pair of brown canvas trousers, a red and white striped t-shirt, and a pair of sandals. He laid them on the stone bench under the gallery, and told the boy to put them on when he was finished, then come around to meet him at the cafe.

Juan Carlos climbed out of the cool water after splashing himself down and rubbing the street filth off, and put the clothes on. They weren't brand new, but they were in better condition than anything he had ever owned, and they were clean and had a smell like fresh picked fruit. The sandals were uncomfortable, but he put them on and walked slowly to get the feel.

He had never worn shoes before in his life. His young feet were thick and hard, like dark dried leather on the bottoms, but the sensation of having a strap between his toes and not being able to feel every grain of sand under his feet was unusual. He couldn't understand why people needed shoes.

He made his way back out to the alley and around to the front, and found Don Ramon sitting at a small table in front of the cafe. He approached the table, as he had a thousand times in his life to beg for spare change or a scrap from rich people who ate in cafes. The Spaniard motioned for him to take the chair across the table from him.

"I will allow you to sit at the table with me today because we have business to discuss, but this will be the only time you will sit with me. It isn't proper for a young boy from your class to sit with a man of my class. Do you understand?" he said.

The boy nodded his head, but in truth, he didn't understand any of this. He was just hoping to get one good meal. At the very least, he could make off with a fresh set of clothes.

"As I told you, I am Ramon Banu Lasso de la Vega. Do you understand what this name means?" he asked.

"No, Señor," Juan Carlos said.

"Banu was my mother's surname. She was from a very important family in Seville, in the south of Spain. Do you know where Spain is?"

"No, Señor," the boy answered again. Where he might have normally lied to any adult in order to please them or trick them, he felt compelled to be truthful to Don Ramon.

"Spain is the greatest country on the other side of the world. Lasso de la Vega is my father's family name. He was a Viscount, a nobleman, and very important. All that you need to remember is that I am of noble birth." He could see the boy didn't understand anything he just told him, but he continued. "There was a great war in my country many years ago, and things are difficult there now. I came here to Bolivia, to regain honor for my family."

Juan Carlos understood nothing this man was talking about. His entire life had been spent within a ten-block radius, living on stone streets, fighting, and stealing food or something he could trade for food. The words this man was using were out of his realm of comprehension. His ignorance was written all over his face.

The Spaniard continued, "What you need to know, young lion, is that I own this three story building, and this cafe. And before long, I will control everything in this barrio. One day, I may control all of La Paz. You are here, because I will need young men with courage to stand beside me. You will help me, and I will always take care of you and protect you. We will be like family."

To a starving, lonely boy on the streets, the words were like gifts falling all around him from heaven. He didn't understand it all, but he felt a warmth rising up inside, and a glimmer of something he had never experienced before; hope.

A meal of roasted lamb and potatoes was brought to the table and placed in front of Juan Carlos, and his belly growled with anticipation. He looked at the food, then looked up at Don Ramon. It didn't matter what this giant man was talking about, he thought to himself, he was going to do anything he wanted him to do.

RAMON BANU LASSO DE LA VEGA

Ramon Banu Lasso de la Vega was born into the family of a gentleman. But even though his father had the title of Viscount, a lower level Spanish nobleman, he was a bit of a rouge and a gambler. And living his life the way he did, he had to become proficient with the use of weapons in order to keep himself alive from time to time. He favored the folding navaja style knife for its easy concealment beneath his fine silk clothing, and spent more time caring for his knife and his clothing than he did raising his son.

He didn't even like talking to him. He mostly ignored him, and when he tired of the boy's talking he would turn his right side in his direction, as that ear had been nearly deafened in a bar fight years before. "I didn't hear you boy, you were talking into my bad ear," he would say, as young Ramon chattered for his father's attention.

When Ramon reached his fourteenth birthday, his father thought he should learn to defend himself with a sword or knife. Being a fine swordsman was still considered a worthy, and very traditional skill for men in the noble class, and Ramon hadn't shown much inclination to do anything else very well. It was also a splendid excuse to get the boy out of the house, so he sent him off to board and train at the finest knife fighting school in Seville for the next four years.

Ramon fell in love with the training, and the close bonds between himself and his masters. Even though the training was hard and sometimes violent and painful, he relished the attention and recognition; something he never got from his own father.

The masters at the school were more like family than his own. They taught him, disciplined him, congratulated him when he did something well. They even encouraged him to be his own man and gave him the confidence to go out into the world. They took a boy who had been submersed in a world of indifference to his presence, and made him feel worthy of something more.

In 1914, when the first Great War broke out in Europe, Spain made the decision to stay out of the fray. But their economy, in particular in Andalusia in the south of Spain, plummeted, and food riots were happening almost every day as the poor people in this region faced starvation.

Many of the young noble-class Spaniards were itching to get into the war, and Ramon, young and hot-blooded as he was, decided he would make his way to France through Pamplona in the Basque country, and volunteer to serve in the French Foreign Legion.

He was determined to distinguish himself in battle, and thought surely this would win the respect of his father. He traveled back to Cordoba to tell his parents what he was going to do, and ask for their blessing.

He arrived in the afternoon to find his father gone, and the servants having no idea of his whereabouts. His mother was taking a long afternoon nap, and could not be disturbed. So he went to his room to gather a few small things to take with him to war. A small folding field knife with a corkscrew on the handle, and a silver cross on a chain that his grandmother had given him as a boy, were the only things he deemed worth carrying.

Since he was fourteen when he was sent away to the boarding academy, none of his old clothes or boots fit any longer. He would go off to war with only the clothes he wore. The French Foreign Legion would issue him a uniform and supplies anyway, so better to travel light. Then he waited alone in the drawing room until dinner was served at 10:00 p.m.

It was a small room, but felt large because the ceilings were tall. The walls were covered with ornate tapestries, the floor was intricately inlaid parquet, and the ceiling was painted with depictions of Moorish legends. He sat alone on a large red sofa that looked out into the garden.

His mother came down the stairs promptly at the dinner hour. She seemed mildly surprised that her son was home.

"Hello, Ramon. I wasn't aware you were coming home from Seville," she said.

His mother had never been very warm or affectionate. Where his father was often openly hateful to him, his mother usually treated him with disinterest. But then, she treated almost everyone the same way.

"I came to tell you and father that I am leaving for France, to join the war. I thought you might like to see me one more time before I left, and I hoped father would give me his blessing."

"Well, yes, it is nice to see you. Your father hasn't come home in several days, and I don't expect him home anytime soon. But you may as well join me for dinner before you leave," she said.

They sat together at the long mahogany table in the formal dining hall, his mother sitting at the end where she always sat, and Ramon sitting to the side in a middle chair. His mother delicately slurped her first course of gazpacho, then moved to the second course of thinly sliced Iberian ham which she sliced into tiny bites with the sterling knife in her right hand, and skewered neatly with the three-tined fork in her left.

She lifted each bite and placed it almost apologetically into her mouth, and chewed slowly until it was fully dissolved before swallowing, staring blankly forward at the empty chair on the opposite end of the table. She glanced in Ramon's direction and smiled once or twice, but never offered a word of conversation or interest in anything he had done or was about to do.

She lifted a small silver bell with a long handle from the table each time she was ready for the next course, and gave it a jingle to alert the kitchen staff. When she was done, she faintly tamped her mouth with a green cotton napkin, and stood and said, "Goodnight, Ramon." Then she turned and went up to her bedroom without a word more.

Ramon spent one last night sleeping in his old room, and hoped he might hear his father stumbling in the door. Drunk or not, he wanted to show him that he had grown, and was about to go off into the world and face danger like a man. But his father never returned. He woke the next morning, ate a light breakfast in the kitchen with the house staff, who treated him kindly, then saddled his horse and rode north.

DURING HIS YEARS in the war, he became known as the "silent assassin." He was fearless and cunning. He possessed the nerve of a young man who has no concept of the finality of death. Often sent into enemy encampments during the misty hours before dawn when the grip of sleep and exhaustion was heavy on the soldiers; he would slip in among them and do his work with nothing more than a finely edged weapon.

He cut off the officers' rank insignias from their uniforms to lay on his commander's desk, then he severed the left ears and thread them on a hanging string outside his tent. His comrades all thought it was a twisted way of showing his bravado, but it might have had something to do with his father.

When the war ended in 1918, Ramon felt almost a little cheated. He had grown fond of the killing. He relished it, like a fine meal washed smoothly down with a glass of Malbec from the high country. The killing made him famous, and much more to his liking, feared.

When the French government disbanded his unit, his life of glorious purpose ended. The very thing for which he had been bred and carefully crafted no longer existed. He was a man without prospects or recognition. A man like any other man, and he hated it.

Ramon wandered aimlessly for several years. He worked odd jobs here and there, but was never able to find a profession that suited a man of his upbringing and his particular skills. At last he decided to make his way back south to his family's estate in Cordoba, walking the desolate war-torn road through the Basque region between France and Spain.

He begged for rides on trucks and wagons, and food along the way, and lived only by the grace of the poorest people along the path. The Basque spoke a language very different from his own and they were nearly starving, having been beaten down by both the French to the North, and the Spanish monarchy from Madrid. But they were an honorable people and they harbored a deep respect for any young man who had volunteered to fight the German invaders. They never failed to share a portion of what little they had.

As he came through central Spain, he found his own people, the nobles, less appreciative of a young man who had defied his own government to run off and fight with the French. He walked for six weeks along the road from Madrid to Cordoba through the dry rolling hills; often sleeping under a bridge or in an abandoned barn during the scorching days, and walking under the starlight.

Sometimes a carriage or one of the early motorcars of the rich would clatter past, but none offered assistance to the man in dirty, tattered clothes. The trail home wore a deep resentment into the pit of him. Resentment for the nobles who ignored him like a piece of trash on the road, and resentment for the poor who showed mercy.

Mercy was a sentiment that never sat well with him. He felt no mercy for anyone else, and when it was shown to him in his own dark hours, it made him feel weak. By the time he reached home, he had found hatred in his heart for almost everyone around him.

When he finally walked up to the broad iron gates outside Cordoba that marked the entrance to his father's estate, they were rusted and hanging askew from broken hinges. He walked up the long gravel road to the white mansion and found it dilapidated and crumbling.

The white stucco was peeling and chipping away to reveal the bare stone walls, and many of the Portuguese clay tiles on the roof were broken or missing. The gardens were burned brown and weeds sprouted where flowers once grew in the large stone-lined planters, and the magnificent orchard of olive trees on the southern hillside were bare and grey.

He paused for a moment, and remembered the last time he saw his mother. She was standing by the planter in her silk morning robe, cutting flowers for her breakfast table as he mounted the black horse and rode off to war. She had looked up at him, given a faint whimsical smile, and went back to her flowers as if his departure didn't have any significance.

Standing at the front door, he called inside but no

one answered. The servants who kept the house, and raised him as a boy, had long since gone.

"Father!" he called as he stepped inside. His voice echoed into the hallway and up the stairs. The rugs and tapestries that used to line the walls and floors were gone, and every small sound ricocheted across the marble and stone.

A low voice growled from the salon, "Who is in my house?"

"Father, is that you? I've come home," Ramon answered.

He walked slowly into the room that had once been his mother's favorite sitting area. Now it was dark from the dirt and dried leaves plastered over the windows, and the light flickering in illuminated the blue-grey smoke from his father's pipe and particles of dust that swirled in the current. The air was dank and musty from the leaking roof, and the floors felt sticky and stained under his feet and smelled like stale sherry.

"Where is mother?" Ramon asked, as he entered the room.

His father was in the shadows, leaning back in a large black armchair, and he stared at Ramon for a long moment before answering.

"Did you bring back any money? Surely you must have taken a few coins from those bastards in the North."

Ramon felt that deep resentment growing larger

in his belly. He hadn't expected much of a welcome from his father, but he hoped at least that he might be happy to know he was still alive. It was too much to hope for.

"I said, where is my mother?"

"I sent that bleating cow back to her family in Seville. A letter came last year, seems she died from the diphtheria," he said. "I traded her furniture last month for beef and sherry, but now the sherry has almost run out. I'll sell her jewelry next month, unless you have done something useful for a change and brought back something valuable."

What small piece of his soul that might have remained, sank away as his father glared back at him. Ramon drew a deep breath, and his hand moved forward to the long blade in his waistband and his fingers wrapped tightly around the worn handle.

His father was old and drunk, but his eyes caught the movement to the knife, and his right hand slid instinctively into his front vest pocket and tapped the folding knife tucked inside at the ready. Then Ramon sighed heavily, and retreated two steps backward before turning and walking up the stairs.

His father had given away a crucial bit of news; his mother's jewels were still here. He went straight to his mother's room on the second floor and twisted the elegant crystal handle on the door, but it was locked. He didn't have the patience to search for a key, so he moved across the wide hallway and rushed into the door with his shoulder and crashed through.

The room was filthy and the walls etched with black mold, and it showed the ransacked evidence of his father's drunken rage. His mother's clothes and fine things were scattered about, but Ramon knew exactly where she kept her jewels. He went to the large chest in the corner and pulled it aside to reveal a folding panel in the oak floor, and pried it open with the tip of his knife.

Concealed below the floor was a beautifully carved rosewood box, trimmed in silver with the Banu family crest engraved on the seal. He reached in and carefully lifted the box out, then sat it on the floor next to him. He tried to open the lid, but it was locked, and as before, his impatience seized control of him.

He grabbed the box and smashed it against the mahogany chest. It shattered and splintered, and the remains of his mother's dowry scattered onto the dusty floor.

He picked up the rings, sparkling necklaces and jeweled bits and shoved them into his pockets, but when he stood and turned to leave he found his father standing in the doorway to the bedroom, staring back at him. He had a cold, murderous scowl across his face, and the long navaja unfolded and locked ready for killing in his hand.

"After all I have done for you, you grew up to be nothing better than a thief."

"What did you ever do for me, you wretched old man?" Ramon shot back. "You are a worthless drunk, and now even your noble title is worthless! I'm going to take what is mine before you waste it on sherry."

His father yelled back in a rage, "I will kill you before I let you steal from me, boy!"

The old man lurched at his son and thrust the point of his blade straight at his face. Ramon leaned back just out of reach of the sharpened steel, but lost his footing as he slipped on the fragments of the broken jewelry box. The wood splinters and silver trim screeched when they ground into the oak floor under his boots as he caught his balance, and his father came back again with a backhanded slash.

This time, Ramon was ready. He raised his arm and blocked the incoming strike, then grabbed his father's knife hand and twisted it backward and down to the floor until the ligaments in his wrist let go with a loud "pop". His father grimaced, but never made a sound. Ramon wrenched the navaja away, grabbed the old man by the back of the neck with his left hand, and coming in low with his right, he drove the folding blade all the way to the polished ram horn handle, deep into his father's liver.

He held the blade in, leaned close to his father's face, and stared into the vile old drunkard's eyes as they winced, then glazed into a foggy blankness.

"You've killed me, boy," his father said, as he slumped to the floor.

Ramon stood over him still holding the navaja, coated in the black livery blood of a man who spent his life drinking. He stayed there for several minutes; silently, patiently watching him pass on to the next world, and never felt the slightest trace of remorse.

RAMON TOOK his mother's jewelry and made his way quickly to the port town of Málaga, nestled on the Mediterranean shores near Gibraltar, and paid for passage on a steamer to South America. He landed first in Venezuela, but it was crowded and already under heavy control, so he continued on through the countryside until he found himself in the small city of La Paz, Bolivia.

Money and immigrants were beginning to trickle into the country, and the poor and middle-class barrios around the outskirts were a ripe place for a man with talents and nerve. It was the perfect place to set up shop and build his own little seat of power and influence.

Ramon was going to rebuild the fortune his father squandered using the same methods that noblemen had acquired wealth back in the old country; by taxing the poor and the working-class who wanted to live within their domain. He was going to claim dominion over a ten square block barrio to begin with, and squeeze the local merchants, cart vendors, market operators, and anyone else who earned a coin, for a piece of it.

In exchange, he would keep their streets safe and any unwanted competition out. If another patrón threatened them, and there were others in La Paz, he would defend them as a shepherd would defend his flock. But first, Ramon would have to convince the locals that his patronage was something they desperately needed. The perfect opportunity presented itself at the cafe that would soon belong to Ramon.

He had wandered into a cafe one day, and lucked into it; the perfect setting to display his capacity for greater violence. Three bandits were holding the cafe owner at knifepoint, and ravaging his food stores. The man had no money, so the food was all they could steal.

When Ramon boldly walked into the cafe, they turned and laughed at him. Laughed at his fine clothes and his arrogant swagger. They had no clue about the man they were facing. He moved like a streak of lightning from one to another. They never clearly saw the blade that killed them because it blurred through the air with a whistling hiss.

He dispatched the lot of them so fast the cafe owner wasn't quite sure what happened. Then he began the negotiation.

"It looks like you need protection from bandits," he said to the owner.

"I can't afford to pay for protection. I barely make enough to feed myself because no one comes here to eat. I own the whole building, but the criminals have taken it, and the people in the barrio are afraid to come to my cafe. If I had any money I would just abandon this place and go somewhere else," the man said.

"If you are going to abandon it, then why not sell it me?" Ramon said. "I will give you two large rubies, worth more than you could make in a year, for the whole building. And I will accept you as my partner in running the cafe. I will make sure people come to eat, and you can keep twenty percent of the profits," he bargained. "And I promise, you will never be robbed again."

For an instant, the cafe owner thought he was being swindled, but then he considered his options and looked at the still-bleeding corpses scattered around the floor.

"I accept. But sir, the criminals in the building; they won't just leave for you."

"By morning, the building will be empty. You will need to clean it out for me before I move in," Ramon said. The owner found it a strange request, but agreed.

In the early hours of the morning, after the nightly drinking and fighting in the upper floors of the building had dulled to an uneasy quiet, the silent assassin crept through the alley doorway. He drifted patiently like a night shadow, from one room to the next.

When the sun rose on a new day, no one was alive to see it. On the corner of the building, dangling from a rusty nail was a string with sixteen cleanly severed left ears, threaded like hot peppers to dry in the heat. Ramon's reputation swept through the barrio, and by the end of that new day, the legacy of Don Ramon was born.

THE MAKING OF A BLADE
MASTER

In the weeks, months, and years that followed, it became obvious why Ramon had chosen Juan Carlos to become his first young lieutenant. He had needed young men who were quick and agile, calm in the face of danger, and fearless in a fight. It takes a very special character to become a master of the blade.

He woke the boy early in the morning, before the faintest glow of daybreak slid above the snow-capped peaks that surrounded the sprawling city. They walked each and every street and alley together, and memorized the buildings, shops and people.

Juan Carlos followed Ramon so closely that he never left the boundary of his shadow fall. Taking three quick steps with his little legs to match one of Ramon's, and a run or a skip to keep from being left behind, he was determined to never lose sight of him.

He was no different than an abandoned little dog, shown a bit of kindness, and clinging desperately to the giver.

And for a time, Ramon treated him with those odd moments of kindness that kept him at heel. They would be standing on a street corner watching the people, and for no particular reason, Ramon would reach down and touch his shoulder, then catch his eyes as he looked up and give him a warm smile. A single smile from Ramon would keep him happy for days.

In the early years, Ramon handled all of the negotiations and collections himself, and Juan Carlos and the boys who joined him were his eyes and ears on the street. Nothing happened in the barrio without Ramon knowing about it very quickly.

As Juan Carlos grew and Ramon began to trust him, he sent him to make the most simple of collections. If a local shop owner or street vender decided not to pay his taxes, Ramon would come to personally collect his due, and maybe an ear as a sentimental trophy.

He walked the streets like a Spanish peacock, in white silk shirts with lace collars, and tight fitting pants and polished boots. A proud bullfighter in the midst of rag-wearing peasants, but he felt no pity or compassion for the common people in the barrio. He seethed in being denied a truly noble life, feeling as if he had been exiled to this underworld of the old Spanish colonies.

WHEN JUAN CARLOS turned fourteen or there about, as he really didn't know how old he was, Ramon began his training in the art of knife fighting. The changing face of La Paz demanded it.

As it happened, Ramon wasn't the only Spanish castaway with skills in the fighting arts to reach the Americas. A great many fortunes were lost to the war, and many others just like Ramon came to the colonies to lay claim to a new aristocracy. Venezuela, Brazil, and Bolivia were awash with peacocks and freshly painted family crests on the sides of crumbling buildings.

They all had their own tales of heroics and tragedy, and many were trained in the same deadly arts as Ramon. So many young Spaniards came and spread these same fighting skills that it became known as *El Legado Andaluz*, "The Andalusian Legacy". If Ramon's small soldiers were going to help him claim dominion over La Paz, he would need to train them well.

For the first year, they trained with dull wooden knives. Juan Carlos learned the foundations of footwork, thrusting, slicing, and defending. He learned where to cut an opponent to cripple him, bleed him, or kill him as needed. In some cases, it was considered preferable to leave your victim disabled or with a gross deformity to spread your message far and wide.

"Leave him with an arm that hangs like a limp withered stocking full of cherries, and everyone will remember you," Ramon used to say.

People would forget about the dead soon enough, but a man who limped through the streets everyday, crippled from a knife fight, was a constant reminder. A reminder that this barrio belonged to Don Ramon Banu Lasso de la Vega.

As his speed and control improved in the second year, Juan Carlos was allowed to train with a real blade, albeit with a slightly dulled edge. The weight and balance were different, and it takes time to learn how to pull a knife cleanly from a hidden sheath as a reflex.

The knife Ramon gave him was common and ugly compared to his own. The knife he carried was a Toledo dagger made by one of the artisan blade smiths in Spain, and it was elegant and beautiful, like Ramon. A long, polished and engraved blade that came to a slender point, with an extended hilt to protect the hand, and a handle of golden ram horn, finely wound with silver wire. A nobleman's blade.

But the knife he gave to Juan Carlos was one more suitable to a street boy. A discarded old carving knife, blackened with age and abuse. The tip had been broken and refiled and shaped, and the handles were common ash wood, faded to grey.

Ramon made Juan Carlos carry the knife with him everywhere, even as he slept or bathed in the fountain in the courtyard. If he saw him put the knife down on a table or a bench, he would beat him until the lesson was learned. He might take his clothes off occasionally, but the knife had to remain lashed around his waist. It became as much a part of his body as one of his arms, and just like one of his arms, he came to control it with the speed of subconscious thought.

In his third year, the training became brutal. Ramon sparred with him daily using a wooden knife that was placed with the tip and edge in a bed of burning coals until they glowed red and on the verge of bursting into flames. It was the final lesson that insured Juan Carlos understood this was not a game.

Pain makes a lasting impression on a young mind. Every slash or thrust that Juan Carlos failed to block or defend would sear his tender young flesh, and leave the rank smell of burning skin and hair in the dark confined room where they trained. He bore the scars on his neck and forearms from countless days of Ramon's teaching.

It didn't take long before Juan Carlos was nearly as lightning quick with a blade as his master, and he became a feared soldier in the streets of La Paz.

As THE TERRITORY of Ramon expanded outward, one

block at a time, there were inevitable clashes with neighboring gangs and patróns; and on every new block there were young men left with scars or poorly functioning limbs after an encounter with Juan Carlos.

He had grown nearly into a man now. Not tall like Ramon, but tall for a Boliviano. He was lean and strong in the waist, with quick spinning speed. Fast legs for lunging, jumping, and dodging. And a supple and flexible upper body that could bend like a stalk of wheat in the spring wind. His hair had grown out now, long and black, and he kept it tied back and braided with a fine leather cord.

He was fierce in the fight; Ramon had chosen well in that regard. But deep down in the core of him, there was another shade of man. A shade that didn't enjoy the violence and infliction of pain. He saw it as the means of his survival, as he had since he was a small boy orphaned on the streets. But he never took pleasure in it, as his master Don Ramon did.

And to this point, he had deliberately avoided the one threshold from which there was no return; taking a life. Ramon knew it too. He knew this would be the final test for his young pupil, and it would be the moment that anchored Juan Carlos firmly into the life. The life from which there is no going back. No changing who you are, or who you want to be. Murder for personal gain is the barrier into the abyss.

THE OTHER, more remarkable event that marked a change in Juan Carlos' life during that same year, was the appearance of Gisele.

He came into the cafe one evening to report and deliver the daily tax collection to his patrón.

"Don Ramon, we collected everything due from the fruit vendors on General Roca Avenue. But there was a new cart working at the end of the street that we have never seen. Someone from another barrio moving in," he said.

"Did you tell him that he has to pay a special tax to work in my district?" Ramon answered.

"Yes, Don Ramon. I told him that this barrio was under the protection of Don Ramon Banu Lasso de la Vega, and if he wanted to sell his fruit here, he would have to pay a tax."

"And what did he say?" Ramon asked.

"He said he didn't pay taxes to anyone, not even a Spanish lord."

Ramon's eyes flashed with fire for an instant, then he asked, "What did you do then?"

Juan Carlos smiled, "I slammed his face into the cobblestone and left a scar on his neck to remind him of who you are. Then I had Rico take his cart full of mangos and lock it away, and told him he could have it back when he paid for two months tax up front."

Then he reached into the front pocket of his

baggy pants and pulled out a beautifully ripened mango, and leaned forward in a respectful pose and presented it to Ramon.

Ramon raised his eyebrows in curious amusement, and he laughed at the thought. His young pupil was beginning to take initiative. He was beginning to feel his power growing, and he wasn't afraid to hurt a man if he felt the need.

"YOUR DRINK, DON RAMON," came a whisper-soft voice from behind Juan Carlos.

He turned and looked directly into the eyes of a young girl, fifteen or sixteen years old perhaps, walking up to the table with a cool alcohol drink made from fermented corn. She glanced at him, then quickly diverted her eyes back to the front, and placed the drink on the table without ever looking at Ramon directly. Then she shrank backward and disappeared quickly into the kitchen of the cafe.

Juan Carlos followed her movement until she vanished behind the bar, then he turned quickly back to look at Ramon with a look of astonishment across his face, as if he had just seen a mythical creature passing before his eyes.

"Her name is Gisele," Ramon said. Then with a sterner look he said, "She belongs to me now, and she works in the cafe."

It was said with the hint of a warning, and Juan

Carlos understood clearly. But the warning wasn't enough to wash the image of the girl from his mind. Mostly, it was the image of her incredible eyes that gripped him. He had never seen anything like them.

All of his life he had only seen the dark brown or black eyes that are native to Bolivia, and maybe a few that were a lighter shade of brown, like Ramon's. But Gisele, she had eyes like the deepest blue pool of mountain water. Like the blue of the late day sky as the sun slides below the hills. And long straight hair the color of aged honey that was silky and shiny. She was taller than a local girl of the same age, and graceful. She couldn't be from here, he thought.

To THIS POINT in his life, Juan Carlos had been concerned with the most elemental needs of survival. Food, a dry place to sleep and stay warm, and the teachings and direction of his master. There had been little time for anything else. He had never known the affections of a girl, and never taken much notice of them. They were more of a distraction. But for the first time, he felt an uncontrollable ache in his stomach that had nothing to do with hunger. It was a craving for something unknown to him.

He walked the streets everyday now with the dulled edge of distraction. He heard whispers in his ears, and turned to see no one there. He saw colors in the buildings and shops and people's clothing that he never noticed before. A palette of colors more brilliant than the rainbows that hung over the mountains to the West after a drifting rainstorm. And the blues, all shades of mystical blues, would hypnotize him for minutes at a time, or until one of his friends would snap him back to the world.

"Juan Carlos, wake up!" Rico yelled in his ear. Juan Carlos jerked his head around to see his three bunkmates, Rico, Pancho, and Santi laughing at him. They were the four foot soldiers of Don Ramon, but only Juan Carlos was allowed to enter the cafe, so the other three had never seen her.

"What were you thinking so hard about?" Rico asked.

"Nothing. I wasn't thinking about anything," he responded. He didn't want anyone around him to know that he was not the same anymore. That he didn't have the same focus. He couldn't understand it himself, but he felt impaired. His focus only became clearer as the hours passed and the time drew near every day to go back to the cafe and hand over the taxes.

He came into the cafe and scanned the room like he was searching for Don Ramon, but he knew his master always sat at the same long table by the back wall. He lingered and dallied, hoping for a glimpse of her, until Don Ramon would finally tell him to leave.

He climbed the stairs to his room late every night and sat on his bed by the window above the cafe. He leaned out with his elbows on the sill and his chin cradled in his hands, closed his eyes and listened. He listened intently to the sounds of men eating and drinking, laughing and arguing. And occasionally, he thought he could hear the movements of the young girl, Gisele, passing through the room and laying drinks on the tables.

He was probably just imagining that he could hear her, because she moved as lightly across the floor as a butterfly. Lighting here and there for only an instant to place a bowl or plate on a table, and then she would disappear into the wind.

Sometimes he would hear her groan and strain, as a drunken merchant would grab her by the waist and pull her into his lap, or slap her hard across the bottom as she passed. It made him burn with anger at the thought of what she endured in the room just below him. It made him have thoughts of taking the final plunge into darkness, and killing a man. Any man who laid his hands roughly on the beautiful young girl that held his fascination. But he knew Ramon wouldn't approve of him killing a taxpayer in the middle of his cafe, so he remained silently by the window.

THE RAY OF SUNSHINE

From the instant Ramon pulled the starving little waif Juan Carlos up from the cobblestone until now, he had been the only man who ever seemed to care about what happened to him. He kept his word. Juan Carlos never faced another day from that moment with the pain of hunger.

He gave him clean clothes that kept him warm, and a comfortable place to sleep that was safe. He could close both eyes at night and not fear that some evil would catch him while he slept. And as Ramon gathered more boys to join the ranks they became like a family, the only version of family that he had ever known. In some twisted sense of the word, it was love.

Not so much like the love we all like to think about between a father and son, and surely, Ramon had never experienced it himself. But more like the love that binds a mildly neglected dog to its master. If you feed it, give it a place to sleep, give it a task like guarding your yard, and pat it on the head every now and again; the dog will interpret those things as love. You may give him a beating here and there, and he will still love you, because he treasures the few times that you pat him on the head and tell him what a good dog he is.

Juan Carlos had spent these years like a faithful canine. Dutifully guarding Ramon's territory, and treasuring the brief moments of praise when they came. He had grown content with his lot in life, until the young girl, Gisele, came into the fold. Without meaning to, she triggered something deep inside him.

Gisele presented something bright and beautiful in a world that he had known to be only dark and grey. She was the single column of golden sunlight that pierces through the center of a storm cloud and illuminates a field of flowers. She made him believe that there was beauty in this world, and he had passed it every day, blind to it. And he wondered perhaps, if Ramon was the man who kept him blind to the world.

JUAN CARLOS LIE awake on his straw bed thinking about last week, and unable to sleep. His life had changed in an instant. Pancho and Santi lie curled and twisting in their beds; one grunting and kicking his legs like a small dog chasing a creature through the woods in his dreams. The third bed was empty now, until Ramon could replenish the ranks.

The boy who used to sleep there, Rico, was dead now. Rico had been Juan Carlos' best friend, if such a thing as friends really existed in their world. After all, they were members of a gang; a militant tribe controlled and directed by an alpha male who ruled their very existence. And when young boys are raised and ruled in that way, every aspect of their lives under control, they revert to the most animalistic behavior. They become a pack.

Individuals in a pack work in perfect synchronicity as long as their lives are being well orchestrated, structured, but they are always trying to reaffirm the hierarchy of the pack. Constantly seeking balance like an Archimedean level. If one leaves or dies, there will be some fighting among those below his station to see who is going to move up the food chain and take his place.

But little Rico had been the outlier in the pack. More like the runt of the litter, who would normally have been killed and eaten by the rest, were it not for Juan Carlos.

Rico wandered into Ramon's barrio when he was ten or eleven years old, frail, starving, and pitiful. Ramon wasn't inclined to take him in, but Juan Carlos convinced him that the boy would make an excellent spotter, being unassuming and able to move freely in and out of the barrio without much notice.

Rico bonded to Juan Carlos instantly, and shadowed him as Juan Carlos had once shadowed Ramon. The boy had no real interest in becoming a street fighter in a gang, but having Juan Carlos as his protector ensured his survival. He was probably more like a pet than a pack-mate, skittering around Juan Carlos as he walked, and constantly hoping for a kind word.

As he gained a few more years and became stronger, he stayed close to Juan Carlos and guarded his back while they collected the taxes, and sometimes confronted other gangs. He was with Juan Carlos the week before, watching his back, while the fish vendors from the river pushed their carts in from the edge of the barrio.

Ramon bought fresh fish for the cafe, and he had finally persuaded the fish sellers to move their market within the area he controlled. He charged them a lower tax, because they brought other business with them. While they were watching the carts rolling by, they were attacked from behind by two knife-wielding rivals from another gang. They sprang from an alley that bordered Ramon's territory with another patrón, and came in for the kill without a sound.

"Juan Carlos!" Rico shouted, before he was cut down and fell silent.

Juan Carlos then took that fateful step that he had avoided for so long. He killed.

The rival who stabbed Rico was tall and muscular,

with a sunburned red face and wild, tangled hair. After dropping Rico to the street, he rushed at Juan Carlos with his knife high, and lunged in a downward stab. Then, the years of Ramon's brutal conditioning came to bear.

No conscious thought, just deeply engrained responses. He stepped lightly to the left and parried the strike, and in less than a second, he pulled his blade and closed the distance and sliced across the left side of the boy's neck. He followed up quickly with a backhanded "X" slash across the right side, dropped low with his knees, and drug the blade deeply across his belly.

The second attacker, a smaller and younger boy, fled in terror.

The tall boy collapsed to his knees and gripped his belly to keep it from bursting, and the blood from his neck splattered and showered the street in front of him in quick pulses. Juan Carlos grabbed him by the tangled locks on the top of his head and looked deeply into his eyes with a vacant calmness, and realized he had seen him before.

It was the older boy who had beaten him into unconsciousness on the cobblestone street in front of the Franciscan Mission, all those years ago.

His old enemy sank to the ground, and Juan Carlos turned to his friend, Rico, who was lying on the street heaving in gurgling breath. He had been stabbed high in the chest, and the blade had punctured his esophagus. He couldn't speak, but his eyes were pleading for understanding.

"Why did this happen to me?" they begged.

His eyes turned from confusion to fear. He knew he was dying and the terror washed across his face as his complexion paled to an ashen color. He tried to cry out, but could only utter a croaking sound as the blood bubbled up from his throat.

In his final moment, he looked embarrassed, having shamed himself in the arms of his hero, and he gathered his courage as the light faded. Juan Carlos cradled his head above the cold stone street, and tried to comfort him as he drowned in his own blood.

The vendors and people in the barrio scattered and fled into their homes, and Juan Carlos was left on the street alone with Rico. He picked the slender, gentle boy up in his arms and looked around desperately for help, just as the last doors were slamming and locks bolting shut. He walked for eight blocks with Rico, never pausing or letting his body touch the street again.

Odd thoughts came to him as he slowly carried him home.

"I forgot to collect the taxes from the fish vendors. Ramon will be angry," he thought. "I have blood all over my shirt. How am I going to explain to Ramon that I need a new shirt?"

Then the most perplexing thought of all, "I should be crying for Rico. Why can't I cry?"

When he finally came to the cafe with Rico's body in his arms, Ramon came out yelling. "Why did you bring <u>that</u> back here? You should have left it in the street!"

To Ramon, when the weak perished in the street, they should be left in the street like road kill. You don't bring road kill home to mourn its passing.

IT WAS STILL long before the sunrise, but he eased out of the bed and slipped his feet instinctively into his sandals in the darkness. Then he moved quietly down the stairway and out into the moonlit courtyard. He bent over to the fountain and reached down and cupped some cool water in his hand, and splashed it lightly on his face and dampened his hair and smoothed it back.

For the first time in his life, he was afraid. Not of the violence, or of being killed in the streets, but afraid of who he was going to be from this day on. He should have felt something when he killed the tall boy. He should have cried as his friend died in his arms.

But there was nothing. He was afraid that he had lost his soul. That he was nothing but a shell, with a great dark chasm where his heart should be.

Ramon made a great celebration of the killing. He

brought Juan Carlos into the cafe that night, and made toast after toast to celebrate the victory of his greatest pupil. He let Juan Carlos sit at the big table and eat his fill, and let him drink with the men.

But the evening unsettled him more than anything. He was being recognized and admired as a killer. Covered by Ramon in a new layer of expectation. The expectation that he would kill again and again, until Ramon ruled all of La Paz.

The only consolation from that night, was that he saw Gisele passing closely all night long. So close that he could smell her sweet scent, even among the drunks and fumes of cigars. Close enough that her small bare arms braised against him, exactly four times, as she passed with drinks. And once, as she spun quickly to avoid the groping hands of a drunkard, her long braided hair whipped around and lashed Juan Carlos across his neck. He saw it coming, but didn't move away. The sensation felt as intense as Ramon's hot wooden blade that seared the skin, and it made him shudder.

HE WAS SITTING on the edge of the fountain, when she spoke to him.

"Hello, Juan Carlos," came the soft voice from the shadows beneath the gallery.

He looked up and searched the darkness, but

couldn't see her. Maybe her voice was just a dream.

"I'm here," she said. Then she stepped out into the moonlight.

"Gisele! What are you doing out here?" Juan Carlos said.

"I like to come here when everyone else is asleep. It's the only time I can use the fountain to wash myself, without someone watching me."

"I'm sorry. I didn't know," he said. "I will leave now."

"No, please don't," she said.

She came over and sat next to him on the basin of the fountain, and reached down and lightly wet her fingers and dabbed the cool water on her neck. The summer heat made even the late night air warm and sticky.

"Where are you from, Gisele?" Juan Carlos asked. "You can't be from Bolivia."

She smiled, but hesitated, and dripped another bit of water across her shoulder and arm.

"Don Ramon bought me from the Franciscans. My mother brought me here to Bolivia two years ago, but she left me at the mission one day, and never came back for me. I was born in a country called Argentina. Do you know it?" she asked.

"No, I don't know much about the world outside of La Paz. Only a little about Spain, that Don Ramon has told me."

Then she continued, "I grew up in a land very far

from here, called Patagonia. It's a land of mountains and rivers, and beautiful horses. My father was an important gaucho on a very large estancia."

"A gaucho?" he said. He had heard legends and stories about gauchos, but never met anyone who actually knew one. La Paz was not a place where gauchos existed.

"Yes, I grew up with horses, and sheep and cattle. It was a wonderful life. Until my father died. Then my mother brought me here."

JUAN CARLOS LISTENED INTENTLY for the next hour as Gisele described the jagged mountain peaks and snowy volcanoes, the broad river valleys that flowed around them and off to the sea, and the brilliant red skies at the end of long summer days.

She talked about the gauchos and their lives on the open range in the saddle. Green pastures with grass as tall as a man's waist, with ten thousand sheep grazing in a flowing flock as far as the eye could see. And she told him how men worked and earned their own puesto, a home for themselves and a place to raise their own family. Her richest memory from when she was a little girl on the puesto was of her father's horses.

"I've never seen anything so large and powerful, but so beautiful at the same time. They can be fierce and wild, but when you look into their eyes you feel something. Something you can't feel when looking into a person's eyes. It is pure truth. My father used to say a horse's eyes never tell lies."

"I've never seen a horse," Juan Carlos said. "But I have seen eyes that make me feel something I have never felt before." It just leapt from his mouth before he could stop it.

She tilted her head slightly and smiled, and the moonlight sparkled in her hair. Juan Carlos felt the flush of embarrassment and fear run across his face. He had never said anything like that before. He had made himself vulnerable for the first time in his life, and it terrified him.

"Where is Patagonia? How can you get there from here?" he said to change the subject.

She looked up into the night sky and found the Southern Cross hovering above. "Just go that way," she said as she pointed south. "Follow the condor winds along the foothills of the Andes Mountains, until the rivers and grass turn green and you find the land of the seven lakes."

"You know which way to go by looking at the stars?" he said.

"Yes, my father taught me when I was little. The people who live there all know how to find their way by the stars."

"But how do you know these stars? The sky over La Paz must be different from the sky where you came from," he asked.

She smiled and started to laugh, but she caught herself. She didn't want to mock his ignorance. He was a fully-grown man, hardened and tempered by Ramon through a ceaseless process of battle and corruption. A finely honed and sharpened instrument.

But deep inside remained the innocent and unworldly mind of a child. A beautiful, untempered soul that still retained a sense of wonder about the world.

"I used to think that too," she said. "But then my father showed me how the sky moves around the whole world every night, like a giant spinning wagon wheel. And now I know it's true, because we are very far from Patagonia, but this is exactly the same sky I used to see back home. It followed me here."

When the glow of the sun reached into the courtyard, they realized it wasn't safe to be seen together. Ramon had made it clear that Gisele was his property, and Juan Carlos didn't dare risk being found with her. They both agreed it would not be a good idea to do this again. And yet, they both knew they would be anticipating the next early morning in the courtyard.

So this became the nature of their love. Stealing away in the early morning hours while the rest of the world was asleep, to sit and talk, and dream of someplace else.

Juan Carlos had never had dreams of anything other than the life he knew. He knew of nothing else.

He didn't even know anyone, who knew of anything else. Other than Ramon, no one had ever entered his life who could lend him a vision of other vistas, or people, or animals, or anything different from what existed in this barrio of La Paz. As far as he could tell, every other place in the world must be just like it. And everyone else's lives were filled with the same endless threats of violence and survival.

Gisele's stories and the things she had seen and done, flooded his mind with possibilities he didn't know existed. And listening to her as she described life in this other place, and the way people lived, would wash away some of the filth and corruption that covered him every day of his life in the barrio with Ramon. He bathed in her voice every night while the rest of Ramon's dirty world slept around them.

Over the following year, Gisele painted a landscape in his mind that awakened him. It stirred him into vivid, colorful dreams of mountains and horses, and a life in the open spaces where people lived in harmony with nature, instead of in conflict and pain.

It made him consider if there was a chance, even a small one, that he might be a different man deep down inside; different from what life in the barrio had made him. It awakened something else in him too. A growing desire to escape the wretched violent world of Don Ramon.

SINS OF THE FATHER

L ife in the barrio was much the same from day to day, and Juan Carlos began to realize that his life here would never change. Not in the world of Don Ramon. Ramon was the master of this little world that now covered a quarter of La Paz, but as his power and influence grew, Juan Carlos' life just became harder, and more dangerous.

Their boundaries were starting to push against the territory of another outcast from the Spanish nobles who was, by all accounts, as fierce a man as Ramon. They had kept an uneasy truce for the last year, not pushing any farther than the Catholic Church that stood on the block between their domains. But Ramon was never content, and his discontent turned to rage on the day of the wedding.

The other patrón, Don Miguel de Aragon, who

hailed from Jerez at the very tip of Andalusia, was about to take a bride. Her connections would expand his reach and power far beyond his current thirty-block domain. She was the descendant of an original Spanish lord who came at the behest of the King of Spain in the early days of the colonies, and her family held political positions throughout Bolivia.

Don Miguel de Aragon would be an unstoppable force when he gained access to the military and police who favored his new wife's family. They were to be married in the church that bordered the two territories, and the local Bishop was going to personally conduct the ceremony. It was more than just a wedding. It was a show of force. And that the bridal party intended to enter the church on the neutral side, and exit onto the street in Ramon's side, was a clear threat.

On the day of the wedding, Ramon gathered his gang before sunrise and moved carefully through the streets to the church. He thought Don Miguel de Aragon might send some of his own street soldiers to the backside of the church, his side, in the early hours to protect him and his wife as they proudly walked down the steps into Ramon's backyard.

They saw nothing out of place when they arrived at the back of the church. No sign that anyone feared a reprisal from Ramon, and that made Ramon even more angry.

Ramon positioned his young soldiers around the church and gave them instructions, but instead of letting Juan Carlos lead his own small group, which he normally did, he asked him to stay by his side.

"Stay with me Juan Carlos, I want you here. We will win this together. We belong together," he said, in an unusual tone.

He reached out his hand and gripped Juan Carlos by the shoulder, and smiled. He looked at him in a way he never had before. It was a distracted glance, but with a reflection of something new. Something akin to pride. Juan Carlos smiled back and nodded his head.

At 11:00 in the morning they could hear the great procession coming to the entrance of the church on the other side. They listened as the crowd of guests chattered and laughed and mingled, then took their seats and spilled over into the front courtyard because they numbered so many.

Ramon gritted his teeth when he heard the bellowing pipes of the church organ announce the moment of the bride's arrival, and then fell silent as the Bishop raised his hands and asked for all to be seated.

The Bishop made a grand display of the union, and Ramon grew more impatient as he listened to his groaning voice through the stained glass windows. It went on, and on, until he couldn't take it anymore. He started pacing furiously on the street in front of the exit doors.

Then, he heard the great cheer arise from the crowd as the new couple was officially presented. When the exit doors opened, Ramon was standing ready to face his foe.

Don Miguel de Aragon and his beautiful bride in a white floral dress from Madrid, emerged from the doors and paused on the tiled landing. Several young men who worked for Miguel moved quickly around them and positioned themselves along the sides of the marble steps.

Hundreds of guests came running around from the front of the church to form a gauntlet of well wishers and rice throwers. Miguel looked down from above and made eye contact with Ramon, and he smiled. He smiled broadly and showed all of his teeth. Then he laughed as if he had just conquered the world.

CHAOS ERUPTED.

PEOPLE WERE SCREAMING and scurrying in all directions like roaches in a dark room, suddenly flooded with light. Blades were drawn and blood was spilling. In the center of it all, at the bottom step of the church, was Ramon and Juan Carlos.

They came back to back and fought like a matched pair of flashing blades. Spinning and wheeling, they moved up the steps as one living fighting machine, each keeping tabs on the other through their sweaty backs.

The bodies fell around them as they inched upward and closer to the bride and groom. In one instant of pause, Ramon turned his head and looked at Juan Carlos and beamed like a proud father.

"Ha! We have them on the run now!" he yelled.

Don Miguel de Aragon and his bride stood perfectly still throughout the fight, with the Bishop huddling in their shadow. He wouldn't give an inch of ground or an ounce of satisfaction to his rival. When the duo of Ramon and Juan Carlos reached the top step, Don Miguel made his final play.

He reached into his formal wedding vest and drew a Belgian made revolver. He knew Ramon would only fight with his elegant blade, his one symbol of Spanish nobility. But Miguel was a more practical and modern Don. He was interested in the end and not the means. He embraced the efficient killing power of the pistol over the romantic history of the blade.

"You are a fool, just like your little cockroach of a father!" Miguel laughed as he brought the gun up from its hiding place. "La Paz will be mine!"

The sight of the gun coming out in Miguel's hand

made Ramon more angry than before. It cheapened the victory, or defeat, he had imagined in his head; one blade-master against another. He stood tall and stared into his eyes as Miguel raised the revolver and aimed at the tip of his nose. But Miguel hadn't fully anticipated that he was fighting two blade-masters, and not just one.

Juan Carlos, the young wraith from the dirty streets of La Paz, didn't hesitate. He dropped and rolled in from below, then leaped upward and slashed completely through the elbow ligaments of Don Miguel.

The gun, and the hand that gripped it, twisted awkwardly to the left and was pointed directly at the floral white dress when it howled with yellow flame, then flew loose in the air. Ramon jumped forward and drove his dagger deep into Miguel's chest and finished the fight. He glared into Miguel's stunned eyes for just an instant, before he collapsed next to the woman he had married only a minute before.

The Bishop stood alone now, his brilliant purple robes splattered in red, and stared down at the bodies at his feet and strewn down the stairs to the church. He was shivering with terror, but he needn't have been concerned. Ramon wouldn't go that far.

RAMON SURVEYED the scene of his triumph. He

calmed the Bishop, and assured him that large contributions would be made to properly restore the honor of the church, and in time, people would forget all about the gore and remember only the legend of Ramon.

And of course, the fact that the Bishop survived in the center of the battle was a clear sign that God had kept him from harm. He would forever be remembered as God's beloved messenger, and the Bishop seemed content with that.

His boys were cut and battered, but none had died. Further proof that Ramon was not only the better fighter, but also the better teacher. It pleased him even more than vanquishing his rotten enemy who brought a foul weapon to an honorable contest of nobility.

The gun made his victory feel different than he had hoped. It made it ever so slightly hollow, without the satisfaction he deserved. Like the same lack of satisfaction he felt when he killed his father, who was greatly diminished by age and sherry at the time.

"Even when I risk my life in combat, this world never gives me the honor I deserve," he skulked, as he led his group of boys and young men back to the cafe.

Juan Carlos, who had been a swift, cold machine in the battle, was breaking apart inside. Seeing the woman in the white dress die as a result of his swift strike on Don Miguel, was ripping his heart from his chest.

He couldn't shake the vision of her dark brown eyes staring blankly up at the sky, and the startling contrast of crimson red soaking into the delicately sewn flowers on the snow-white dress.

He had become what Ramon always wanted him to be, an assassin. A ruthless butcher. He was praying for the numbness to take over his mind as he walked through the streets back to the cafe, but it wouldn't come.

He felt like falling to the cobblestone and letting the tears that welled and burned like acid, flood into the street. But La Paz, and Ramon, had sealed that exit of emotion many years ago. So he carried the pain with a face of stone.

WORD of the fierce battle and Don Ramon's victory over Don Miguel de Aragon reached the cafe long before the clan arrived. When they turned the corner onto the final block, the street was full of merchants and men and women cheering Don Ramon home.

He walked slowly down the street with his head held up, reveling in the moment; but he knew these people despised him. They stood and cheered and clapped, but in their faces he could see how much they hated him. They lived in a barrio that was more like a prison, and he was the cruel warden. He demanded homage, and inflicted pain on anyone who failed. They cheered out of fear.

On this rare occasion, he invited all of his boys and young men into the cafe to drink and eat their fill, and he made a particular fuss over Juan Carlos. He ordered drinks for everyone and stood up on a chair where they could see him.

"A toast, to Juan Carlos, the second best blade-master in all of Bolivia!" he announced to the crowd.

Juan Carlos smiled lightly and tried to act happy, but to him the cheering and backslapping only heralded his falling deeper into the pit of hell. For a moment in the battle, he had seen Ramon look at him, and it felt paternal. He felt a connection that he had longed for his entire life.

But then only a few seconds beyond he was standing in the midst of a murderous scene, leaving a beautiful woman in a white dress on her wedding day, splayed out on the steps of the church. He felt sure that he was damned.

Ramon ordered the glasses kept full, and he sat at his corner table and watched the room as the night wore on. He watched as Gisele came back and forth from the kitchen with trays of liquor, dodging the gropes and grabs and pinches. And he watched as Juan Carlos' eyes followed her every move across the floor. He could see his longing for her to come closer, and his anger swelling, biting his lips, when he saw another man touch her.

Ramon scowled and muttered under his breath, "I've warned the boy. I gave him every chance in the world. I told him she belonged to me. Why couldn't he listen to me?"

Ramon felt no love or affection for Gisele, in truth, he felt no love for women in general. He had been spurned by women, even his own mother, from the day he was born. He was handsome, strong, and powerful. He was born a nobleman, and yet, no woman had ever loved him. So he treated them all like either property or trash.

Gisele had been property. Duly purchased from the Franciscans. But as he had watched Juan Carlos slipping deeper into her grasp and away from his own, it was a crushing blow. A stupid young bargirl holding sway over the boy that he had raised and trained. She wielded a power that he couldn't understand.

By the early morning hours the great celebration had ended. Many were drunk and passed out on the tables and floor. Juan Carlos had slipped away early and gone to his room, and Pancho and Santi followed shortly after and collapsed into their beds.

Ramon remained until the very end, drinking and rocking slowly back in his chair until it tapped the wall behind, and then fell slowly forward, over and over. He stared through blurred spinning vision at the young girl, Gisele, as she tried to pick up the remains of the glasses and trays, and stepped roughly over the bodies and smashed a few drunken fingers for the pleasure.

Gisele went out the side door of the kitchen in the alley and tossed a large pail of dirty water and vomit into the street. She turned the pail up on its edge against the building, stood and stretched her aching young back and looked up at the stars.

"Soon," she whispered under her breath.

Then she turned and walked back into the kitchen, pulled off the apron wrapped around her and hung it on the wall, and opened the small door that led into the little closet where she slept. It was just big enough for the small bed against the wall, and a single chair where she sat to take off her shoes and clothes. A tiny glass window was on the alley side of the closet, and it let a constant ray of starlight come in, so that she could always see without a lamp or a candle.

As she opened the door, a looming darkness greeted her. There was no starlight in the room tonight; only the towering shadow of a man, Don Ramon. She gasped with sudden fright, and Ramon reached forward and grabbed her by both arms, lifted her into the air and flung her onto the bed.

He was staggering drunk, and he stumbled in the small dark room and reached out to the wall to catch his balance and stood there for just a second. This wasn't the first time Ramon had attacked her, but he was more drunk than usual. Gisele gathered her wits quickly; she wasn't startled anymore, she was ready to fight.

She was on her back on the bed with Ramon standing in front of her, so she drew both her knees up, and with the force of a stallion, smashed her heels into his groin. The air in his lungs erupted from his mouth in a violent bark, and the impact doubled him over and sent him staggering backward through the doorway. He tumbled over the chopping block in the middle of the kitchen and crashed to the floor.

When Gisele came running from the room, Ramon was writhing in agony on the floor, and heaving out all of the alcohol he had been drinking through the night.

"I'll kill you, you little bitch!" Ramon wailed.

"Not tonight you won't!" Gisele yelled back in his face.

She spun around and grabbed an iron skillet from the stove and swung it with both hands. The blackened skillet sang out like the Sunday church bell when it ricocheted across Ramon's skull and knocked him flat to the floor. The ringing sound reverberated through the walls and into the room above, and two young men who were fitfully dreaming about a bloody church massacre, bolted straight up in their beds with eyes as wide as saucers.

Gisele ran back into her dark little closet, and pulled a bundle, tightly wound with a blanket and rope, from under her bed. She paused for a second and looked down at Ramon laying spread out on the stone floor before fleeing through the alley door.

"It wasn't supposed to happen this way. Dear God, please let him be there waiting for me," she said. Then she slipped out the side door, and off into the night.

ESCAPE

J uan Carlos and Gisele had hatched a plan to flee together. By terrible luck, on the same day that Ramon took his clan to the church. The plan seemed simple enough. Gisele remembered at least some of the journey from when her mother brought her north.

She knew there was a train that ran from a lake town, called Oruro, just a few hours to the south of La Paz. They could hire a boatman to take them downriver to the town without being seen. Then, they could jump aboard one of the long trains that carried open containers of corn down to the border town of Villazón.

They would have to make their way through the jungle and around the guards at the border crossing, but then it would be easy enough to come back to the road that leads to the town of Salta in northern

Argentina. They would still be very far from Patagonia, but there were roads, and new railways being built by the British, and they should be able to find work here and there along the journey.

Somehow, they would make it.

The journey itself to Patagonia would be long and dangerous. Over 3000 kilometers of jungles, deserts, mountains and rivers; and people who might be dangerous too. But none of it made Juan Carlos afraid, in fact, he was excited about seeing so many new places and things. The only thing that made him afraid, was Ramon.

Ramon was not a man to ever let go of a thing, once he possessed it. And Juan Carlos and Gisele were things to him, and nothing more.

When one of his young soldiers was killed in the street by a rival, he never mourned for the boy. He was angry that his gang had been made to look weak. He could replace and train new boys with little effort. But he grew furious when he lost something he had invested time and effort into developing.

They would need to be most careful about their plan to slip away without anyone suspecting they were going to do it. As much as Juan Carlos looked forward to his early morning rendezvous with Gisele, he told her they had to stop meeting in the last week before the day they would leave, so not to risk getting caught.

They would both have to steal away a few coins here and there, and stash it safely for the journey. But not so much that Ramon would notice the money from taxes and the cafe was light … just a small amount, each day.

In the final week before they planned to leave, they each packed a roll of a blanket and a light jacket that Ramon had given them for winter. That, and the clothes they had on their backs, were all that they owned. They were leaving in the spring, so the weather would be warm, with only light rains they thought, so blankets to wrap around themselves at night would be enough.

JUAN CARLOS WAITED until he could hear Pancho and Santi snoring deeply and rhythmically before he reached under his bed and pulled out the blanket roll, and crept slowly to the door. The door was never fully closed and locked, so he touched his fingertips to the edge and gently pulled it open just enough to squeeze through, then floated down the stairs like a ghost.

He reached the door to the alley and leaned out to see if anyone was there, and when he was sure it was clear, he moved quickly down the side street. At the end of the block, he turned left and broke into a dead run down the street.

He and Gisele had made a clever plan. He would leave through the alley and make his way down the back streets. Gisele would leave through the kitchen entrance on the side of the cafe, and follow the main street east, then take the fourth road to the right. They would meet a few hours before daybreak, right in front of the old Franciscan Mission.

From there, they could head straight to the river and meet the fisherman who sold fresh fish to the cafe. Gisele had made a deal with him. He would take them in his long canoe down river to Oruro during the early morning hours, for the price of fifty boliviano coins.

Juan Carlos arrived first, and he came down the alley behind the mission and slowly moved up to the edge of the building, where it opened into the plaza. He leaned against the drain pipe coming down the corner of the building, and thought briefly about all the times he had been here as a small boy; drinking rainwater from the rusty pipe and waiting for a meal to be tossed into the streets by the friars.

The clouds scattered into clusters and moonlight broke into the plaza. It was a scene of black and grey shadows, damp cobblestones, and eerie quiet. He couldn't see any signs of Gisele yet, but he had left earlier than he expected, and he thought it might take her longer to get here. An hour passed and she didn't arrive. Then nearly another hour.

He walked out into the center of the plaza, thinking Gisele would be less afraid if she saw him there waiting when she came up the street. Then he saw movement in the side street on the far side. Two shadows moving. Then they stepped out into the low light. It was the two other boys who shared his room, Pancho and Santi.

He was confused for a second. How did they see him leave? How did they follow him when he was moving so quickly and quietly? Why were they here?

Then it all became clear. From the main road to the West, Gisele stumbled into the plaza, with Ramon following closely and holding her from behind by her long hair with her head wrenched slightly backward. He was sober now, and angry, and his hair was matted with his own blood, dried into a sticky scab.

He had known for days that Juan Carlos and Gisele were planning to slip away, and for months about their secret nightly rendezvous. He thought perhaps the battle at the church had changed his mind, when Juan Carlos leapt forward and stopped Don Miguel from killing him with the pistol. He beamed over the boy like a proud father.

But then he watched the two of them in the cafe, and he knew. He knew Juan Carlos was leaving and taking her with him. Why couldn't he just be an obedient son?

"Did you think you could just run away from me, boy?" Ramon said in the darkness. "And steal my property for yourself?"

Juan Carlos was speechless, and trembling. Not trembling out of fear for himself, because he had lost any fear of pain or even death many years ago. Boys who grow up on the streets of La Paz become fearless, or they perish. He was trembling with rage. Rage at the man who was gripping his love like she was a filthy stray cat.

"She's not your property, Ramon. I love her, and we are leaving this place!" he said.

Ramon felt the sting of disrespect when Juan Carlos no longer addressed him as "Don", and he jerked Gisele's head back sharply until she cried out. Pancho and Santi looked startled and confused, and glanced quickly back and forth between Ramon and Juan Carlos. Juan Carlos had been like their big brother and their protector. They trained together, patrolled the streets together, and lived together.

But Ramon was their master, and they feared him more than they loved Juan Carlos. Juan Carlos looked at them and slowly moved his head from side to side, "Don't do it, brothers," he said.

Ramon signaled the two boys to attack.

Without hesitation they pulled their knives and came as a pair, but they never had a chance. Juan Carlos moved like the wind. No blade strike ever touched him. He countered and slashed Santi's throat, and he fell to the stones and made no more sounds but a gurgling death note.

Pancho came in for a low swipe at his stomach, but he pulled him down and thrust his knife into the base of his neck, and twisted it quickly to severe the spinal cord; just as Ramon had taught him.

Ramon raged. He threw Gisele facedown into the street, and ran at Juan Carlos. The long Toledo dagger was spinning and twisting and flashing like blue sparks in the moonlight. He hadn't been the "silent assassin" for many years, but he was still the most lethal Spanish blade-master in all of La Paz.

As Ramon reached him at a full-on death charge, Juan Carlos dove straight down and through his legs, as he had done in this same plaza years ago to seize a drumstick. It was a move he had learned in the hardened streets, and not one that Ramon had taught him, nor had he ever seen it in the fancy knife fighting schools of Seville.

As he passed through Ramon's legs, he made one deep slice with his blade across the inner thigh. Ramon was quick, he leaped and managed to cut Juan Carlos across the lower back as he passed under him, but not a fatal blow.

Juan Carlos slid through his legs then jumped to his feet and spun around to face Ramon. Ramon stood like a frozen specter in the fading moonlight, facing the old mission with his back to Juan Carlos.

"You've killed me boy," he said in a whisper.

Juan Carlos could see the blood coursing from the severed femoral artery, and pooling rapidly in the cracks in the cobblestone between Ramon's feet.

Ramon tilted his head downward to look at the growing silvery pool in the grey light, and laughed faintly to himself. Then he sunk to his knees, and gently laid his dagger on the street in front of him.

He felt a sense of satisfaction coming over him. He had finally met an equal blade-master on even terms. It felt oddly enough like a victory, as the man who killed him had been his greatest student. He had actually killed himself, he thought.

His blood and his life left him in ever-quickening pulses. His vision blurred and his mind grew calmer with each surge of his heart. His life had come full circle back on itself.

He had taken the young boy from the streets and treated him as much like a son as he was capable, and heaped many of the same cruelties on him as he had known himself. He trained him in the fighting arts as he had been trained; and now the boy had stolen something from him to go off and make a new life for himself. Ramon had fully reaped what he had sown.

In his last moment in this world, he stared at the grand oak doors of the Franciscan Mission. He imagined his mother might come through those doors and cradle him in her arms and comfort him, as he often dreamed of when he was a young boy in Cordoba. He called to her. But the doors remained sealed, and he was completely alone when the darkness took him.

Juan Carlos didn't wait to see the ending. He ran for Gisele and scooped her up from the street. "We have to go now!"

The two young lovers raced through the night until they reached the docks at the river. The fisherman was standing there waiting, but he looked startled to see Gisele and Juan Carlos.

"I..I..didn't think you were coming," he stuttered.

It was pretty obvious why. He had told Ramon about the plan to escape. He feared Ramon as much as any other man in La Paz.

"Ramon is dead. I killed him," Juan Carlos said as he stared into the fisherman's eyes. "You'll keep our bargain. Or you'll join him."

The fisherman didn't speak another word. He pulled the ropes loose from the dock, and offered his hand to Gisele to help her into the flat canoe, and they pushed away into the dark current and drifted down river, leaving the dull glow of La Paz behind.

A FACE OF STONE

J uan Carlos was fascinated by the night sounds along the river, and even the sounds of the water moving beneath them and the gentle rocking of the long canoe. Every shape, every sound and movement was a completely new experience.

He had spent every minute of his life walking on cobblestone or brick streets. Hearing only the sounds of city life and people and lonely dogs barking in the night. He knew there was a river near the city, but he had never ventured that far to see it, and he couldn't swim so when the canoe tipped and wiggled to stay balanced on the water, it frightened him a little.

As they passed under the stars from the open plains and entered a more densely jungled landscape, he heard the sounds of animals singing and chattering at the moon. There were fish and other water creatures splashing and moving in the river all around them.

He was drifting into an alien world, and trying to keep a brave face for Gisele. But the farther they drifted from the city, the closer they came to the world Gisele was familiar with.

The fisherman broke the silence, "Is Don Ramon really dead?" he asked.

"Yes," Juan Carlos answered, without turning to look at him.

"Won't the others who work for him, the young dangerous ones; won't they come for you?"

Juan Carlos stayed quiet, staring ahead into the darkness of the river.

Gisele turned around and looked into the fisherman's eyes, "They are dead too."

She could see the fisherman's face turning pale in the faint starlight, and the glimmer of his crooked front teeth as his jaw fell limp and his mouth came open. After a long moment, his eyes blinked rapidly and his head jerked as if he were startled awake, and he took a deep breath. His pace on the oar quickened.

THEY REACHED the outskirts of the town just as the morning sun crested the tree tops. Juan Carlos looked around and marveled at the enormous canopy of trees, again something he had never seen before. The stories that Gisele shared, prepared him only vaguely for the visual experience.

"I don't want anyone to see me bringing you into the town. Every policeman in Bolivia will be hunting the gang who killed Don Miguel de Aragon and his wife at the church. They will hang you if they catch you, and anyone else they think is helping you," the fisherman said. "You need to go ashore here, and walk along the river. The railroad tracks pass close to the river not far down, and you can jump on the train when it goes past."

The long canoe glided up onto the muddy riverbank, and Juan Carlos climbed out and held the canoe steady as Gisele cat-walked along the center of the canoe to the front, then handed their two small bundles to him. She turned again and looked at the fisherman. The sun had brought the river world into an orange and yellow haze and she could see him clearly now, her bottomless blue eyes pierced through to the heart of him.

"You don't need to pay me ... I ... I'm pleased I could help the two of you escape," he said, in a quavering voice.

"We made a bargain," she said. Then she reached out and rolled fifty boliviano coins into the wet bottom of the canoe by his feet. "But you will not speak a word to anyone about this."

"No. No, of course not," the fisherman answered.

Juan Carlos looked directly at him now, his hand

wrenching around the handle of the knife at his waist, "Don't ever make me come back here."

The fisherman shivered as if the dagger had just been plunged into his belly. He shook his head in response because his voice choked. He slid the oar down to push backward against the muddy bottom after Gisele stepped out; then he spun the canoe back upriver with a quick twist of the oar and stroked with all his might.

THEY MOVED QUIETLY DOWN along the waterline and caught the early morning train shortly after. Gisele knew Juan Carlos had been cut in the fight with Ramon, and as they walked along the river bank, she gathered herbs that she recognized and a bit of the silty mud from the bank and wrapped them in large leaves from the shore plants.

They could hear the train churning along the tracks and climbed easily onto the back of a box car as it moved past, and huddled together for sixteen hours until it came to the border town of Villazón.

During the ride, Gisele tended to Juan Carlos' wound.

"Take your shirt off and let me clean the wound on your back," she said.

"I'm fine. Don't bother."

"Juan Carlos, we will be going through wet jungle

tomorrow, and that cut will get infected and you will die. Take your shirt off, please."

Juan Carlos pulled the shirt up over his head and turned where she could see his back, and the story of his young life was laid bare. His body was a war map. A sculpted record of the cruelty of the world he had grown up in.

Lashes from ropes and belts at the hands of the Franciscans. Scars around his hairline and his shoulders from beatings in the streets. And the scars from Ramon's hot training blade, scattered across his arms, neck, and around his waist and back. She reached out and softly ran her fingertips over the burn scars that healed in raised knotted lines, and she could feel his pain in the deepest part of her soul. The tears came flowing down her cheeks.

"I thought it was so unfair when my father died, and when my mother took me away from my home and abandoned me. I thought the world was being cruel to me. But now I see what cruelty really looks like," she sobbed.

Juan Carlos turned and looked into her eyes, "We all have scars, Giselle. Some on the outside, some where they can't be seen."

Ramon's blade had left a sweeping, ten inch cut across Juan Carlos' lower back, from the point of his left hip up to his ribs on the right. It was open and lightly seeping blood, but not terribly deep. She took the herbs and mud from the leaves and made a soothing poultice, and coated the wound. Then covered it with the leaves and tore a strip from the bottom of her ragged skirt to wrap around his waist and hold it firmly.

They held each other tight, and gently rocked from side to side as the train slowly swayed under its heavy load.

Juan Carlos had not spoken a word for hours.

"Juan Carlos, you are so quiet. Are you in pain?" Gisele asked.

"No. The wound feels better after you treated it," he said. "I'm thinking about Pancho and Santi. They didn't deserve to die. They were my friends."

"No, they didn't, and I'm sorry you had to kill them. They were good boys, but they would have killed you just the same," she said.

And after a moment she added, "I'm happy you killed Ramon." It would be the last time she ever spoke his name, and her tongue burned as it slithered through her lips. It left a caustic, bitter taste in her mouth.

Juan Carlos couldn't shake the vision of the woman in the white dress. Every man or boy he had killed had been trying to kill him; but not her. She had been standing there on the steps of the church on the happiest day of her life, a vision of purity. Until his blade severed the arm of Don Miguel and sent a bullet piercing through her body.

And what was it for? To save the life of a monster.

A monster he ended up killing himself only hours later.

It gripped him as tightly as Gisele's blue eyes had done the first moment he saw her. And as Gisele's eyes often washed away the dirt and evil that shrouded his soul every day, the vision of the white dress would be the stain on his soul that could never be removed. A permanent tarnish that resists all attempts to polish it away. It would be a blemish, an imperfection, that he would have to accept and learn to live with. Or the blemish would spread like a cancer and slowly consume him.

"When I was young, I thought Ramon was going to be like my father. That he would protect me," Juan Carlos said. "But he was just as evil as the friars who used to make us fight for food. The only good thing he ever did was bring you close to me."

For years, Juan Carlos had wondered who his real father might be, and what he was like. Maybe he had been a wandering Spanish nobleman, like Ramon; or maybe a merchant or a friar. He wondered how different his life might have been if he had known him.

But then, his life might not have been any different at all, because almost every man he had ever met was the same. If he wanted his life to be different, he would have to change it himself. He would have to become something other than what Ramon and the world had shaped him into.

But he was wound tightly in the cerements now, the cloaks of La Paz and Ramon. It would take all of his will and the hand of an angel to pull him free of the tomb where he now lay in his mind.

"I will never kill again, Gisele," he said. "Not a man, not a dog, not a spider crawling on the wall. I'm done with it," he said.

Then, he felt the earth spinning around him. Spinning as it did when he drank in the cafe until he was drunk the day he killed the tall boy. His stomach twisted and wrenched, but there was nothing in it to come up. A wave of panic swept over him, it induced an uncontrollable tremble in his hands.

He looked into Gisele's deep blue eyes and felt like he was falling into them. Falling into an ocean-colored abyss. The face of stone, that firmly sealed vault of emotion, finally cracked, and he fell forward into her lap and sobbed until the tears ran dry.

THE LONG JOURNEY

As the train neared Villazón and slowed to a crawling pace, they gathered their few things and jumped into the long grass field at the edge of town. They walked along a dirt road into a square where market vendors were selling fruits and fresh vegetables, and Gisele took a few bolivianos and bought some things for the next part of their journey.

They kept an eye out for police and avoided them. Gisele knew about the telegraph offices, and suspected the police might have already sent word out about the church massacre.

They didn't know that in the midst of the fighting at the church, only Ramon had been identified by the Bishop. He didn't know or care about the boys who followed him. When they found the body of Ramon and two of his young soldiers in the plaza at the old Franciscan Mission, everyone just assumed that Don

Miguel de Aragon's men had settled the score. With Ramon dead, they stopped looking for anyone else.

The detour to avoid the guards at the border crossing into Argentina, through the swamp and jungle, was the most difficult. They pushed and clawed their way through the dense wet jungle, and Juan Carlos hacked at the thorny vines with his knife, but it was slow.

The air was thick and moist, and the mosquitos tormented them endlessly. Their thin leather sandals were worthless in the thick black mud of the jungle, and the ants gnawed at their feet and legs with every step.

Twice, they came across the path of deadly brown vipers, the first snakes Juan Carlos had ever seen, and they circled wide around them and lost their way. It was impossible to see the sun or the shadows to know where they were, under the dense canopy where only filtering rays of light flickered through as the wind swept the tree tops in great waves.

They heard a faint mechanical rattling once, and headed in the direction of the noise and soon they could see the tree canopy opening in the distance. When they reached the open clay road that lead to Salta, they knew they had made it safely into Argentina.

The clatter turned out to be a Citroën U23 flatbed truck; blood red color beneath the fine orange dust of the dirt road. It was carrying half a load of crated vegetables, bouncing and clattering with every bump. The truck's thin hard tires were mired deep in a mud hole, and the lone driver was helpless to break it free.

Juan Carlos marveled at the sight of it. He knew automobiles existed in La Paz, but Ramon had never allowed them to enter his barrio, because they moved so fast he couldn't catch them to demand a tax from the drivers.

"Hola!" the driver said as he saw the two young people emerging from the jungle.

"Hola," said Gisele. Juan Carlos was uncomfortable speaking to someone new, but he walked around the truck and ran his fingers along the smooth metal frame with great fascination. He kept a close eye on the driver as he walked.

"Do you think you might help me? I've been stuck in this mud for an hour. Where are you going to? Salta? I am taking vegetables to market there, and I could give you a ride on the truck, if you can help me free it from the mud," he said in a nervous jitter as he watched Juan Carlos.

"Yes, we can help you," Gisele answered.

They used their hands to dig out the watery mud that had the tires glued in place, and gathered sticks and rocks from the jungle to give them traction. Then, as the driver started the engine and put the Citroën into gear, they pushed with all their strength as the wheels spun and clawed their way out of the hole.

For an instant, they thought the driver was going to drive away and leave them as he accelerated out of the mud and continued on for a way down the road. But he stopped when he was sure the truck was on dry ground.

"Jump on the back!" he yelled, as they came running up to the truck.

They stretched out on the wood flatbed, and laughed as the truck revved and lurched forward and bumped along the dirt road. Their first experience in Argentina was thrilling. The fear of the unknown that Juan Carlos felt the night they left, was turning to excitement now. With every new hill they crested and corner they rounded, there were new sights and sounds, and magnificent mountains, and finally his first contact with new people.

After two hours on the road, the driver stopped the truck to rest the engine and his aching back. They sat under a broad acacia tree alongside the road and started a small fire to heat water in a little iron pot and make tea from a local herb that Juan Carlos had never tried, yerba maté. It was bitter, but it made his stomach feel better because he was very hungry.

"Do you have family in Salta?" the driver asked.

"No, we are going back to our home in Patagonia," Gisele said.

"Patagonia? *Que linda*! But you aren't going to walk all the way there. How will you go?" he asked.

"We will find a way." Juan Carlos said, with a sense of surety in his young voice.

The driver could tell from his accent that he was Bolivian, but the girl sounded Argentine so he didn't pry.

"You know, the British have built a railroad that goes all the way from Salta to Neuquen City in northern Patagonia. It doesn't take passengers yet, but you might be able to find some work for the railroad to get you down there." Then he said, "Do you know anything about horses? My cousin works on a repair crew for the railroad, and they are always looking for a gaucho who can wrangle horses for them."

"Yes! Juan Carlos knows horses very well! And me too!" Gisele said, shooting a glance to Juan Carlos to back up her lie.

"He could probably get a job with them, but I don't know if they would hire a girl to travel with the repair crew."

He could see their faces shrink from excitement to a look of desperation. Then he leaned back against the tree and looked up at the sky, and said as if he were talking to himself, "I'll bet they would hire a strong young horse wrangler, and let him bring his little brother along, though."

When they finished the long drive into Salta, the truck driver dropped Gisele off by the street markets to shop for a few used clothes, as he knew the weather going south would be much cooler than what they were prepared for. He offered her a few Argentine pesos as fair payment for helping him out of the mud hole. Then he took Juan Carlos to introduce him to his cousin, who in turn introduced him to the engineer of the repair crews.

As it happened, there was a track repair crew heading south along the line in a week, and they needed a horse wrangler to manage a dozen animals on the route for a two-month trip. They used three or four horses each day to pull and move the railroad ties with harnesses and blocks and tackle, and the horses had to be cared for and herded all the way to Neuquen City. Juan Carlos lied about his familiarity with horses, but he looked the rugged part, so they hired him on. He asked if he could bring along his "younger brother" with him.

"Sir, I have a little brother to care for. Our parents are dead, and I can't leave him behind. He doesn't eat much, and he can help with the horses for free," he pleaded.

The railroad engineer was an orphan too, and he agreed, "Alright, but keep him out of trouble and away from the crews."

Gisele tied her hair into a tight knot on top of her head and pulled a large wool hat down over her head so far that it even covered her ears. She kept a light cover of road dust and a little grease, rubbed on her face to conceal any hint of femininity. They bought an old worn poncho to drop over her and hide her body, and a pair of canvas breeches and saddle shoes.

She made sure Juan Carlos was properly outfitted with bombacha riding pants and a pair of well-worn boots, and a black boina hat just like her father used to wear.

For years he had worn his knife lashed to the left front of his waist by a leather cord, and never took it off. The leather had hardened in place and the knot was so tight that it couldn't be untied. Gisele had to gently cut through the cord and free him from the instrument.

It felt like cutting loose a chain that had bound him for years. He took a deep breath as she cut it, and as she pulled the cord away from his skin it left a deep crevice where it had been for so long the skin was trying to grow around it. She pulled it free, and he took a step and wobbled, then put his arms out to catch his balance. The small bit of weight had always been there and his body adjusted for it.

To keep him looking the part, Gisele found a decorative wool sash that Argentine gauchos often wear around their waist, and showed Juan Carlos how to carry his knife tucked neatly under the sash in the small of his back. It felt a little odd at first, but he enjoyed being able to pull the knife and sheath out and lay them someplace away from his body at the end of the day.

The next leg of their journey would span nearly

one thousand miles. Much of the railroad was being built to follow alongside a cleared dirt and gravel road that wound its way south, following the foothills of the Andes Mountains and the westerly sea breezes that Gisele called the "condor winds."

It was labeled as Ruta 40, as it was the fortieth major road project in Argentina's history. It connected the far north of the country all the way to the South, and also provided a very strategic travel route for a defense line along the border with Chile.

Most days the railroad crew made about fifteen miles of progress and sometimes over twenty. As the days passed into full summer, the temperatures soared past one hundred degrees in dry desert landscape, and the dust from the road swirled and blew and reached into every crack and crevice in the train cars, boxes and tools, clothing and human bodies.

They passed small creeks and streams once or twice a week, and Juan Carlos would take the horses down to the water in the evenings to cool them down and wash the dirt from their coats and faces, and they loved it. Gisele would slip out of the tent when the sun was low, trying not to be seen by the workers, and come to the streams with Juan Carlos to bathe and wash the dirt from her long hair.

While most people find the first sight of a thousand pound horse a little frightening, Juan Carlos found it glorious. He loved the horses, and they loved him back. It was his first encounter with any creature, except Gisele, that showed itself to the world with complete honesty.

If the horse was afraid, it showed him clearly that it was afraid. If it was happy to see him, it came and rubbed its great head against his body. And if it was angry, it stamped its hooves and warned him plainly not to keep doing whatever he was doing. He told Gisele once, "They live with their souls on the outside." It was a way of living he greatly admired.

Horses, and many other animals in this world, can see through the cloaks and layers of men, to the very core of you. To the essence of who you really are and what manner of spirit you possess. Their spirits can also be shaped and cloaked by the cruelty of men, so that they lose themselves; but when they are left to their own devices without men, or treated kindly, their pure souls are always visible.

Gisele had years of experience around horses, having been born to the gaucho life and raised on a puesto. So she was able to help Juan Carlos learn to handle them very quickly, but she had to be careful about the repair crew seeing her do too much, and she stayed as far from them as possible. From a great distance, she looked like a boy in her dirty clothing and it was better to keep it that way.

Juan Carlos and Gisele rode side by side herding the horses well behind the work crew, who traveled in a small coal-fired train car on the track with a bunk and tool car attached. Each day when they reached a place where wood ties needed to be replaced or moved, Juan Carlos would bring up fresh horses and harness them up for the day's work.

Gisele stayed back a half kilometer behind with the other horses finding graze or water. At night, they camped back away from the crew in a small canvas tent and built a fire, and sat out looking at the stars that filled the wide-open sky. Juan Carlos was eager to learn how to find his way by reading the stars, so he could always find his way back to Gisele. The first night they spent together in the tent, was the first time they consummated their love.

IT WAS late in the evening when they doused the fire with water from the tin pot, and Juan Carlos pulled the tent flap open for Gisele. Then followed her inside and tied it shut behind him. It was dark, with only a hint of light from the Milky Way filtering in through the brown canvas. She went in and pulled her dusty coat off and laid it in the corner. The crew foreman had given them several thick sheepskins to lay on the floor of the tent to insulate them from the cold ground, and two blankets each to fend off the mountain chill.

Gisele pulled off her sweater, then untied the rope that held the waist of her breeches snug, and stepped lightly out of them. She looked up and saw the shadowy outline of Juan Carlos standing perfectly still, staring at her, although he couldn't really see her. She pulled the sheepskins into a large single pile and lay down, pulled the blankets over her. Then she pulled the corner of the blanket back open and beckoned Juan Carlos to join her, "Come lie with me, Juan Carlos."

Of the two of them, Gisele was the only one who had experienced the physical part, of what should be love. But for her it was not. It had been forced on her when she was a younger girl; several brief and cruel assaults at the hands of Ramon. But the assaults had shaped her. Shaped her into the kind of girl who could kick a man in the groin and smash a skillet over his head. It made her fierce.

But deep down inside she knew that it could be different with a man she loved. And with a man who loved her back. She loved Juan Carlos and she longed for him.

He was excited and shivering with fear in the same instant. Even facing death, as he had many times, didn't frighten him this much. He took off his boots and his trousers, and kneeled down to the bedding and lay close beside her, and she pulled the blanket over his broad shoulders. He could feel the tip of her nose touching his and her warm breath washing across his face, but still he couldn't clearly see her in the darkness, and he didn't know what to do next. She reached up and touched his face, drew his lips to hers, and led him where he needed to go.

IN A WEEK'S time they passed the city of Mendoza, which stood in the shadow of the tallest mountain Juan Carlos had ever seen. It went all the way up to the heavens, so high that the clouds couldn't go over it, they just gathered and circled it in a swirling mist.

"Gisele, do you know the name of that mountain?" he said.

"Yes, it is called Aconcagua. It is one of the highest mountains in all the world."

As they traveled south of Mendoza, they saw small farms growing apples and pears and peaches all along the railway line. The British who built the railroad years before had helped the farmers get started in this valley. The trains would carry equipment and materials and supplies to the towns sprouting up in the West, and they thought in the future they would be able to haul train loads of fresh fruit to markets in the East to keep from going back the other way empty. Juan Carlos and Gisele detoured here and there into the orchards, as they never saw anyone tending them, to fill their ponchos and pockets.

After seven weeks of work and travel, the dusty road along the desert foothills turned to rolling green hills; and quickly from hills to canyons and mesas with raging rivers. When they reached a wood and iron bridge that spanned the gorge before a village called Zapala, Gisele remembered this place from her trip north many years before with her mother. She knew they were on the northern threshold of Patagonia.

"Juan Carlos, I know this place!" Gisele said. "They were building this new bridge when we came through here years ago. I think we are only a few days ride away from my home!"

Juan Carlos was gazing to the South now, and staring at a shining white point that just barely pierced the blue sky above the hills.

"What is that over the hills, Gisele?"

"That's the old volcano, Volcan Lanin!" she said. "We have made it."

For the first time since they fled La Paz under the cover of darkness, he felt the fear of reprisal slip away. He had been excited with all of the new sights and experiences along the journey, but he never completely stopped worrying that someone would be coming for revenge. In his mind, he had to reach this place called Patagonia before they would be safe, and now they were here.

On the second night encamped in Zapala, the railroad foreman gave Juan Carlos an order that he just couldn't obey. He had been tending the horses day and night for nearly two months. They were worked hard, and often poorly fed, and Juan Carlos struggled to keep them going some days. They needed rest and good graze for at least a few days, but the foreman was a brutal bastard.

"Juan Carlos, take those two old horses down to the river tonight, away from camp, and cut their throats. They can't work anymore, so at least we can cut them up for some fresh meat," he said.

He went back to their camp in the afternoon, knowing that he could never do what he had just been ordered to do.

"Gisele, how far do you think we are from the next town?" he said.

"Two days riding on horse, maybe," she responded. "Why are you asking? Do we need to leave?"

"The foreman just ordered me to kill the two grey horses. But I won't do it. I won't!" he said. "They just need a little rest and good grass, and they will be strong again. But he would rather kill them and eat them, than let them rest."

"The railroad tracks turn east from here, Juan Carlos, but straight south and down through the steep valleys, there is sweet grass that grows high. And there is a beautiful river with trees and wild fruit. We could walk the horses there in a day, then let them rest and feed. The rail-roaders have to go on east tomorrow, they will never come after us; not for two old horses," she said.

So once again, Juan Carlos and Gisele were forced

to plan a late night escape. He went out alone, leading the two grey horses just before sunset and made his way down to the river. An hour later, after the sky was dark, Gisele followed with their two blanket rolls slung over her back and a large sack with several days' worth of fruit and some dried meat.

She had to stop twice before reaching the river, feeling sick along the way. Juan Carlos had noticed how hard the two-month journey had been on her. She had trouble keeping food down sometimes.

They took the two horses and walked under the starlit sky until dawn, stopping for a short rest every hour. When the eastern sky cast an orange glow over the landscape, they found themselves looking out on a valley that stretched for twenty miles across to the next mountain range. A river flowed through the valley floor that Juan Carlos thought was so big that it must be the ocean. The hillsides were green and yellow and red and purple with early morning wild flowers, and they could see flocks of birds, thousands upon thousands of birds, wading and chattering in the shallows along the edge.

Juan Carlos sat down in the thick wet grass, and pulled his knees up and rested his chin on them and looked out over the valley.

"I didn't think it was real," he said. "All this time, I thought your stories might just be stories. I came because I love you, Gisele. But all of your stories are true."

Gisele sat down next to him, and looped her arm through his and leaned her head over onto his shoulder. The horses grazed in the thick sweet grass and snickered and snorted with contentment. They all felt the same powerfully stirring emotion. They were home.

"I hope we can find our very own puesto, in a big estancia with tall trees," she said.

"And, my father's name was Pablo. When our son is born, I would like to call him Pablo," Gisele said as she stared out over the valley. Then she turned to look at Juan Carlos, and smiled.

It took a moment to set in. He was young, and still something less than worldly. Then he sprang to his feet and looked down at Gisele.

"Our son?" he asked.

She laughed and nodded her head.

A NEW BEGINNING

J uan Carlos pulled the blanket off and rolled slowly over in the wet morning grass, then he draped the blanket over Gisele to keep her warm. He stood and stretched his back, and reached around to rub the soreness out.

The dagger wound was almost healed now, but it still hurt like hell when he bent over or turned quickly to one side, and the scar would stretch to the point of tearing open again. And every time it hurt, he saw Ramon's angry face in his mind. He pictured him clutching Giselle by her hair and tossing her to the street. But Ramon was dead. Almost everyone he knew from his life before was dead. And he had been the one who killed them.

He was still trying to process the idea that he was going to be a father. Gisele had told him three days ago when they first came to the broad river valley, and the news still hung suspended in his brain like a foggy dream. He was happy, but mostly he was terrified. He had never had a father, and he really didn't know how to be one.

The closest thing he had to a father growing up was Ramon. A man who beat on him, scarred him, and pushed him into a life of crime; and Juan Carlos ended up killing him. He hoped that wasn't the final destination of fatherhood… to have your son grow up and kill you.

After slipping away from the railroad crew with the horses, he and Giselle had made a simple camp along the river shoreline, up in the edge of the forest where the gravel turned to green sweet grass, and the two grey horses had been grazing and rolling in the sun. It was the first time in his life he had spent a couple of days doing absolutely nothing but lying around. He didn't have to find food, he didn't have to do any hard labor, and he didn't have to hurt anyone. It was his first vacation.

The horses were rested and healthy now, so they could ride across the river today and with a little luck, find the dirt trail leading to San Martin de Los Andes. He was obsessed with finding work now, any kind of work, to take care of Gisele and his son who was on the way, so getting to a town would give him the best chance. He had managed to work for the railroad for two months without having to pull his knife and kill anyone, so he hoped there would be a chance to find another peaceful job in the town. But he would do whatever circumstances dictate he do.

"Is it hurting this morning?" Gisele asked. She was looking up at him from under the wool blankets with a sleepy smile on her face. Her hair was tangled with leaves from the lenga tree they slept under, and loose strands dangled in her face.

"Not anymore, you have healed me," he said. "In more ways than one."

He knelt down beside her and brushed the hair away from her eyes, and stared. He always stared into her eyes. They were the center of his world. The place he came to for solace, for understanding, for direction. They were powerful, and peaceful. Her eyes were his connection to God, if there was such a thing.

His early life at the hands of the Franciscans hadn't convinced him God really existed, but her eyes fostered a belief in something bigger than he could imagine. They gave him faith that purity, kindness, and beauty flowed into the world from somewhere else. He saw it in her eyes, and he could almost taste it in the crisp mountain air. He could taste it in the cool night sky, the sweet flavor of a presence, a magical force, that settled on the tip of his tongue.

"I THINK the horses are strong enough to ride today. Is it safe to cross this river?" he asked.

"Yes, we can go upriver where the valley is very

wide, and the water is low. We will find a shallow vado to cross over," she said. "I think we are still two days riding from San Martin, so I hope we can find some food along the way. 'Pablito' is telling me he is hungry this morning."

She smiled again at the thought that she was carrying a child and rubbed her belly as though it were big and round, even though it was still very flat. They had only three apples left from the food they brought with them when they left the railroad crew in Zapala. Juan Carlos had grown up in the city and was proficient at stealing food or fighting for it, but he didn't know anything about finding food or hunting in the mountains. He had a lot to learn.

He gathered the two grey horses and put the bridles on them. They had no saddles so they would have to protect the horses' backs with the sleeping blankets and ride gently. He lifted Gisele up onto the mare, then grabbed the reins of the other and jumped and swung his leg quickly over the horse's back.

The horses clopped slowly along the high water line of the Limay River where centuries worth of driftwood and debris from the mountains was pushed into a bulkhead, and below it was a gravel beach swept clean from the lapping waves of the river. The water was running crystalline and cold. It was late summer now, and the snowmelt was almost gone and the river was shallow.

They found a wide place, and directed the horses

into the water, which they seemed to enjoy as they splashed and pranced on their way across. They leapt out of the cold river up a steep muddy bank, and stopped to shiver the water from their coats. Soon after reaching the other side, they found a well-worn animal trail that followed the southern shore.

"We must be on a private estancia, this trail is used everyday," Gisele said. "And I see signs of sheep and cattle."

The trail broke away from the river for a while, and as they came over a steep hill, the river had looped back in front of them. Grazing along the north slope all the way down to the waterline was an enormous flock of merino sheep. Then along the ridge-line to their left, Juan Carlos saw a rider coming. A lone man on a huge black horse coming at them at full gallop. Juan Carlos pulled his horse in front of Gisele to protect her, in case the charging rider attacked, but they had nowhere to run to, so they stayed in place.

As the rider drew closer, they could see he was young, maybe early twenties, about their age. He wasn't dressed like a working gaucho, but was wearing glossy black boots over his bombachas, a white shirt and wide brimmed hat, and a particularly long knife tucked in his belt. He was an outstanding rider, and was coming along a narrow section of the ridge at a fearless speed.

As he approached, he pulled back hard on the

reins and the black horse threw his head up and came sliding through the grass on his haunches with his hooves tearing a groove through the soil. He had a serious, stern look on his face, and he took a long moment to look at them before speaking while the black horse stomped and pawed at the ground.

"This is private property, what are you doing here?" he demanded.

Juan Carlos stayed quiet. He was entirely focused on the knife and contemplating his next move if the young man made even the slightest threatening motion.

"We are lost," Gisele said. "We are trying to find the road to San Martin de Los Andes."

Her soft voice calmed the young man almost instantly. His posture changed, his chin dropped ever so slightly, and his arms relaxed and loosened the reins. Even the black horse seemed to calm. He ceased the stomping and shook his great head, then reached down and grabbed a mouthful of sweet grass and dandelions and began to chew around the bit.

"We have come a long way, all the way from Bolivia. I lived on an estancia very near to this place when I was young, and we have come back to live here," she said.

"Where did you live? I know all of the estancias in this region," the young rider asked.

"The owner of the estancia where I was born was an Englishman, Señor Bruce. I was born there, my father was a gaucho. But he died, then my mother took me to Bolivia and abandoned me," she said. Then she added, "I just want to come home."

The young rider nodded his head. "I knew the Bruce family, but they don't live here anymore. A German bought the estancia and lives there now. I am afraid you don't have a home to come back to."

Gisele and Juan Carlos looked at each other, and the young rider could see the girl's heart sink at the news.

Juan Carlos spoke up, "Is there anyplace I can find work? I am good with horses, and I work very hard."

The rider had noticed the horses the two were mounted on. No saddles, worn marks on the horses shoulders and rumps from wearing pulling harnesses, and heavy tack bridles. They weren't normal riding horses, and he thought they might be stolen. The very reason he had come charging down the ridge at the sight of the two is because poachers and thieves had been stealing and butchering sheep and cattle from their herd.

"Can I ask where you got the horses you are riding now?" he said with a wary stare.

Juan Carlos looked him in the eye and told him the truth, "We have been working for the British railroad engineers for almost two months, taking care of the horses for the repair crews. When we reached Zapala, the engineer told me to take these two horses and kill them." Then he paused, and reached down and stroked the neck of the speckled grey horse he was on, "I wouldn't do it," he said.

The rider thought about it for a moment, and knew at least the man had told him the truth when he could have told a lie. He had basically admitted to stealing the horses, but at least he was honest about why he did it. He turned back to Gisele, "You say you grew up on the Bruce estancia; do you know anything about caring for sheep and cattle?"

She sat up straight in the saddle, "Yes!"

"We might have work for you here. We have two thousand merinos and one hundred head of beef cattle. My brother and I do most of the work, but we had a gaucho who left us last month and it is too much for us now. My father would have to approve of you though," he said. "What are your names?"

"I am Gisele, and this is Juan Carlos," she answered.

The young rider pulled his horse closer and reached out his hand, first to Juan Carlos, then to Giselle and shook them firmly. "My name is Guillaume. Welcome to Estancia Ballofett."

THEY FOLLOWED Guillaume across several ridges and pastures, and picked up a wagon road leading to the main house of the estancia. When they arrived, they tied the grey horses to the corral post and waited a respectful distance from the house, while Guillaume went inside to speak with his father about them.

The house wasn't grand by the standards of some of the foreign landowners in this area, as a few rich Europeans had come and built monuments to their family's wealth and heritage. But it was beautiful, and a bit intimidating to the young couple who had known only the crumbling adobe brick buildings of La Paz, and a canvas tent.

The owner of the estancia was Claude Ballofett. Born in Paris, and brought to live in Patagonia, Argentina as a boy by his father, who was one of the original settlers in this area. He had helped carve this land from a raw wilderness into a place suitable for raising livestock and harvesting timber for construction. He was proud of his French heritage and had returned to France to fight during the first Great War, and spoke Spanish with a strong native French accent. But Patagonia had taken ahold of him. He loved this part of the world more than any other, and chose to raise his own family here.

Claude came out of the house with his son following behind and walked directly at them, stiff and deliberate, as if he were walking in a parade. He made strong eye contact with Juan Carlos first and extended his hand and introduced himself, delivering his full formal name. Juan Carlos responded with simply, "Juan Carlos" as he did not know his last name, or if in fact he had one.

Then Claude Ballofett turned to Gisele, and softened his gaze and smiled. He came another half step closer as he took her hand, and leaned forward and kissed her right cheek as he introduced himself formally to her. It was a gesture of kind civility that crossed the barriers of social class. Claude was a man of kindness, unbound by rigid social etiquette.

"My son tells me you are looking for work. Will you work hard?"

"Yes, señor," Juan Carlos answered.

"He also tells me you took two horses from the British."

"I refused to kill the horses, señor," Juan Carlos answered, and offered nothing more.

"So the horses deserted the British, and chose to come with you then?" he said with a smile. "I don't want to explain to anyone why I hired a horse thief. I have lived here a long time and raised my family here, I have a reputation to maintain."

Claude Ballofett was an astute man, as most men who survive in trench warfare are. The kind of war where men are fighting with bayonets and swords, and hand-to-hand in the mud. It's an awareness of the slightest of movements and sounds that keep men alive. He noticed as he said the word "family" that Gisele had unconsciously brought her hand up to her abdomen for an instant, then pulled it down and held it behind her back. She was hiding something.

"I will try you out for a month to see if you can

handle the work. There is an old cabin near the pasture around the hill, in the forest. You can stay there," he said.

"Thank you, señor!" Juan Carlos said. "I will work very hard for you."

Claude Ballofett turned to Gisele, "I will expect you to work hard as well, señorita. But not so hard that you hurt your child."

She was startled, but simply nodded her head.

GISELE AND JUAN CARLOS followed Guillaume on the trail up through the forests and across a large green pasture, then to the cabin that was built in the trough of two small hills. It was surrounded by apple and pear trees and had a small corral and a barn for horses, and a fire pit for cooking outside. It was made from pine logs, stripped and honed by hand and interlaced and chinked.

It was small for a family, but large for two people; and to Gisele and Juan Carlos it was a castle. They had dreamed of such a place, but never allowed themselves to believe it would come true.

"This was my grandfather's first home," Guillaume said as they walked in the front door. "He built it when he came here in 1898, in-between the two hills for protection from the wind. He planted all of these trees as seedlings. I think you will enjoy it here. Be ready for work early tomorrow; my father will be testing you quickly to see what you are worth."

Then he set down a large woven basket he had carried up from the main house, and tipped his hat as he left.

Giselle walked over to the table and lifted the lid on the basket, then she turned to Juan Carlos and her face was glowing. In the basket were a full loaf of fresh baked bread, two large dried salamis, a large wedge of wonderful smelling goat cheese, and a small decanter of table wine. Don Claude Ballofett was a serious and hard man when it came to protecting his property and his family, but he was also generous.

The old man could see how hard life had been on them. They were thin, and their clothes were nearly rags, and on top of that he had seen clearly that Gisele was expecting a child. Whether they worked hard and stayed on at the estancia, or not, wouldn't stop him from being kind to them right now.

They had done what they set out to do. They made it all the way to Patagonia, and now just as they arrived, nearly broken and hungry, the world rewarded them. Juan Carlos wrapped his arms around Gisele and held her, and for the first time, she cried in his arms. She cried tears of joy.

NEVER KILL AGAIN

One doesn't choose to be a gaucho. It's a life that chooses the man, not the other way around. Juan Carlos gave himself fully to it, and it embraced him. It nurtured the best parts of him, and starved the evil remnants of his life in La Paz. He rose before the sun, and worked until there was no light left to see.

The sheep needed moving to different parts of the estancia every few days, and there were regular dippings and trimmings, separating rams, and shearing. The cattle had to be worked in much the same way, and there were over a dozen working horses that needed feeding and grooming and care.

Then there were fences to be repaired and watering channels to be dug, and many other daily chores. As winter drew near, firewood had to be chopped and split and stacked under the wood barn, enough for six months, and cleaning and building fires added more hours of work every day. And he loved every moment of it.

He loved the mountain air and skies around him so open he could see for twenty miles. He loved working with the animals, especially the horses. The sensation of rolling gently in a saddle and feeling the horse's footfalls as it climbed a rocky trail. Feeling its deep breath between his boots, and a snort and powerful shudder that ran through its body when a fly tickled its nose. He loved bending over to a clear stream and cupping clean water in his hands to drink, and watching the trout sipping mayflies from the surface in the late afternoon.

Sometimes he would sit by the river, looking at the endless volumes of pure water running to the sea, and think about how desperately thirsty he had been sometimes as a boy; drinking water from muddy puddles in the street, or from rusty drain pipes. He loved everything about his new life, and missed nothing from the old.

Gisele helped out with the animals too, until the baby growing inside her wouldn't allow it anymore. So she helped with some of the cleaning and cooking chores in Claude's main house sometimes, and kept the cabin feeling like a real home.

When news came that the annual Puestero was going to be held in Junin de Los Andes, she was ecstatic. Some of her most wonderful memories of her childhood were from the Puestero. When Claude told her they would all be going together to represent the Estancia Ballofett, she was over the moon.

The Puestero is the rendezvous of all the gaucho families that live and work in the remote puestos on all the estancias spread far and wide across the Patagonian countryside. For one week, they come into the small village of Junin de Los Andes to buy supplies and sell artisan crafts that they spent all winter working on. They also buy and sell horses and livestock, and compete in rodeos and horses games; and at the end of the week they hold a grand dance festival.

It's a time when the men can drink and laugh and brag with friends from other estancias; and the women can reconnect with family from all over and catch up on the news they have missed.

Being the generous man he was, Claude gifted Gisele with a beautiful blue dress that had once belonged to his wife, for the event. And he made sure Juan Carlos had a fresh shirt and bombachas that matched the Estancia Ballofett family colors.

For the first few days of the Puestero, Juan Carlos had been too busy worrying about Gisele to enjoy the events. The town atmosphere and large crowds unnerved him, and he didn't want to leave her side for a moment. And he fretted constantly about her delicate condition. He insisted on putting her into the wagon to ride even a few blocks, rather than letting her walk.

"Juan Carlos, I am fine!" she snapped at him finally, while he was hovering around her.

"I am going to sit here in the park and listen to the guitar music. You should go away for a while. Go have a drink with Guillaume," she demanded. Guillaume grabbed him by the shoulder and pulled him down the street towards the cafe where the gauchos always gathered. Juan Carlos turned back to look at Gisele three times with pleading glances, but she refused to look his way.

"She is a Patagonian girl born and bred, Juan Carlos. She doesn't need your protection every second. Come on, let's go have a drink and laugh for a while," Guillaume said.

In the first day or two of the events, the cafe was always a happy place. Men who hadn't seen each other in a year were ready to tell stories and lies, and have some fun. But by the third day, old grudges sometimes came to the surface, and when men with grudges get drunk, things go bad very quickly.

Gauchos are affable men, until one insults another, or insults his horse, or his woman. Then the knives come out. In the very olden days, it didn't stop until someone was dead. But in the new enlightened years, it was 1940 after all, they played by more civilized rules. The fight stopped when first blood was drawn. A winner was declared, no one died, no one went to jail.

The moment Guillaume and Juan Carlos entered the cafe, it started. From across the room came a bellowing curse, directed at Guillaume.

"Bastardo!"

Guillaume turned to the left and saw the tall brutish man in the corner, pointing at him.

"There you are! You stinking French woman!" he yelled.

Three or four drunken men around him laughed, and the rest of the room came to a screeching silence. Guillaume couldn't even remember what the original argument had been about. A horse. A girl. Who knows, it was years ago when it happened, but apparently he was still sore about it.

Calling out Guillaume in public could only go one of two ways. Guillaume could walk away and be branded a coward; a reputation that would follow him for the rest of his life, and tarnish the Ballofett family as well. Or, he could accept the challenge and draw his blade. Guillaume was young, but he was no coward.

He took one step forward, and the crowd scattered to the outer edges of the room, leaving an open circle in the middle. He turned quickly to Juan Carlos, "I am sorry to get you into this Juan Carlos, but I need a second. Will you stand with me?"

"Yes, of course. But...Guillaume, I have promised

Gisele that I would never kill another person," he said.

"You don't have to kill anyone, Juan Carlos. Just don't let him kill me if I fall."

Juan Carlos nodded, then stepped back to the edge of the crowd. Guillaume stood in the center of the room now, and drew a beautiful nickel coated dagger with polished ivory handles. He pulled the bright red poncho that was draped over his left shoulder, and quickly spun it around his left arm.

The tall brute came forward with his drunken cronies following closely behind. He also wrapped his poncho on his arm to defend attacks, and pulled his long puñal style knife with an engraved sterling silver handle. He was an experienced fighter, more experienced than Guillaume, and he was looking forward to spilling his blood.

They inched closer to each other, and the tall man faked a lunge and half-hearted jab with his blade. Guillaume jumped back two steps, and the drunkards laughed. "He is afraid!" they yelled.

Guillaume stepped forward, determined not to retreat again. This time, he lunged and slashed with his knife, but the tall man blocked it with his poncho wrap. Then he shook the poncho loose on his arm, and whipped it around and lashed Guillaume across the face.

Guillaume twisted his head to shield his eyes when the heavy wool came burning across his skin and stung his ears, then the tall man came in fast. He rushed forward and buried the point of the puñal deep into Guillaume's thigh, then gave it a twist and pulled it free to let the blood flow, eliciting a painful scream from Guillaume. Guillaume's wounded leg buckled, he dropped his blade and grabbed his leg with both hands and hobbled to keep from falling.

A well-mannered fight should have ended there, and the crowd started to rush in, but the tall man wasn't done yet. He kicked Guillaume's wounded leg out from under him, sending him to the ground, then stomped on his belly with a hard boot heel, knocking the wind from his lungs in a gush. Then he yelled another insult over the noise of the raging crowd, and bent over and slashed the helpless Guillaume across the chest. His shirt was split open and a deep red stain started spreading immediately in the fabric.

The tall man raised his blade again, then his attack came to a sudden crashing end.

Juan Carlos came flying across the room and smashed his shoulder into the tall man, sending him flying back into the group of drunken friends, who caught him before he hit the ground and stood him back to his feet. He threw his arms out and roared, and his eyes were wild with rage. No one would dare get in the middle of his fight. No one but Juan Carlos.

"The fight is over, you have won. Now let him be!" Juan Carlos said, as he stood over Guillaume.

"It's over when I say it's over! And now my fight is

with you!" he yelled as he came bounding back into the circle.

He slashed at Juan Carlos' face as he came running in, but Juan Carlos drew back like Odysseus' bow, and the silver knife sliced through the vacant air. Then Juan Carlos reached back, and pulled his blade. The old blackened steel that Ramon had stitched to his body from the time he was a boy. The blade that sent Ramon and many others to their graves.

He never wanted to draw this blade against another man ever again, but the violent side of life wasn't done with him yet. Life was determined it seemed, to drag him back into the raging torrent.

He thought of Gisele. He thought of his unborn son. Then the calm focus came over him.

"Look at that piece of shit knife the little boy has in his hands!" the tall man yelled to the crowd. "That wouldn't cut the balls off a sheep!"

And the crowd laughed and pointed at Juan Carlos and his crude knife, as if both were grossly overmatched. Guillaume had dragged himself to the edge of the crowd, and he watched what happened next with astonishment.

The tall man came again, screaming and slashing back and forth with the long shining puñal. Juan Carlos moved at a speed that rendered him nearly invisible. Like a wisp of smoke. A wraith. First he was in close, cutting and slashing across the man's chest and his belly; then suddenly behind him, cutting and striking. He made a dozen strikes on the tall man before he knew what hit him.

Then Juan Carlos dropped low, and swept both of his feet out from under him and sent the big man crashing on his back into the dirty wood floor. It cracked and splintered as his head whacked on the yellow pine planks. Juan Carlos stood over the top of him, staring into his eyes with a lethal calmness.

The tall man's shirt and pants were shredded from slashes and stabs from the crude blackened blade that was as sharp as surgical steel. But he hadn't cut his skin a single time. His skill was so complete, that he bested him without actually hurting him. He had kept his promise to Gisele. The tall man lay on the floor with his ears ringing from the blow to his head against the floor, and fear in his eyes. Someone in the crowd yelled, "There is no blood! The fight isn't over!"

And with the cry for blood, Juan Carlos plunged the blade swiftly downward, and stopped as the tip barely penetrated the flesh, just below the man's left eye. He drew it back an inch, and a teardrop of blood ballooned to the surface through the nearly imperceptible puncture. The tall man emitted a whimper, then fainted and went limp on the floor.

Again the crowd erupted with cheers.

Juan Carlos reached down and pulled Guillaume to his feet, then over to a table in the corner of the room. Guillaume's wounds were slight, and needed only a little whiskey poured into them and a few quick stitches with a needle and gut thread, which elicited another embarrassing squeal.

The cafe had seen a number of fights this week, and the local doctor was on duty and assisted the wounded for the price of a drink. When he saw Juan Carlos striking and slashing his way across the tall man's body, he thought for certain he was witnessing a killing. But his services weren't needed.

After that night, Juan Carlos was no longer the unknown Boliviano who worked for the Ballofetts. He was a living legend among the gauchos.

"Thank you for saving me, Juan Carlos," Guillaume said. "He was going to kill me. I owe you a great debt."

Juan Carlos, in his usual quiet way, merely nodded and smiled. Guillaume had not forgotten the hint of his past that Juan Carlos let slip, about promising to "never kill another person". He decided perhaps repaying his debt should include keeping the young man's past, in his past.

From the moment he first encountered Juan Carlos and Gisele on the hillside as they crossed the river and entered the family land, he had only seen the quiet, hard working side of Juan Carlos. A man who was respectful and caring, and spoke softly to his woman. A man who sat by the river in silent contentment, and seemed to be speaking to God on his own terms. He brushed the dust from the horses in the afternoon, and cared for them as another person might dote on a child.

But Guillaume knew now that there was more to Juan Carlos. There was something fierce in him. Something dark in his past life. And he was trying hard to bury that something away deep in the ground, but it would always be hovering just below the surface, waiting to be unleashed on the world.

The stories about what happened in the cafe would spread fast, but Guillaume downplayed it, for Juan Carlos' sake. He told his father it wasn't as dramatic as everyone said it was. That the tall gaucho, and everyone in the cafe, were too drunk to really see what happened. That kept Claude from being too concerned about the young man living on his property, but there were many in town who knew what they had witnessed, and the stories wouldn't die.

On the long ride back to the estancia the next day, Juan Carlos was feeling the old familiar fear. The fear that his soul may have been forfeited many years ago in La Paz. He had drawn his blade too quickly. Couldn't he have just talked to the tall man instead of going for the knife? True, he didn't kill him, and he felt some satisfaction in keeping his promise. But in the calm, blank moment of the engagement, his instinct was to kill. The dark voice in the back of his mind, Ramon's voice, was whispering to him; telling him to go for the sweet spot.

He hadn't said a word about what happened in

the cafe to Gisele, but a story like that doesn't stay hidden. As they rode slowly along the trail, he turned to her.

"Gisele, I need to tell you about something that happened," he said. "I am afraid it will make things difficult for us here. I am afraid I ..."

"I know about what happened, Juan Carlos," she said, cutting him off. "I am proud of you."

"Proud? I drew my blade on another man. I couldn't stop myself. How could you be proud of me?" he said.

"I am proud of you because you faced danger to save your friend. And not every man would have done that. You are brave, and you are loyal. That's why I am proud of you." They rode on in silence for a minute or two, then she added, "And besides, the way I heard it you could have easily killed the man, but all you did was humiliate him. That man owes you his life. You saved two lives. You have taken a deadly skill and used it to save lives instead of ending them."

She pulled the reins back and stopped her horse, and Juan Carlos stopped his. Then, she looked straight into him with those piercing blue eyes, and smiled, "You have finally beaten him. That Spanish noble bastard. Truly beaten him."

PABLITO

It should have still been cold and wintery in the river valley, but a strong, rare wind from the North came ripping across the high desert mesa and crashed against the Antarctic cold front. It was a *zonda,* the hot wind that appears when no one expects it to, and from a place that no one knows. It just appears. And along with the hot *zonda* came sudden melting snow and rushing rivers, and spring flowers, and bright sunshine, and the birth of Pablo Gonzalez. It was an amazing day on the Estancia Ballofett.

Claude called for two midwives to come for Giscle. Guillaume had insisted since this was the first child to ever be born in the original Ballofett cabin, they should make sure it happened properly. He organized a grand asado in the fire pit in front of the little cabin, and the men gathered day and night outside; eating, cooking, drinking, and taking turns sleeping in rolled blankets in the horse barn. Juan Carlos paced furiously to the cabin and back to the fire pit, until he wore a trench in the ground a foot deep; while inside the cabin Gisele labored.

"How long is this supposed to take?" he said to Guillaume. "Is this normal? Is something wrong?"

"Calm down, Juan Carlos, it is fine. Babies come when they are ready, and not a minute before."

From the time she began her labor it was nearly forty hours to the birth of little Pablo. The sun was just starting to glow on the eastern horizon, the coals in the fire pit were waning and cool, and the men were huddled around in their ponchos and nodding in and out of sleep when the door to the cabin finally opened. A woman in a plain grey dress with her hair wrapped in a white scarf stepped out.

"Juan Carlos, come inside and meet your son," she said.

Juan Carlos, who had been going back and forth to the door all night, was suddenly frozen. Guillaume pushed him forward. "Go! We all want to see him, but you have to be first!" he said.

He walked slowly to the cabin and stepped inside. The midwives had moved Gisele's bed into the living area to have more room to work around her, and she looked up at Juan Carlos, cradling their baby in her arms. She was exhausted, and she could barely speak.

"Come hold your son, Juan Carlos," she said in a wispy voice that was hoarse from childbirth.

He took three quick steps, then hesitated. Then he took one more, and held his arms forward to receive his son. Gisele couldn't sit up, so one of the midwives cradled Pablito and lay him into Juan Carlos' arms. He looked at Gisele, and could see she had reached the limit of her strength. Her eyes had always been piercing and strong, but now she was struggling to keep them open.

"She needs to sleep. Take your son out and introduce him to the world," the midwife said.

He stood motionless for a long time, holding the baby and transfixed by the idea that it was his son. His skin was so pale and soft, and his fingers and features so delicate and tiny. The arms and hands that held him were dark and calloused, and scarred. Juan Carlos thought how ugly his arms and hands looked, holding this little thing of real beauty.

He heard the groaning and loud throat-clearing behind him, and turned to see the faces of all the men crammed into the open doorway. He smiled and walked outside, and they circled around him and stared at the baby. A half dozen rough and calloused hands all reached in to offer a finger to be grabbed, and to touch his little toes. Pablito wrapped his hand around Guillaume's finger and clung to it, and he looked up at Juan Carlos and said, "He is going to be a strong one!"

"Stronger than I am, I hope. And a better man," Juan Carlos whispered to the baby boy.

THE MONTH after Pablito was born, a traveling minister was making his way though the small towns and estancias in northern Patagonia. He came through once or twice a year to help the believers keep their faith and occasionally convert a native to Christianity. He depended largely on the generosity of the wealthy landowners for board and food and travel from one stop to the next. Claude Ballofett, being a devout Christian, had invited him to stay at the estancia for a few days to recuperate from his long journey.

He was a young minister. Pale and thin, but he loved the great expanses of the frontier. He would spend hours walking along the river and sometimes sit and write poetry in a small notebook that he showed to no one. If his superiors found out he was writing poetry rather than spending all of his time preaching and converting, or gathering charitable donations for the church, they would be very harsh.

Juan Carlos was riding along the ridge one afternoon and spotted the young minister sitting in the long grass field above the river. He had been introduced to him two days earlier, so he knew who and what he was, and given his history with the Franciscans he should have been uneasy around him. But instead, he found the young man pleasant and simple. He approached and stepped off his horse.

"Señor, may I join you?" he asked.

"Of course."

Juan Carlos sat in the grass next to him and looked out far across the river, remaining silent for a long time. Then he spoke.

"Señor, can a son be born with the sins of his father?"

He had been thinking about this from the day that Pablito came into the world. Worried, that for all of the things he had done as a young man in La Paz, his son might be damned along with him.

"I don't think God will hold a son responsible for his father's sins, Juan Carlos."

"Even if the father has done terrible things? Things that are unforgivable?" he asked. His head slumped down and he stared at the ground as he waited for an answer.

"Every man answers for his own sins, and he can ask God's forgiveness. Nothing you have done will put your son at risk with God, Juan Carlos. But we can hold a baptism here at the river for your son, and make sure he starts out with a clean slate. Would that make you feel better?" he said.

"And then nothing I do will hurt him?"

"Only what he chooses to do with his own life will matter in the end," the minister said.

TWO DAYS LATER, Gisele and Juan Carlos met the

young minister along the shores of the Limay, and watched as he performed the ritual to cleanse Pablito's soul and present him to God. Juan Carlos felt a great relief when it was done. The burden of his past had never left him. It was a weight that hung high in his chest, and when his mind drifted there, it pulled down and squeezed his heart until it felt like it was going to burst.

His most fearful dream, besides the one he still sometimes had about the woman in the white dress, was that his son might have to carry the same burden. At least now, he thought, Pablito could be his own man.

Had he known at that moment what kind of man Pablito would become, he wouldn't have worried. They never took notice, but the world around them had already recognized their infant son. As they passed through the fields on the way to the river, the swallows came in a large flock and swooped and pivoted in the air to get a closer look at the bundle in Gisele's arms. Three red deer came to the edge of the forest, and followed them at a safe distance, and as the minister waded into the river with the child in his arms, the trout rose and rolled all around him. The natural world saw something familiar in their baby.

A WORLD AT WAR

On the other side of the world in the homelands of many of the Patagonia settlers, Adolf Hitler had been signing treaty after treaty with the British, the Russians, and the French. The ink was hardly dry on each of them before he launched full-scale invasions that violated those treaties. Invading Czechoslovakia after signing the Treaty of Munich; then Poland, Norway and Denmark.

He unleashed the blitzkrieg on Holland and Belgium and reduced Rotterdam to ashes. British soldiers and a small number of remaining French were driven to the sea and pulled from the beaches by private seamen and shipping companies at Dunkirk. About 140,000 French escaped and became the foundation of the Free French army.

Then, Marshall Petain signed an armistice with Hitler, essentially submitting France to German occupation and removing them from the war. But the Free French army, and all of the Frenchmen living abroad would not be easily defeated.

Men of French heritage enlisted in the armies and air forces of Allied nations in droves. Often having to subvert the political allegiances of their new homelands. The sons of French settlers in Patagonia were among them. Using any and all contacts to gain travel visas to the United States and Canada, they defied the ruling Peronist Party in Argentina, which sympathized with Hitler and the Axis powers.

The two young sons of Claude Ballofett, Guillaume and Patrick were desperate to fight. They followed two other young men from the neighboring estancia, Cerro de los Pinos, and joined the Royal Canadian Air Force, making their way first through New York and on to Canada. Claude Ballofett had returned in his youth to fight for France in the first Great War, and he was proud to see his sons honor their heritage. He feared for them, but he knew all young men have a craving for glory, and France needed them, so he supported their desire to answer the call.

The days and months passed agonizingly slow after the boys left for the war. The house was empty and silent and Claude rarely slept well, thinking about his sons. News about the war was scarce and slow to reach the provinces, and as he lost himself in the pit of worry and loneliness, he also lost interest in the day-to-day workings of the estancia.

He sat in the shadowy confines of his study, reading newspapers from London and New York that were months old, over and over again. Finally, he decided to leave the solitude of the mountains to stay with family in Buenos Aires, and be closer to the news that arrived more regularly from the war front. His home and land, sheep and cattle, and his life's work, would be left at the mercy of marauders and thieves and the degradation of the harsh Patagonian seasons.

He had built his home lower on the mountain and closer to the river, using large stones dredged from the Limay and timber harvested from the first pine forests planted by his father. It was a modest house compared to other estancias in the region, but he was a modest man. His office was a small room, barely large enough for the grand mahogany desk he had shipped all the way from Paris, and two small but elegant armchairs of the same wood that sat in front.

He had two, grainy black and white photographs on his desk. One of his wife, Francoise, who had left him almost eight years ago to return to her life in France which she adored, and taken their daughter, Louisa, with her. They wrote to each other on occasion, but he had not received any news of them since the armistice, and had no idea if they were still alive. The other was of his two sons, Patrick and Guillaume, taken on the riverbank as they were fishing one day, by a visiting friend with a German Rolleicord camera.

He was sitting at his desk and packing a few items, including his two photographs into a leather traveling case when Juan Carlos called to him from the open front door.

"Don Claude. I have come as you asked," Juan Carlos said.

"Juan Carlos, please come to my office," he answered.

He scrubbed the bottoms of his boots back and forth on the thick woven coco mat in front of the door, then lifted each up to inspect the bottom before entering the house, because the oak floors were always kept meticulously cleaned and polished. He pulled his boina hat off and walked back to the office door, and waited again to be invited beyond.

"Buen día, señor," he said as he arrived at the office door. He knew that Claude would be leaving this day for Buenos Aires, but he had no idea what that would mean for him and his family. Would the estancia be abandoned? Would he be forced to leave and find another place to live? He didn't know, and the uncertainty was troubling him.

"Hola, Juan Carlos," Claude said with an easy smile. "Please come in and sit with me."

He took two steps into the office and sat carefully down on one of the fine chairs, testing it before fully committing his weight. It appeared so fine and delicate that he was afraid a rough man like himself might break it. He settled, then balanced in the chair with as little movement as he could.

"Juan Carlos, I have a great favor to ask of you, even though I have little right to ask it. I don't know when I might return, nor if my sons will ever return; but my family has been here for many years and worked very hard to build this estancia," he said.

He paused for a moment to look again at the photograph of his sons, then he continued, "You have been with us for a short time, only a little more than a year, but I have sensed from the beginning that you are a young man with honor and courage just like my two boys. Because of that, I am entrusting everything I have here into your hands. I know it is more than one man can handle alone, and I know I am asking you to protect something that doesn't belong to you. I only ask that you do the best you can."

Juan Carlos was shocked by Claude's request. Not so much the magnitude of the request, for one man to take on so much responsibility; but shocked that he trusted *him*, and believed he was honorable.

"Don Claude, I will do everything I can to take care of the estancia; and whatever I must to protect it. I swear it," Juan Carlos said. "But there are things that I don't know how to do, like the auctions for the wool and cattle, and paying for supplies."

"I have hired an administrator from the town to oversee these things. But running the estancia will be completely in your hands." Claude continued, "You know, the small cabin that you and Gisele and little Pablito are living in was built by my father when he first came here and settled this land. He cut the trees with an ax and honed them one by one with a drawknife. He planted all of the fruit trees that surround it. I watched those trees grow and ate fruit from them when I was a boy, and I slept in the same room where little Pablito sleeps now. My family's history here in Patagonia began in that little house. I am very happy that a man like you is living there and raising a family of your own. As long as you do your best for me, you will always have a home here."

WHILE THE VIOLENCE of war raged across Europe, the ripples of war stretched out all over the world, even to the far reach of Patagonia. Shortages in basic supplies were followed by shortages of food. The thieves and poachers made regular raids on estancias that weren't guarded by hardened men. Luckily for Claude Ballofett, he had left a very hard young man in charge of his property.

Gisele was now busy keeping a home and caring for a baby, and Juan Carlos' days became longer and harder than before. In addition to taking on the work normally accomplished by three men, tending to sheep, cattle and horses, and maintaining the estancia;

he also had to protect it. And as the next few years wore on, that became a challenge for every estancia in the province.

Poverty drove many people to the last resort of stealing for a living. Livestock poachers and thieves were swarming in from the North and from across the border in Chile. Moving along many of the new roads the government built in recent years, they could easily travel along the edges of the estancias and kill a wandering cow or sheep when no one was around to see, then move off quickly in carts and wagons on the road.

If a house was left unattended, like Claude's, the thieves would ransack it in an hour and haul off everything worth stealing. There were great distances between homes and estancias, and the odds of getting caught were slim.

The other danger, was from the less scrupulous landowners. There were many old enemies in the valley, including Germans who fought against the French in the first war. They were cordial in town or at an asado, but they hated each other. There were even rumors circulating around Argentina that the Germans were planning to capture all of Patagonia, then use it to annex the rest of Argentina.

The Argentine government at the time, had shown unusual sympathy to the Axis countries and the Nazis, and it stirred the rumor mill. Claude and the other French often called them the *boches*, a rather derogatory term, and both the Frenchmen and the Germans living in the province delighted in showing off war trophies from the First World War. A French infantry helmet with a prominent bullet hole through the center of it, sitting on the fireplace mantle. A German officer's helmet being used as a pot for geraniums on the front terrace. They antagonized each other almost constantly.

When word got out that Claude Ballofett had left for Buenos Aires and his two sons had gone to fight in the war on the side of the Allies, his property became a target.

Juan Carlos patrolled the vast estancia alone all hours of day and night. On occasion, he might catch a man or a few who were trying to steal a cow or a few sheep. Usually a forceful tone and maybe a threat was all that was needed to deter them. His reputation as a fighter and a master with the knife still lingered, and no one was eager to challenge him.

One time he found a small family, a young man and woman, and two small children camped along the river's edge with one of Señor Ballofett's sheep roasting over a fire. He started to drive them off at the point of his blade, but realized very quickly that they were not bad people, they were just starving. The children were thin and frail, and the man looked worse than the children.

He begged Juan Carlos, "Please just let my children eat one good meal, and then we will move on. I won't eat any of it!" he said. Juan Carlos knew that even if Claude was here himself, he would have pity on them.

"You have already killed the sheep, so stay and eat. Let your children fill their bellies and rest a day or two, but then you need to move along."

There were a few other times when the simple warnings weren't enough, and one in particular that caused a small uproar in the community.

He was riding the fence line one day making sure there were no cuts or breaks, and he came down to the front gate of the property at the main route. The gate was open and he could see the fresh tracks of an automobile entering the road and leading up to the main house. He heeled his horse into a full gallop up the road and as he came over the hill the obvious treachery was right in his face.

A long black truck with an oak bed and side rails was backed up to the front door of Claude's house. The front door was hanging out of kilter to the side after being bashed open and off the hinges. And even over the clatter of his horse's hooves pounding forward against the gravel road he could hear the thieves inside the house yelling and laughing and smashing.

As the black gelding locked all fours and skid to a stop in front of the truck, Juan Carlos was flying from the saddle and pulling his blade in midair. He was still being propelled forward by inertia like a supernatural being as two of the thieves came waddling out the open doorway with Claude Ballofett's mahogany desk in their hands, one holding each end.

The lead man was walking forward and carried the front of the desk against his butt as he walked straight ahead. He was short and stout, with sun-parched skin and short black hair, and a typical gaucho's boina hat that had probably once been black but was now faded to a mottled gray color. He was laughing as he passed through the doorway and out onto the porch, likely at something vulgar his partner was saying about the Frenchman who owned this house.

He looked up just in time to see the blur of Juan Carlos' fist as it connected with his left temple, then the lights went out. He hit the ground like a dead man, even though he wasn't dead. Yet. He was fortunate Juan Carlos chose to hit him rather than cut him, or he might have cleanly separated his head from his neck.

The young guy holding the back of the desk was tall, slender, and had the telltale fair complexion and shaggy blond hair of an Aryan. He stood out like a sore thumb in the midst of the dark-tanned workingmen who lived in the saddle. He was quite obviously one of the *boches* that Claude had spoken of with such displeasure. As Juan Carlos would later find out, he was actually the grandson of the instigator of this crime, and the truck belonged to his grandfather.

When the man who was keeping the front of the desk elevated went suddenly to sleep and dropped his end of the desk, the tall blond man folded under the weight of it. He lurched forward, then his skinny white legs buckled, and the desk, which weighed almost as much as the truck they were trying to load it into, pinned him to deck of the front porch. It also cracked his femur and made him howl like a banshee.

After the sound of one body thudding to the ground and the laughter being replaced by howling and crying, a third thief came running from inside the house to the aid of his compatriots. As luck would have it, it was an old acquaintance.

Through the broken doorway stepped the same tall, brutish gaucho that had challenged Guillaume at the Puestero the year before, and ended up at the fainting end of Juan Carlos' blade. He worked for the German neighbors and he had volunteered for this little raid in the hopes of running into Juan Carlos one more time. His defeat at the hands of a smaller man and the crude looking knife had been the ruin of him. His friends abandoned him, and people laughed and snickered in his presence for months after that night. His standing among the gaucho community had been greatly diminished. He wanted with all his heart to kill Juan Carlos.

His patrón's grandson pinned under the mahogany desk was screaming, "Help me! Get it off, get it off!"

But the tall man was locked in a death-stare with Juan Carlos and his pleas fell on total deafness.

"I have been waiting to see you again, and this time I am not drunk," he said as he glowered at Juan Carlos. "I am going to kill you and feed you to the hogs."

"Surrender now, or I will spill more than just a drop of your blood this time," Juan Carlos said in a low voice.

But the tall man wasn't interested in surrendering. He taunted Juan Carlos even further, "I hear you have a pretty woman and a baby out here somewhere. I can't wait to visit her after I put you under," the brute muttered. Then he smiled. Smiled a big, wide, grey-toothed grin just like the smile that Don Miguel de Aragon had made that triggered Ramon's revenge.

Juan Carlos didn't make another sound, like the dog that's done barking and has decided it is time to bite. He felt the calm, blankness set in. The windless eye of the storm. His blade hand came smoothly to the front and his boots found their grip in the dirt. He waited for it.

The tall man pounced forward with a thrust of his familiar old puñal dagger and stomped his boot against the wood planking with a loud "clap", expecting to make Juan Carlos retreat. But the calm wraith stood perfectly still, un-rattled by the false charge. Then he jumped from the porch down to the dirt and feigned left, then right, then came straight ahead slashing and waiving his knife like he was painting a figure eight in the air with a long trailing ribbon.

Juan Carlos stepped left and parried the slash, and their blades clashed and clanged like long slender cymbals. The tall man spun around and slashed again, aiming for Juan Carlos' throat and missed by only the tiniest of margins. But as the blade passed, the tall man's flank was exposed for just an instant, and he paid the price.

Juan Carlos sliced him cleanly between the ribs, not deep enough to kill him, but deep enough to filet open the soft meat that held one rib to the next. The man winced and gritted his teeth from the lightning bolt of pain that shot through him, but before he could spin and slash again, Juan Carlos dropped low and hacked through his Achilles tendon, which collapsed him instantly to the dirt. Then, with the butt of his knife handle in his fist, he cracked him over the top of this head and sent him facedown into the dust.

Again, he had bested him without killing him, albeit with more lasting damage this time. The man should have never mentioned Giselle.

IT CAUSED a great buzz among the people of Junin de Los Andes when the three men came riding into town on the back of a Gendarmerie truck, two in need a serious medical attention, and the third with his face swollen like an over-ripe tomato. After receiving a note from a passing truck driver, the Gendarmerie had arrived at the Estancia Ballofett to find the three tied and bound, and their wounds lightly bandaged. Juan Carlos was working to repair the front door when they arrived, and they didn't seem particularly shocked by the story.

The three men had been drinking liquid courage the evening before their raid, and talking loud enough for others to hear. The Gendarmerie were actually surprised to find them alive, knowing at least a little about who was guarding the place, and they really didn't care to get too deeply involved in the affairs of the gauchos or in the middle of frontier justice. They took a few notes, filed a report, and never came back.

When an old German landowner began asking about what might have happened to his shiny new truck, the one he had leant to his grandson for a "night on the town", no one had seen it. It turned up the next year though, when the Chimehuin River blew out from winter snow melt and washed its carcass up from the deep pool above the single lane bridge and onto the gravel bank.

TOKENS

B ehind a large home in the Palermo district of
Buenos Aires, Claude Ballofett was sitting in a
wooden chair in a small garden, surrounded by high
brick walls that were draped in green English ivy. The
home belonged to his cousin, Guy. The grass was
manicured and the shrubs and flowers cropped, and a
small fountain sat against the wall and the white-
capped sparrows came every morning to splash and
bathe in the cool water.

He sat here every day, reading the latest papers
from New York and London, which were already two
weeks old by the time he received them, scanning for
a mention of the Canadian Royal Air Force
squadrons his sons were assigned to. The papers had
to be smuggled into Argentina, due to the censorship
of information about the war.

Patrick had gone to Bombing School in Quebec,

and was then sent to his Operational Training Unit in Britain. He was assigned as an Air Gunner in a Vickers-Wellington bomber. He sent letters home nearly every week for the first six months, then they came less frequently over the following two years. It had been eight weeks since the last arrived.

Guillaume had been trained to fly a Typhoon fighter. He didn't give many details of his experiences in his letters, but Claude knew that he had been involved in battles in France, Italy, and Malta. He kept in touch with his brother when they could, but they never saw each other after being deployed to different bases.

There was a loud clatter at the front gate of the house and the brass bell rang three times in quick succession. Claude could hear it, but he remained in his chair. The housekeeper walked out along the brick pathway to the gate, and returned in a few moments. She held two Postal Telegrams in her hand.

She looked frightened, as anyone in these times looked if a telegram was delivered to their home. These two were addressed to Sr. Claude Ballofett. She stepped forward and handed them to him, as he remained unflinching in his chair, and she looked down at her feet to avoid looking at his face before she turned and went into the house.

He held the telegrams face down in his lap for an hour. Then he stood, unsure for an instant whether his legs would hold him, and walked into the home and placed them on the table next to the entry. They lay there for the next ten days untouched. He knew what they would tell him, yet he waited for ten more days in the hopes that a letter might come from one of his sons that would give him hope, but none came. In the morning on the eleventh day, he gathered himself and walked to the table and read the first telegram.

Post Office Telegraphs

FROM: WAR OFFICE LONDON

TO: SR. CLAUDE BALLOFETT

WE DEEPLY REGRET TO INFORM YOU THAT LT. PATRICK M. BALLOFETT WAS KILLED IN ACTION 26TH JANUARY, 1944.

LORD MONTFIELD EXPRESSES HIS SYMPATHY.

. . .

SECRETARY WAR OFFICE

HE DREW A DEEP, slow breath and braced himself to read the next telegram. His hand trembled as he shuffled the bottom paper to the top. The second telegram read nearly as the first, save for the name and date assigned to Guillaume's disappearance after his fighter plane had been shot from the sky by German forces.

Post Office Telegraphs

FROM: WAR OFFICE LONDON

TO: SR. CLAUDE BALLOFETT

WE DEEPLY REGRET TO INFORM YOU THAT 2ND LT. JEAN GUILLAUME BALLOFETT WAS REPORTED MISSING IN ACTION AND PRESUMED DEAD 4TH FEBRUARY, 1944.

LORD MONTFIELD EXPRESSES HIS SYMPATHY.

. . .

SECRETARY WAR OFFICE

CLAUDE LAY the telegrams back on the table, then slowly sank to his knees on the dark oak floors.

ON THE 15TH of May in 1945, one week after the Allies accepted the unconditional surrender of the German forces in Europe, Claude Ballofett arrived at his estancia on the banks of the Limay River. It had taken six days, in a combination of trains and bouncing automobiles, to cross the country and reach the Andes Mountains. He carried two small boxes with him, one for each of his two sons.

He had clung to a small hope for the first few years of the war that they would both return. Return to the estancia they loved so much; marry fine young women from prominent French families; and raise their own children, his grandchildren, here in Patagonia. But it was not to be.

The boxes contained only small trinkets and items from the boys' childhood days growing up on the estancia. A small wood carving of a horse and a little yellow handled pocket knife; a few brilliantly colored river stones, pulled and polished from the Limay; an ancient arrowhead found on a high mountain trail, and the desiccated shell of a beautiful green beetle bug. Things that boys pick up and store in their pockets for adults to find. The boxes were all that Claude had to place in the earth on a special part of the estancia, and say his final farewell.

When he arrived at the large wooden gate off Ruta 40 that marked the entrance to his property, he fully expected to find it destroyed. Chopped down for firewood perhaps, or merely out of spite by one of the angry *boches* who lived in neighboring properties. Instead, he found it standing straight and clean and the gate firmly latched as it had always been.

The road up to the main house had grown grass, as no vehicle or wagons had passed over it in the years, but there was a neatly worn horse trail in one lane of the two-lane path. As he passed the first line of pine trees planted for wind-breaks and dropped into the shallow valley looking out over the river, he rejoiced at seeing his giant flock of merino sheep grazing their way slowly up the eastern slope. And when he came over the rise, his house stood before him with the afternoon sun making the logs glow with a burnished-orange cast, and horses gathered in the front lawn. It was like nothing had changed since the day he left for Buenos Aires.

He could see a faint white smoke floating up from the stone chimney, and a lamp glowing in the window by the front door. As he approached, the door opened and Juan Carlos stepped out to greet him.

"Señor! Welcome home!" he said. "A telegraph

came to the office in San Martin de Los Andes that told us you were coming home. Gisele said we should come and build a fire to warm the house for you, as the cold and rain have started early this year."

He reached out his hand and grabbed Claude's, and Claude Ballofett threw both arms around him and hugged him like he was family. Little Pablito came running out and slid to a stop in front of the old man. He had heard stories about the kind man who owned this land, but never expected to see him; and this grand estancia that he was growing up on didn't feel like it was owned by anyone, but more like he and his family belonged to it.

Gisele stepped out onto the front porch carrying a baby wrapped in a merino wool blanket, and she smiled and beckoned Don Claude into his home. Claude leaned forward and kissed Gisele on her right cheek, and with only his finger he gently pulled back the edge of the blanket to reveal the face of the sleeping baby.

"Our family at the estancia is growing!" he said. Then he turned and smiled at Juan Carlos. "What is your new son's name?"

"Carlos. After his father," Gisele answered. "But we call him Carlito."

He entered the house and found it warm and comfortable, just as he had remembered it these years he had been away. Gisele had cooked a small hen with some potatoes just for Claude, and she served him dinner at the large table while Juan Carlos sat by the fireplace and held the baby, and Pablito laid out across the thick rug and fell asleep. After finishing his meal, Claude sat in the large leather chair and asked about the past four years.

"I imagined that I might come home to ruins and rubble, Juan Carlos. It wasn't that I doubted you; but I have heard stories of others here whose homes and businesses were destroyed by poachers and thieves. How did you manage this by yourself?" he asked.

Juan Carlos stared into the stone fireplace and reflected before he answered. "Don Claude, no man was ever more kind and generous to us than you have been. You gave me an honest job. You gave us a home to raise our family. I just did what a man must do to repay a debt of honor," he said. "You may hear stories about me, about things I did to guard your property. All I can say, is that they were necessary." He offered no other explanation, and Claude nodded his head with understanding.

"I will ask one more favor of you. Tomorrow I would like to take these boxes to the meadow by the river, and bury them," he said, as he reached over to the table and lay his land on one box, then the other. "This is all I have left of Patrick and Guillaume. Will you please come with me?"

During his journey from Buenos Aires he had thought of having a great gathering of his old friends and neighbors for a proper funeral for his boys. But as he sat in his house, with Juan Carlos and Gisele, he realized he wanted only a peaceful, quiet goodbye.

"Of course, señor," Juan Carlos said.

The following day, Juan Carlos, Gisele, Pablito and Carlito all joined Claude as he walked the long path down the hill and through the forest until it opened into the grassy meadow that overlooked the river. Juan Carlos dug two deep holes in the rich dark soil where Claude chose, and they placed the boxes in and covered them. Claude had intended to say many things as he buried the small tokens of his sons, but the only thing he said was, "I miss you both. But I will be with you again someday." Then he turned and they began the long walk home.

FACÓN

On the day they buried the two small boxes in the meadow, as they walked together along the trail to the house, Claude took notice of Juan Carlos' worn clothes. They had been stitched and sewn and patched with stray cloth over and over again during the last four years to keep them together. His boots had strips of rawhide stuffed in the soles because they had worn through, and calf gut stretched and tied over the shredded toes.

And besides his clothing, Juan Carlos' body reflected hard wear. He was thinner than when he had seen him last, and his hands were thick and fingers swollen from never ending labor with tools and animals and wire fences. The evidence of hardship and sacrifice was everywhere he looked.

And yet, Claude's home was as he left it. The garden was kept clear of weeds and vines, the wood was sanded and lacquered, and the rich-grained oak floors were clean and polished. He had nearly as many cattle as the day he left, twenty head of sheep more, and sixteen nicely broken horses in the front pasture. Juan Carlos had taken his charge to heart.

Then, for some unknown reason, Claude became fixated on Juan Carlos' knife. The same old blade he had been given by Ramon Lasso de la Vega as a boy, tucked into the brown leather sheath in the small of his back. It was a blackened, crusty looking knife with a plain wood handle. Unlike the pedigreed dagger carried by Ramon, it was common and crude. It had probably started its life out as a kitchen tool for carving or some other mundane function. But even the common can have a purpose. This knife had at its core the soul of a killing blade, and it was well "blooded".

The meager salary Claude carried in his pocket for Juan Carlos suddenly felt incomplete. He would appreciate it, and he asked for nothing more, but something more was necessary in this case. Something for a true gaucho, he thought. A blade worthy of a worthy man.

THE GAUCHOS of Argentina carried many different types of knives. Some served only a very utilitarian purpose in the field each day, and others were used both in the field and as a defensive weapon. The oldest and most elegant type of knife was the facón. It was long and slender, and usually had an edge on only one side. In the earliest days, they were fabricated from the steel of the finest swords and sabers that found their way from Europe to South America.

There were many laws that prohibited men from wearing swords, so they cut the best weapons down to a size that could be carried more easily or even concealed. But fine swords were rarely available anymore, and most of the knives were now made from whatever scrap steel left over from the war could be found and reforged. Claude had in mind to reward Juan Carlos with something special.

In the corner of his office, was a long cypress chest. Golden colored wood with black shadows, copper fitted edging and latching, and a once brilliant brass lock, which was now a pleasant green from the effects of air and age. Claude took the small iron key from the top drawer of his desk, knelt down in front of the chest and put the key into the slot and twisted and jiggled it until it popped open. He lifted the lid and the hinges whined lightly from having been closed for many, many years.

On the very top of the things piled in the chest was a uniform, folded neatly and pressed. It was thick heavy wool with decorative brass buttons that were now almost brown with patina, but hidden away in the cypress chest, the uniform had held its beautiful celeste blue color. He pulled it out and laid it on the floor next to him. What he was looking for was much deeper in the chest.

He pulled out a shiny black military belt with a French Lebel revolver; and a box that held numerous ribbons. All of the things he brought home after his service as an officer in the French Army in the first Great War. And in the bottom of the chest he found what he wanted. A long slender object wound snugly in a light grey cloth. He lifted it out with both hands and laid it across his lap, then carefully unrolled the cloth to reveal a long, straight sword.

It was a French infantry officer's sword tucked in a steel dress scabbard, made in Klingenthal, France, the famous "Valley of the Blades". He drew the sword from the scabbard with his right hand and held it out in front of him, pointing towards the light that emanated from the window, and peered down the length of it. It was still as straight and true as the day it came to his hands. The blade was long and stiff, and formed a neat point at the tip. It had a unique oval shaped cross section and less of a taper than normal, which made the blade even more stiff, and perfect for what he had in mind. The upper part of the blade was ornately engraved, as was the nickel hilt, and the black handle was carved from African buffalo horn and wound with silver wire.

Claude had often anticipated that his sons would someday want to hang his sword in a place where they could admire it, and tell stories about their father to their children. But now there would be no one to ever admire this sword after he was gone. What better way to find a new life for the sword, and to honor a man who had taken up the shield of his sons on this grand estancia, than to forge it into a beautiful facón, as the old blade masters once did, and present it to Juan Carlos.

Claude took the sword to the shop of a Portuguese blade smith in Junin de Los Andes, and commissioned him to make a proper facón, and a matching black leather sheath with elegant silver trim. Through the winter months, he worked to properly cut and trim the blade and hone a razor's edge, and another artisan worked to finish the engraving and silver work.

As the first warm days of spring arrived, and the lupin flowers along the river bank bloomed in brilliant purples, pinks and blues, Claude sent word to his most important friends and neighbors; he would be hosting a grand asado. On the day of the feast, Juan Carlos thought his patrón might be angry with him, because he wouldn't allow him to do any of the cooking or butchering or serving his guests. He asked that Juan Carlos and Giscle be there for the event, but then he hired others to do all of the work.

A large fire pit was dug and ten goats, one steer, and hundreds of pounds of chorizo and sausages were slowly roasted. A wagonload of fresh vegetables, fruits, and exotic cheeses made by the immigrant

Swiss families was delivered all the way from San Carlos de Bariloche. There were so many important guests in attendance that two more long tables and benches had to be made. Claude's cousin from the wine region in Mendoza arrived by train with twenty cases of expensive Malbec and Pinot Noir. While all of the unloading, table setting, cooking and preparation were buzzing around them, Juan Carlos and Gisele watched nervously from the sidelines, not being allowed to work at all.

As the time came to ask everyone to take their places at the tables, Claude called to Juan Carlos, "Juan Carlos, you and Gisele will sit here," he said, as he pointed to the two seats reserved to the right of him, at the head of the table.

They were stunned. Never had gauchos or employees of an estancia been asked to sit at the table with guests, and at the head of the table was unthinkable. "Señor?" Juan Carlos asked with a frightened look on his face.

Claude smiled and nodded, "Juan Carlos, you are the honored guest. This asado is for you."

When all of the guests had taken their seats and were chattering and nibbling on the *picadas*, Claude stood and called for their attention, lightly ringing a crystal glass with the back edge of his dinner knife.

"My friends, thank you so much for coming. I am hosting this asado to repay in small part, a great debt. When the war ended, I returned to Patagonia as a man without sons, and I feared, without a home or property still waiting for me. But what I found was that everything I worked my entire life to build, had been selflessly protected by one single man. Everything you see around you here, I owe to him," he said, as he turned to Juan Carlos and presented him to the guests. Then he continued, "As a small down payment on my debt, I offer this coin."

He opened the wooden box that sat in front of him on the table, pulled out the elegant facón and held it for the crowd to see. Then turned and offered it to Juan Carlos, as he bowed ever so slightly. Juan Carlos was speechless. His hands trembled as he reached forward and accepted the blade.

He had never seen anything like it in his lifetime. He held the scabbard in his left hand, gripped the black buffalo handle with his right and slowly drew the long blade out. The crowd at the table cooed at the sight of the steel glinting in the sunlight. He noticed an inscription on the blade, which was in French, but even in Spanish he couldn't have read it, because Juan Carlos had never learned to read.

He turned and held the blade for Giselle to see, and she marveled at it, but she shook her head and said, "I can't read French."

"Don Claude, what does this say?" he asked with an embarrassed smile.

"It says, 'Avec Gratitude Infinie.' With Infinite Gratitude," Claude answered.

The crowd of affluent men and women at the tables all stood and cheered for Juan Carlos, and he felt as if his heart was going to burst. Never in his life had so many people looked at him. Looked at him with admiration for doing something good for another man.

THE BLACK HANDLED facón became the symbol of Juan Carlos' transformation as a man. A man who honorably protected the home and lands of another who could not protect them himself. The facón signified Juan Carlos as a true gaucho. He would wear it everyday for the rest of his life. And now he had only one small bit of business left to deal with.

He set off early the next morning on horseback. He rode for an hour on the upper mountain trail that lead to the high summer pasture, but he split off from the trail before reaching the top. He tied his horse, then trekked on foot for another hour, to a lake that was nestled into the saddle of the mountain. A bottomless dark pool of water that was dead. No fish, no life, utterly dead. The local natives said the lake was full of evil spirits, because nothing could live in the water, and no one knew how deep it really was. It might go all the way to the pit of hell.

For all these years, and even for the past few when his life was better and he found a worthy purpose, he had still carried with him the old crude blade of

Ramon. That miserable instrument of death. It was the final layer. A constant reminder of every foul thing he had ever done in his life; in his old life.

But now his life was different. He was different. He stood on a cliff that looked down on the great black hole in the earth, pulled the old blade from his pack, and without a second of hesitation or thought, threw it out as far as he could. He watched it spin through the air, then plummet down into the lake and shatter the mirrored surface. Then it sank, and was gone forever.

A GAUCHO IS BORN

Pablito came running into the cabin, "Mama, the black horse is sick! She won't get up from her bed!"

Gisele was cleaning up the breakfast plates and Juan Carlos was sitting at the table, lightly polishing the edge of his field knife across a fine flat stone. They looked at each other and smiled. It was a little early in the season, but they knew she would foal before the last snow came.

"Juan Carlos, take your son outside to see the miracle. I will wrap up Carlito and be along in a bit," she said.

Juan Carlos stood and tucked the knife into his belt and went out the door with Pablito dragging him by the hand. He didn't understand what was happening, but he was about to see the greatest miracle of all. The birth of a living creature.

They had been keeping the big black mare in the stall for a few days now, because she had been showing signs of it coming. She had been restless, and sweating even though the mountain air was still cool, and just yesterday Gisele had noticed her teats beginning to fill.

They walked out to the stall and Juan Carlos turned a wooden bucket over and made Pablito sit where he could see everything that was about to happen. The mare stood up once, then lay back down. Then stood a second time for just a minute, and lay down again. As she laid on her side in the thick straw bed, a great rushing of water came from her, and Pablito jumped up from the stool, "Papi!" he yelled, startled by what he saw. He was frightened and thought the big black mare was dying.

"It's ok, Pablito. She is going to be fine. Sit back down and watch," he said.

Juan Carlos went to the mare and gently pulled her tail up and wrapped it in a cloth to keep the hair from tangling in the birth fluid. Then he went over and kneeled down by Pablito to watch with him. The mare started lifting her head and straining as if she were pulling a heavy weight, and the third time she raised her head and clenched her huge body, two tiny hooves appeared from the back of her. A moment later the little hooves came sliding a bit farther out with the face of a beautiful grey foal tucked between them, and covered in a milky white fluid. Then at once the entire little horse came sliding out into the straw.

Pablito's eyes were as wide as dinner plates, and his mouth agape. He wanted to run over and throw his arms around the baby horse, but Juan Carlos made him stay perched on the stool. Gisele came a moment later with the baby in her arms, and smiled at the sight of the new foal. Pablito was still too stunned to speak.

They watched over the next hour as the mare nuzzled and nurtured the baby, and watched it wobble and stagger onto its thin legs for the first time. Gisele leaned over to Pablito and said, "A horse's spirit is in its legs. They show the world who they are going to be with the first step. She's going to be a powerful horse, just like her mother."

The next morning Juan Carlos was up early, as the faint glow of sunrise came through the pines. He pulled his jacket on and walked out to check on the new foal, and as he approached he could see the mare standing guard over the top of not just the baby, but Pablito curled up with the foal in the warm straw bed. He knew in that instant that his son was born to be a gaucho. A man of the horse and land. He let him stay where he lay peacefully asleep, and went back to the cabin.

"Did Pablito go out with you? He is not in his bed," Gisele asked as he came in the door.

"He is in his bed. He has just decided that his bed is now out in the stall with his baby horse."

IN DECEMBER, after the lupins had bloomed, the time came to take the horses up to the high mountain summer pasture where the grasses grew thick and green and the horses were shielded from the high winds and rain that came through the low valley. The foals would be fat and strong after three months on the mountain.

Pablito was fretting about his little grey foal going up to the pasture with the herd, and being completely out of his sight and helpless. Juan Carlos thought he was big enough now, being seven years old, to join him for the trip up the mountain with the horses. It would be good for him to learn the way and see the pasture, and he was already an accomplished rider.

The morning of the roundup, they were sitting at the breakfast table while Gisele prepared coffee and toast, and a meal to take with them. Juan Carlos, as he did every morning, was insuring the edge on his beautiful black handled facón was sharpened to perfection. Pablito sat across from him with his arms folded across the table, and his chin resting on his arms, watching intently.

"Papi, when will I be able to have a knife of my own? A real gaucho needs a knife," he said.

"You are right, every real gaucho needs a knife. Let's see how well you do today on the roundup, and then we will talk about getting you one, if your mother says it's ok."

Pablito sat up and spun around to look at his mother to gauge her reception to the idea.

"Maybe," she said. "But you know a gaucho has to do what's best for his horse. Even if that means leaving her alone with other horses. Can you do that?" she asked.

His face grew solemn at the thought of having to leave his little grey baby horse up in the mountain pasture, but he really wanted a knife. He nodded his head.

Pablito had been riding for almost three years by now, and he didn't need or want any help from his father, except to put the bridle on his horse, because he wasn't tall enough to reach the horse's head; and to synch the saddle because he wasn't yet strong enough to do it. But he grabbed the reins as they hung to the ground and led his horse, the old chestnut colored gelding, over to a tree stump. He climbed onto the stump, pulled the gelding smartly around close to it, then stepped into the stirrup with his tiny left boot and swung himself up onto the sheepskin saddle.

Once in the saddle, Pablito suddenly ceased to be a seven-year-old boy. He took on the serious gaze of a man. The gelding reacted instantly to his slightest direction and touch. He pulled the reins low and rearward and the horse back-stepped away from the stump. Then he wheeled him to the left a quarter turn, then back to the right; and gave him a heel and leaned forward into a loping gallop down the trail.

Juan Carlos' face lit up, and he turned to Gisele who was coming out the front door with their lunch pack. "Your son was born a gaucho!" he laughed.

She smiled and handed him the canvas pack with the food. "Be careful up there today. I will have dinner waiting for you."

He leaned over from the horse's back and kissed her, then held her face gently with his calloused hand. His hand was rough and the skin around the knuckles was dry and cracked, but it felt warm and tender. Giselle remembered her father touching her small face like that when she was a girl. He held her face for just a moment more to look into her eyes. The rich blue warmth of her eyes could carry him through the cloudiest day.

By the time Juan Carlos rode the short distance from the cabin down the trail through the pine forest and into the main pasture on the hill, little Pablito had all eighteen of the working horses, and a grey burro with a black stripe on his back, gathered and ready to move. Father took the lead down the trail and son picked up the rear, and the horses obediently herded in single file on the narrow trail. They knew where they were going, and they didn't protest.

The trail wound through pine and poplar forests,

planted by Don Claude and his father before him as part of a government program for the first settlers. Then it opened into a forest of the aboriginal Araucaria trees, covered with hard spiny scales like a snake, and some standing over two hundred feet in the air. Their trunks weren't usable for construction, but they were beautiful relics of a prehistoric world. Some had probably stood watch over this valley for a thousand years or more, so they were left alone.

When the forest ended, the trail led down through thorny brush and wild cane, and the pink flowered *Rosa Mosquesta*, the rose hip plants turned loose on the countryside by the Germans. The oils from the plant were a miracle for the delicate skin of European women, but the thorny plant made life a misery for the sheep, cattle and horses.

They reached the rocky shoreline of the Limay and turned east to travel to the wide vado for crossing. The spring water was running fast, and even in the shallowest place it could be dangerous. As they reached the vado, Juan Carlos told Pablito to take the lead across, and reminded him how to lie back across his horse in the deep water, letting him swim freely when he couldn't touch bottom, and hang on to the saddle loop. Juan Carlos would follow from behind, just in case something happened.

As fearless as his father, Pablito lined his horse up to the opposite shore and tapped him into the flowing river, splashing and clacking hooves against the stone bottom until the deep water drowned out the thumping sounds. The rest of the herd hesitated for a moment, then followed quickly into the river in a charge. They emerged on the other side a minute later, Pablito soaked from floating in the freezing water behind his horse, but laughing with excitement. He had passed his first test.

They crossed the gravel road where the motorcars traveled, then took the steep mountain trail up the ridge for another two hours to the summer pasture. The thorny scrub and rosa mosqueta that covered the dry south facing slopes, gave way to a hidden garden at the very top. A flat, rich pasture left behind by the shifting tectonic plates of another era.

Completely shielded from the western winds and storms from the Pacific Ocean by jagged basalt cliffs, it looked like a grand polo field in the middle of a natural coliseum. The storm winds broke themselves against the rock face, then deposited their moisture over the top onto the pasture, and the grass grew thick and sweet.

The horses were weary from the climb, but they knew the place well and loved it. They snorted and danced as they came over the ledge, and raced out into the field. A few flopped on their sides and rolled in the soft wet grass like overgrown dogs. Pablito watched his little grey foal running wide circles around her mother and leaping and kicking her hooves in the air. He knew his horse would be happy here for the next few months, and when he came back to get her she would be twice as big and strong.

Juan Carlos pulled the canvas pack from his saddle and some dried tinder he picked up along the trail, and built a fire in the pit near the ledge. It was a place that had been used for decades by many gauchos to camp and cook, and sip mate. He heated some water in a small blackened tin pot, and poured it into a gourd filled with ground maté herbs and let it seep for a minute before offering the first sip to his son.

He handed the gourd to Pablito, then pulled some bread from the pack and broke a corner piece off the loaf, and brought it to his nose and breathed deeply. He was content now, and hadn't felt the pangs of starvation for many, many years. But still, sometimes when the aroma of fresh warm bread grabbed his senses he had visions of sitting on the cobblestone by the Franciscan mission. The visions never lasted, but he would never forget.

The two gauchos sat in silence, enjoying the bread and maté and having their own quiet conversations with the world; father in the past, and son in the present. Pablito looked out over the green river valley and felt the rhythm of the world speaking to him.

Where most men look and see trees, rivers, and sky; Pablito saw the world in a different spectrum. The river teemed with living things that never slept. The trees danced and whispered in the wind, and all of the creatures that flew and crawled lived among them. And the sky was the most magical place of all. The sky could tell him how the world was feeling and what it was going to do next. The colors, the clouds, the storms, the sun and the moon, and the birds all carried the messages of God. But only children, and a chosen few, can speak the language.

They finished their simple meal and lay back in the warm sun, then pulled their hats over their eyes for a siesta before making the long ride home. When they were ready to go, Pablito walked into the pasture and called his little grey foal with a whistle and lip-smacking sound that she knew was meant for her. She danced over to him, her very best human friend, and he put his arms around her neck and whispered in her ear. Then he patted her rump and she went off across the grass in a trot. He pulled the gelding around to a big rock that he could stand on, again asking no help from his father, and climbed aboard. It was nearly dark when they arrived at the cabin.

"I will take care of the horses, and you go in and tell your mother about your day," Juan Carlos said.

Pablito came into the cabin jabbering, and never stopped through dinner. He told his mother about the beautiful pasture on the mountain, and about his brave river crossing, and his little grey foal racing around. And within minutes of finishing his supper his head was down on the table and his eyes closed. Juan Carlos picked him up and carried him to his bed, and Gisele gently pulled his boots and clothes off and tucked him beneath the covers.

When he woke the next morning he heard the familiar sounds of his mother in the kitchen and his father stroking a steel blade across a wet stone. He staggered sleepily in and sat at the table. Juan Carlos was just finishing with his small field knife, and he wiped it dry and held it to the candlelight, and examined the edge.

It was on the small side for a gaucho's knife, having a blade of only about five inches long, but it had an interesting shape, with a deep belly that tapered up to a fine point. It was thicker than a small kitchen knife, and strong, so it could be used for cutting rope and carving fittings into posts or prying out bent nails, or even digging stones out of a horse's hoof in an emergency. The blade was almost black with age but the edge glistened and it kept its sharpness well. The wood handle had been repaired with a small band of copper wire, but it was sturdy.

Juan Carlos licked the hair on the back of his forearm, and drew the blade across the skin and cleanly shaved a small patch of the hair on his arm with one light sweep. Satisfied that it was sharp enough, he wiped it clean again and pushed it back into the leather sheath, then reached across the table and placed it in front of Pablito.

"You have proven that you are a real gaucho, and

every gaucho needs a knife. This is a good one," he said.

The boy smiled, but he didn't say anything. There was nothing to say that his father didn't already know; and that was the gaucho way.

THE WHITE HOUSE

Four more years had passed. Easy, simple, peaceful years. Years of work, and growing and learning for Pablito and little Carlos (Carlito); and good years for the estancia, although Claude was growing lonely living in the main house all by himself. He missed his sons, and he enjoyed watching the two little ones playing and roaming the ranch, just as his sons did years ago, but it made him sad sometimes. Then one day, he received a wonderful letter.

His daughter, Louisa, sent word that she and her mother were safe, and living once again in Paris. They didn't have the same lifestyle as before, given that her mother's family fortune was devastated during the war, but they were surviving. Claude, being the generous man he was, offered to send them what he could to make their lives easier, and only hoped in return that Louisa would come to spend some time with him at the estancia in Patagonia. He hadn't seen her since she was little, and missed her terribly.

Louisa communicated regularly over the next year, thanking her father for the money he sent, and telling him that she would indeed come back to Patagonia and spend time there with him in the near future, and possibly spend every summer there in the warm South American climate. She could also visit his family in Buenos Aires, which was much like Paris in terms of society life and fashion.

Claude was like a man reborn.

"My daughter is coming home!" he said to Juan Carlos. "I can't wait to have her back in my arms. But, she isn't a little girl anymore. Do you think she will be happy living in my home with me, or perhaps I should build something special, just for her?"

With that thought, Claude set about designing and building a home, just for Louisa, and he knew the perfect place. On the edge of the front pasture, high on the hill, not far from his parents' original cabin where Juan Carlos and Gisele lived now. There was a forest in between so it would still be private, but Gisele could help keep the house for his daughter, which was essential because his daughter had grown up in the midst of the Parisian upper class, and she would never clean her own home. The mountain rose up behind for protection from the winds, and it had a beautiful view of the valley and the mountains on the other side where she could watch the condors soaring in the late afternoons.

He would build it in a style like the cottages of Andalusia in southern Spain, which he remembered Louisa had always admired. She and her mother had traveled many times to Granada and Seville and always commented on the beautiful white cottages in the dry part of southern Spain.

It would have riverstone walls with a white plaster covering, and he would import the best scalloped clay tiles for the roof to make it perfectly authentic. It would have a grand stone fireplace on the west wall with a hearth carved from deep red quebracho wood, and tall ceilings. The front windows would look out over the green pasture and he would place a window in the bedroom on the eastern wall so the early morning light would wake her gently every morning. He knew she would never want to leave once she had seen it.

He found a work crew in Junin de Los Andes to build the house and they worked for nearly a year, hauling the materials up by wagon and working during the week, then returning to their families for the weekends. The house was nearly finished going into the Autumn, and the work crew was tired, but they were determined to be done before the rains started.

Gisele's workload nearly doubled during the construction of the white house, because she was often cooking food and bread and going back and forth from the cabin to see that they were working and had everything they needed.

During the final week, two of the men came back from town sick. They should have stayed home, but they needed the pay and they needed to finish the house in order to get paid. Gisele came with food and maté everyday during that last week, and by the time they left, she was showing signs of being sick as well.

It started faintly, almost gently, as a tickle in her throat. Then the tickle became a cough, and the cough became a fever. In three days, she couldn't leave the bed. The only doctor who lived in nearby Junin had been called away to the South to deal with an outbreak of small pox, so Claude called for one of the local *curanderas,* women who practiced healing for the country folk. They had a very good reputation among the gaucho community, and were often more respected than the doctors. She came to the cabin and put cold rags all over Gisele's body, and smeared a poultice made from herbs across her chest, but three more days passed with little change.

In midst of her illness, the time had arrived to retrieve the horses from the high summer pasture. Juan Carlos wasn't one to ignore his duties, but he couldn't bare the thought of leaving Gisele. He was sitting in a chair beside the bed, holding Gisele's hand and dampening her neck and shoulders with a cool wet rag.

"I can do it, Papi. I can get the horses," Pablito said. He was just an eleven-year-old boy, but in almost every way on horseback he was a full-fledged gaucho, and his father knew it. "Let me go, Papi. I will leave early with the sun, and be back before the moon sets. I can do this."

Juan Carlos turned and looked his son in the eyes, and nodded yes. Eleven was old enough to start taking on greater responsibilities in the life of a gaucho, and Pablito had proven he could be trusted with the horses.

Pablito slept only a few hours that night, and was in the saddle the next morning before the orange glow crept over the eastern plains, aboard his big grey horse. He had watched her come into the world and cradled her, slept with her, and played with her; and now she had grown into his most faithful companion on the trail.

He wrapped a few pieces of bread and a late green apple in a cloth and stuffed it into his canvas saddlebag, pulled his wool poncho over his head and tucked his knife tightly into his waistband. Then he climbed on top of the old tree stump, because as his grey horse grew tall his legs had not and he still needed the stump to reach the stirrup, and he climbed in the saddle and rode off on his first solo trial.

They moved down the path through the forest in pitch darkness, reaching the river in the morning light. A long swim, and two more hours up the steep mountain face brought them to the high pasture after midday. All of the horses and yearling foals were there and healthy, but it took some time to round them all up, as they hadn't seen a human in several months and were a little skittish. He had to catch the lead mare with a lasso, knowing the rest would follow her, and then gather them together.

By the time that was done, Pablito and the big grey were exhausted and needed a rest before they could start the long trip down the dangerous rocky trail and back across the river. He started a small fire and made yerba mate tea, then rolled himself into his poncho on the ground and went to sleep.

PABLITO WOKE WITH A START. The big grey had pushed him with her muzzle to stir him from sleep. He didn't know where he was for an instant, he had been having a deep, dark dream. A dream that left him feeling dreadful. He was shivering like he was naked in a freezing rain, but his skin was scorching hot, and beads of sweat were bubbling to the surface. He couldn't remember any details of the dream, only sounds and colors. He could hear the echoes of wailing and a rhythmic, high-pitched tone that clawed into his head like a rusty nail being drug across a blackboard. He saw pulsing flashes of silver light that blinded him, followed by purples and reds, and a bottomless black canvas.

He jumped to his feet and looked out over the ledge of the pasture and down into the valley. He looked for signs in the river and the forest, but nothing spoke to him. Then he saw something he had never seen before, something that drove a tremor down through the core of him.

In the western sky, hovering above the mountains, the waning moon was burning like fire. Red and orange mirage waves rippled across the face of it as it neared the jagged peaks. And as it was about to fall below the Andes, a giant swarm rose up from the cliffs. A *scarcity of condors*, in numbers he had never seen before, swirling in front with the moon's blood red face looming behind.

The sky was telling him something terrible. As the moon fell below the horizon, the color faded and the great black swarm vanished, but behind them a darkness was swelling over the Pacific. Billowing storm clouds, rolling and boiling and gathering energy for a surge over the Andes.

Pablito swung up fast onto the big grey, gathered the herd and pushed down the mountain towards home. He kept the pace slow but steady going down the steep section from the pasture, as that was the most treacherous part of the trail. One slip could mean a terrible tumble for horse and rider, and almost certain death.

The sounds of the dream in his head and the coming storm on the horizon gnawed at him, and his attention darted back and forth from the narrow trail to the western sky. He was nearly at the last turn of the trail when he made his mistake.

His head was twisted to the right and he was eye-locked on the storm over the mountains, watching the flashes of lightning spider-webbing across the sky. A blinding bolt snapped at the ground, and he reflexively jerked the reins back in his hands. The big grey, obedient as she was, stopped on a dime; and little Pablito came tumbling forward out of the saddle.

He summersaulted over the horse's head and landed on his back on the edge of the narrow rocky trail, and the wind came sailing from his lungs. He was still clinging to the leather reins when he bounced off the edge, and the big grey lifted her head and caught his weight as he swung like a pendulum back into the rock face. His knuckles smashed into the sharp rocks, but he held on, and he looked down for a second and watched his boina hat floating off and disappearing into the darkness below.

He dangled there, gripping the reins and gasping for air for a long minute. As his breath came back, he looked up at the grey, which was looking back at him with wide eyes, and chewing hard on the bit to keep the bridle from pulling out of her mouth under his weight. Without saying a word, he spoke to her, "Back up." He gave her the command with only his eyes; and ever so slowly, she eased backward.

One step, then two, and another; dragging the boy

back up onto the narrow trail. When he came over the edge, he rolled to his back and took deep breathes to calm his pounding heart. His hands were bruised and bloody, and his confidence slightly shaken, but other than that he was fine. He'd survived his first hard-learned lesson. Never, ever, take your eyes off the trail.

They reached the river in darkness, but he knew it well, and he found the wide vado and swam the horses across under the twinkle of stars. They came out splashing and leaping up the high bank on the other side, and he gave the big grey her reins, "Take us home girl," he said to her.

The grey could find the trail home in pitch-blackness, and Pablito trusted her completely. In two more hours they crossed the open pasture with the new little white house shining like a ghost on the far side, and the horses snorted and groaned because they had never seen it. He calmed them, then turned loose the lead mare to take them ahead.

He arrived at the cabin just before midnight. His father came out to greet him in the darkness.

"Did you have any trouble?" he asked. Then he saw Pablito's bloodied hands, "Are you hurt?"

"No Papi, I just hit my hands on the rocks, but I'm fine. My horse needed to rest before coming back down the mountain, and I fell asleep. I'm sorry for being late," Pablito said. He was afraid to ask the next question, "How is Momma?"

"She is still the same as this morning when you left. I have called for a *machi* to come tomorrow," Juan Carlos said.

A *machi*. A native witch from the Mapuche tribe. He must be losing hope if he has taken this last resort, Pablito thought.

In the early afternoon of the following day, the witch arrived. She wasn't what Pablito had expected to see. She was a very young woman, in her twenties perhaps, and not ugly as he thought she must be to be a witch. She lived in a small cluster of huts near the confluence of the Malleo River and the Collon Cura, and she had ridden through the night to arrive at the estancia.

The boiling storm clouds followed her, and they cracked and rumbled as they crossed the mountains and rolled down through the valley. She said nothing to Juan Carlos as she entered the cabin and hid her eyes from him as she passed, almost in fear. It was as if she could smell the lingering odor of death all around him.

But she paused to take a long glance at Pablito, and lightly tipped her head to acknowledge the boy. She sensed something else in him, something deep and familiar.

She stood next to the bed where Gisele lay in sheets soaked with sweat, and reached down to lift one of her eyelids to see her eyes. She let go and jumped back when she saw the deep blue iris, having never seen such a thing before. She looked at Pablito and said, "*Gaulicho* (the Devil) has her!" And just then a flash of lightning lit the world around the cabin, and an ear bursting crash followed that made Pablito jump and Carlito screeched.

The witch began singing a slow, hypnotic song, then burst into a series of violent spams to drive Gaulicho from Giselle's body. The horrible dance went on for an hour, with the storm raging and thundering all around them. It went on to the point where Juan Carlos couldn't stand it anymore and screamed for her to stop. She slowed and slumped from exhaustion, and made one last wave of her willow hoop charm over Giselle's head. Then she stepped backward to the door, and the storm outside grew quiet.

Gisele rustled and moaned in the final moments of the dance, then seemed to fall back into a peaceful sleep.

THE DARK AUTUMN

I t was the first of May, 1950. A day of old pagan celebrations in the northern countries, and a day dedicated to the workers in South America. A day when young and old, rich and poor, gather together for feasts and games before the winter cold arrives. But on this day, the bitter cold and rain in Patagonia came calling early. On this day, Gisele, the girl with beautiful eyes the color of a deep mountain pool, died.

By some standards her life had been short, just twenty-nine years. But in that time she knew the joy of a loving family and a life in the midst of nature's great wonders. She knew the great pain of loss; of abandonment; of cruelty and hardship. Then she found love. True love. And, she found her way back to the place where her heart had always soared.

She knew the joy of having her own home among

the tall trees, and being mother to two fine sons. She had known all of the things in life that were important for her to know, and she lived with joy. So for her, the timing of her death was unimportant.

For Juan Carlos, it was the deepest wound in a life of many. They had fled La Paz together in the dark of night just over eleven years ago. When you are young, eleven years seems to pass like a long, slow walk through the forest. Life feels unhurried and easy.

Young hearts and minds are sponges that haven't yet reached a state of fullness, and so they absorb the sights and sounds, and feelings and passions more deeply. And it feels like it will never end. But now Juan Carlos had reached the end of his walk with Gisele, and it felt like only minutes had passed. It stung with the pain of unfairness.

Claude Ballofett came to the cabin in the trees in the early morning. He tied his black gelding to the rail at the edge of the pasture and walked slowly to the cabin, but stood back from the front door, waiting respectfully for Juan Carlos. He knew his approach would be heard, and so there was no reason to clap or knock or announce his presence. Juan Carlos would come out when he was ready to receive him. This was the gaucho way.

After a time, the steel latch on the door raised and it opened. Juan Carlos stepped out and squinted into the morning sunrise, and held up his hand to deflect the burning light from his swollen eyes. Claude took two steps to the right to take his line of sight away from the burning sun.

He started to speak, then stopped; instead he stepped forward and put his arms around Juan Carlos, and held him as he might have one of his own sons. He held him for a long time. Long enough that Juan Carlos briefly considered that no man had ever held him like this. Then he released his grasp, and stepped back to speak.

"How are your sons?" he asked. He already knew the pain Juan Carlos was feeling, so it was pointless to ask, and Juan Carlos wouldn't have been able to articulate the depth of his feelings. He was a man of few words.

"Pablito is old enough to understand what's happened, but Carlito is confused," Juan Carlos said.

"It will be hard for a while, but they will find their way. They are only a few years younger than my sons were when their mother left, and I remember the sadness the three of us shared. But we had each other," Claude said. Then he continued, "Things must be arranged very quickly, and you need to stay focused on your sons, so please allow me to help with putting Gisele to rest."

Juan Carlos looked vacant, and uncollected. He had never buried anyone before, never been to a funeral besides the burying of the two small boxes of trinkets from Guillaume and Patrick. He had only gone to celebrations when enemies were defeated, and he couldn't respond.

Claude said, "This was Gisele's home, and she should stay here with her family. If you would like her to be in our family cemetery, where my father and mother are resting, it would be fine. But if you would like to lay her someplace else, maybe in a place on the estancia that was special to her, just tell me and I will make all the arrangements."

His mind was filled with a thick fog, but it cleared for just an instant and he saw Gisele sitting in the tall grass field that bordered the apple orchard. She used to love sitting there in the late afternoons, looking out over the Limay River, and watching the condors soaring on the rising thermals of summer. He used to sit with her there sometimes, basking in the warm sunshine and looking over the river to the place where they had crossed the water years before. It was a happy place, with a view to all of the things in the world that Gisele loved.

"The field by the orchard," he whispered. "She would love to be in the field."

Then, his throat clenched and the words ceased. He looked up at Claude, hoping that he would understand where he meant without having to say more; because he couldn't.

"Very well," Don Claude said. He reached out and placed his hand on the young man's shoulder and squeezed lightly, then turned away.

MAY IS USUALLY a month of drizzling rain in Patagonia. The winds from the Pacific have stopped, but the cold and wet comes nearly everyday. On this day though, the clouds broke open and the sun was shining. As the large group walked along the forest ridge, following Gisele in the wagon that was drawn by two bay-colored mares, a covey of quail burst from the tall grass and into the air under the hooves of the horses. They startled for an instant and jerked their heads up under the harness, but the gaucho walking alongside with the reins in his hands calmed them quickly.

Then one bird, a beautiful little cock with a chest as blue as the sky and a little pear-shaped black feather that hung out over the top of his head, circled back and landed directly on top of the long box in the back of the wagon. A woman in the crowd gasped, as if it was an omen, but no one moved.

Then Pablito let go of his father's hand, and walked up to the back of the wagon. He stared at the little bird, and the little bird stared back. Pablito turned around and looked at his father and said, "He is the same color as momma's eyes." The woman in the crowd gasped again and raised her hand over her mouth; and then the little quail flew away.

Maybe it was a sign. Maybe it was a final smile for her son. Or maybe it was just a curious little bird. But it made Pablito happy, and he smiled all through the long sad ceremony. As adults around him wept, he smiled. Sometimes life sends us exactly what we need at the moment. A lifeline. A chance to free ourselves of the disaster our life has become. A compass to guide us to a new course.

Gisele the girl with blue eyes, was placed in the path of Juan Carlos to give him a chance. To give him a glimpse of another world that lay outside the realm of his prison barrio. To let him bathe away some of the layers of filth that weighed him down, and give him the courage to change his course. She gave him something that had never existed in his life before, love. His heart ached so badly now, because it had been caressed back from a cold lump of stone, and now it surged with love and feeling. A lump of stone would have felt nothing.

The uncertainty of life is the powerful force that moves us to take a chance when it comes. To grab the lifeline, or set a new course, and realize that it may not last forever. Forever is a dream of the future, but life is lived in the now. A long life spent dreaming is hollow compared to a brief existence of passion. Gisele had lived a passionate life.

THE CROWD HAD GONE. Don Claude led Gisele's many friends back down the mountainside to his home, where he let them gather and talk and share their stories of Gisele. And there were many stories, because Gisele was loved by everyone who met her. They ate and drank, laughed and cried, and whispered in the corners about what would become of Juan Carlos and his two young sons.

Juan Carlos and his sons lingered for a time in the grassy field before leaving. Eleven-year-old Pablito sat next to his father and looked at him with the same contented smile that had carried him through the emotional burial. The world had reached out to him and given him a sign, and he accepted it. He was more connected to the world around him than any child Juan Carlos had ever seen. He wasn't just born to Gisele, he was born to this place. He was a part of it, and it spoke to him. He had the same calm fearlessness that Juan Carlos had, but his connection to the land and horses and animals was stronger, like his mother.

Carlito was six years old, and though he knew that his mother would not be coming home again, he was too young to really understand what it meant. As Juan Carlos looked at his two sons he suddenly realized that, once again, he had been charged with a great responsibility. To raise two young boys on his own.

A wound as deep as the one Juan Carlos felt now is a dangerous thing. It needs to heal. To mourn and grieve, and slowly heal. It will doubtless leave a scar, but to carry on, the wound has to close. Now he had to face the most dangerous part of the healing equation. He had to make a choice. The choice of embracing the living, or clinging to the dead. The first way leads to hope for the years left to live; the second way leads to madness.

The three of them sat side by side in the damp grass next to the dark earthen mound. Juan Carlos stared out to some unknown object on the horizon; Pablito watched the river below as it swelled with the Autumn rains in the mountains above, and Carlito was occupied with a strange looking bug that clung to a weed stem in front of him.

Pablito broke the long silence, "Momma likes it here," he said. "But she wants us to go home now."

Juan Carlos looked at him and smiled. He didn't doubt his son's connection to the world around him, or to his mother. He longed for it himself. To be able to hear her voice one more time, even if only a whisper in the wind, or through a child's imagination. But he would never hear the same things that Pablito could hear.

"I am hungry, and my pants are wet," came a faint plea from Carlito.

Pablito stood up, then reached down to grab him under the arms and pulled his little brother up to his feet. Then he reached out his hand to his father, as if he had the strength to pull him up from the ground and carry him home. Juan Carlos reached out and took his son's small hand, and was surprised by the force of his grip and the power he felt as he pulled him up.

He was strong indeed. Strong in his soul. He was ready to shoulder some of the load that was holding his father down. They walked back down the ridge and back to the cabin together in a line of three; Pablito in front, holding the hand of his brother, and Juan Carlos following closely behind.

PURPLE FLOWERS

E ven with the noise made by two young boys, the small cabin felt empty and quiet to Juan Carlos. So much of his life had been occupied by his love for Gisele, that her absence left a great void all around him. But somehow in the emptiness, she never really left him. Maybe it was just that his heart longed so badly for her, but he often saw the shadow of her, just a faint outline like a shimmer on the sunrise. He saw her in the moonlight that came in through the bedroom window; and in the flickering shadows of the trees as he stood brushing the dust from the horses in the afternoons.

He laid down at night and blew out the candle by the bed, then reached across to the flat emptiness beside him; but sometimes it was warm, like she had been there, and just stepped away. It frightened him for a while, but then he looked forward to those moments.

When the moments didn't come for a while, he would go alone to the grassy hill and sit next to her. He spoke very little to other people, but sitting in the grass he talked endlessly to Gisele, just like he did by the fountain in the courtyard. He talked about his days riding in the mountains, and about what their sons had done the day before. He talked about the horses and the sheep, and about the flowers she had planted in the garden around the house. And before the winter snows came, he pulled the dried stalks from her favorite purple wild flowers, and carefully plucked the tiny seeds from each and spread them on the ground around her. She had loved all the wild mountain flowers, but purple was her favorite color.

He wasn't sure, but he thought her birthday was in the springtime, so he picked a day. Not a specific day, like everyone else has. Not a common kind of day that came and went without notice unless you lived by a calendar. Not a Tuesday or a Wednesday, but a special day that moved slightly with the seasons. The first day that the purple lupins bloomed alongside the river. That would be the day they celebrated every year as Gisele's birthday.

And this year, the lupins were eagerly leaping from the ground earlier than anyone had ever seen. The flower shoots pushed up from the earth while the remnants of frost and snow were still scattered across the hills and the mountaintops were white. They came up and grew inches every day. And Juan Carlos and the boys went every morning to the river to see them and plan for her birthday party. On November 21st it happened.

Juan Carlos rose early in the morning and came into the kitchen of the cabin and lit a small lamp. He loaded kindling and wood into the iron stove and lit the fire, then left a pot of water to boil on top for coffee. Then he did what he always did in the morning, he sat at the table and laid out his knives and sharpening stone, and rhythmically polished the edges to a razor.

They were usually not far from it when he started, unless he had used them for some hard duty the day before. It wasn't until the pot started whistling and he poured his first cup that he realized Pablito hadn't come up from the bed yet. He was usually up by now. Since his mother died, he had been getting up each morning with his father, and tending to breakfast for the three of them, which is what Gisele had always done.

But today he didn't get up. Juan Carlos walked quietly to the door of the room where the boys slept and peered in. Carlito was sprawled across his tiny bed, his head buried under the blankets and his arms and legs sticking out from the four corners, but Pablito's bed was empty with the blankets pulled up neatly and straightened.

Juan Carlos walked back into the kitchen and looked out the window into the morning glare and saw the dust from a rider, rising through the trees where the trail went down to the river. A second later, Pablito came galloping through the forest on his big grey and pulled up hard to a stop in front of the house. The small boy came flying off the horse before it stopped and hit the ground running to the house. He burst in through the front door.

"They bloomed! Momma's birthday flowers bloomed!" he yelled.

Juan Carlos smiled and said, "Then today we will have an asado and celebrate her birthday."

He had been planning for the asado for several days, as he had seen the lupins coming up and knew it wouldn't be much longer. He had the firewood stacked away and ready, and meats and cheeses prepared and tucked away in the underground cool space. He and Pablito cleared the pit with shovels and started a blazing fire.

They split and stacked the algarrobo wood crisscrossed and let them burn all morning until the pit was deep in smoldering coals. Algarrobo burns slow and hot, then crumbles into large natural briquettes that glow red for hours. They roasted a small goat over the edge of the coals for three hours, then placed chorizo sausages on a wire rack and heated them over the bed.

Pablito and Carlito sat on the bench upwind of

the smoke from the fire pit, and watched as Juan Carlos carefully tended it and meticulously placed fresh glowing coals here and there below the roasting meats. They sizzled and hissed, and filled the air with a smoky fragrance that made their stomachs growl.

When it was near time to eat, Pablito gathered the round wooden plates and utensils from the kitchen and brought them all out to the table in the garden. He poured two glasses of juice that he had pressed this morning from apples he gathered from the trees round the house, and placed one in front of his little brother and the other for himself. Then he poured a glass of table wine from a demijohn for his father, as Gisele would have done. Juan Carlos served his boys from a large wood platter, then sat at the head of the table, with his two sons sitting to his right.

They all looked up for a moment at the empty chair to Juan Carlos' left, and then at each other. No one could remember who had brought the chair out and placed it there, but as empty as it looked, it still felt satisfying to think she might be there enjoying the asado with them. After all, it was her birthday they were celebrating. Pablito raised his glass of apple juice and looked across at the empty chair, and smiled as if he was actually looking at her.

"Feliz cumpleaños Momma!" he said as he raised his juice glass in front of him.

Then they all repeated the happy birthday cheer together, "Feliz cumpleaños!"

. . .

WHEN THE MEAL WAS FINISHED, the boys cleaned the table and took everything back into the kitchen, then both curled up in their beds with full stomachs for an afternoon siesta. Juan Carlos walked alone down the trail through the tall pines and across the pasture, pausing to look at the new little white cottage that sat on the other side. He blocked out the evil thoughts that lurked about the house.

He had looked for someone to blame at first, and looking at the house fueled that rage. He got drunk three times during the winter and went stumbling through the trees with a jug of kerosene in hand, intent on burning the evil edifice to the ground. But the little house was not to blame for Giselle's death.

When he arrived at the grassing field, he sat down next to the lenga-wood plaque he had carved and placed in the ground. The dark mound was sprouting with green grass now, and to his surprise, the seeds he had sprinkled in the fall were already starting to show the tips of wild purple flowers.

He sat there for a long time, speaking softly to her, and wishing for all his might that he could hear her voice, like Pablito seemed to do. He wasn't sure if the boy really was hearing her, but whatever he heard made him happy; it was the happiness that Juan Carlos longed for most of all.

He could see her so clearly in his mind, as if she

were standing right in front of him. He could picture her stepping out into the moonlit courtyard and speaking his name for the first time, " Hello, Juan Carlos." It echoed in his ears and sent a tremor to the tip of his toes.

He could see her, hear her, and remember every curve of her body as it lay against him; but try as he might, he couldn't recover an ounce of the happiness he'd felt in her presence. The happiness was like a vapor that seeped from his pores and would wisp through his fingers as he tried desperately to grab hold of it.

Pablito missed his mother too, but rather than sitting and hoping to hear her voice, he sought her out. He and his big grey horse spent some days racing through the grass fields and up the mountain trails, as he searched. He watched for the signs in the evening sky, and in the flowing river, and in the flowers that waved in the breeze. He felt her presence in this place, and he saw her everywhere he looked. No matter where he was, he knew she was with him.

EMPTY PROMISES

Six months had passed since Gisele left the world, and while things were still difficult for Juan Carlos and the boys, Claude thought enough time had passed to invite his daughter back to Patagonia. Back to the home that he had built just for her.

He knew it might be awkward, and perhaps a bit painful for Juan Carlos to see a young woman, about the same age Gisele would have been, moving into the little white house. It was the house, or rather the laborers who built the house, who passed on the infection that killed Gisele. He knew Juan Carlos hated the house. Resented it standing so fresh and white at the end of the pasture, and having to ride past it every morning.

It was a daily reminder of how he came to lose the love of his life. But Claude was a lonely man, and his daughter was his last hope of having family with him in his remaining years.

Several times during the past year he had sent money to Louisa and her mother through a trusted friend in Buenos Aires. He was able to send a remittance via the French Embassy, which they could receive in Paris. The letters coming from Louisa every month were warm and sweet, and made him dream of seeing her again very soon.

But the estancia was not producing the wealth from wool and beef that it was before the war years. He had spent a great deal of money building the little white house, and his cash reserves were fading. He sent one final remittance, with a letter explaining his situation, and begging her to come to Patagonia.

November 14th, 1951

My Dearest Louisa,

I pray this letter finds you and your mother in continued good health. Your correspondence has been a blessing to me since the passing of your brothers as our family home is an empty shell, absent the sounds of children and laughter. I greatly anticipate your arrival. I have built a wonderful Andalusian type cottage on the high pasture, and it awaits you.

UNFORTUNATELY, the reserves of capital from the estancia have become meager, and I will not be able to send a remittance in the near future. Not until such time as the price of wool and beef have regained their previous levels. Please advise me of your travel arrangements, that I may have someone waiting for you in Buenos Aires to assist with your continued journey to Patagonia.

YOUR DEVOTED FATHER,
    Claude

SIX MONTHS PASSED after Claude sent his note, without a word from his daughter. Her letters abruptly ceased. He wrote four additional letters in those six months with no response from Louisa, then sent several telegraphs directly to her in Paris, thinking perhaps the normal postal services had been interrupted. After another year had passed, her silence became the cruelest response to his pleas.

At first he rationed that his loneliness was no one's fault but his own. Though born in Paris, he had been raised from boyhood on the estancia, roaming the pampas and mountains and valleys, and building the family's fortune through ranching. Growing a vast herd of merino sheep for exquisite wool and beef for the cultured restaurants in Buenos Aires; some of it even making its way to fine tables in Paris. He was born to this life.

He had met his wife, Francoise, during the years he came back to France to fight in the first great war. He fell instantly in love with her and asked for her hand before returning home to Patagonia. He came back to Paris one year later to wed, then to bring his Parisian bride to the south of Argentina, but she never adapted well.

"How foolish could I have been," he said to himself, as he sat alone in the darkness with only the rippling glow of the fireplace for light. "I should have known a woman of her stature and taste could never live in such a remote place, away from the parties and pleasures and luxuries of Paris. It was a fool's dream."

Françoise was a cultured woman who had been raised in the elegant spectrum of Parisian society. Her skin was pale, and perfectly soft and free of blemishes from the environment. She rarely went outside unless fully covered to protect her beautiful complexion, which meant the harsh Patagonian climate was an affront to her nature. The winters were cold. The spring winds would sear the skin of her face into a leathery texture, and she had no affinity for working outdoors under the open skies of summer. In truth, she had no affinity for work at all. But none of this was her fault.

She was the carefully crafted result of her upbringing. She bore their two sons at home on the estancia with midwives, but she returned to Paris to give birth to her daughter. While she was there, she reconnected with the life she missed so much, and vowed to return. Seven years later she did, and she took Louisa with her. Patrick and Guillaume were born to the Patagonian life, like their father, so they stayed.

JUAN CARLOS and the boys came regularly to see Claude at the main house, but as time went by he pulled back deeper and deeper into a cocoon of guilt and quiet despair. His interest in the things that once held his attention waned. Juan Carlos pulled the ten finest rams from the flock to select the one for the breeding in the winter, a decision that Claude had always had a keen talent for, but he only came to the window and glanced at the rams in the front yard, and turned away with disinterest.

His magnificent horses passed by the house each day to feed in the long grass past the courtyard, but he never gazed at them again. Even when the auctions took place for the beef cattle and wool, his interest in the market price and income faded.

It seemed his land and businesses and his money

meant nearly nothing to him now, with his sons dead and his wife and daughter brushing him from their memories like a stray leaf that landed on the shoulder of their silk dress. His many friends in the valley came by with gifts of food and wine, and tried to enlist him for an asado or a game of cards from time to time. He politely refused them all.

If he hadn't been so eager to help his sons slip through the political fences and go to war for a country they had never even seen, they would still be alive. They would be here on the estancia raising their own children by now, he thought. And maybe he could have taken his wife to live with his other family in Buenos Aires, and they could have been happy there. He invented a thousand reasons in his mind that all of his misery was his own fault.

But sometimes, there is no fault. Wars are waged, and young men are born with the hot-blooded heart for battle. They will find their own way to the fight regardless of their father's wishes, and their destiny will find them. And women of culture may try to adapt to a more difficult life and fail, but at least they were game to try. These are the realities of life. Young men die in war, and fair women wither in the sun. The only way to escape it, is to withdraw from the game.

Claude withdrew.

THE LEGACY

T he goings-on of the morning had been particularly interesting. Pablito and Carlos rode down along the shoreline of the Collon Cura River to look for a few stray cows that had wandered away from the herd during the night. They found their tracks leading away from the valley, and it looked like maybe they had been cut off from the herd and run away by a puma or maybe a poacher.

Juan Carlos sent them to search while he moved the rest of the cows over the ridge. Pablito was sixteen now, and handling the regular work of a gaucho on the estancia along with his father. Carlos, who refused to respond anymore to "Carlito" because he was almost twelve and that meant he shouldn't be called by a baby name anymore, was a good rider too, but he didn't enjoy the gaucho work. He was starting to have dreams of life in a town.

Town life was drawing closer by the day. The road that came along the other side of the Collon Cura, now came across by way of a long wooden bridge so that the automobiles and noisy trucks could continue to Junin de Los Andes and San Martin, and even all the way to Bariloche. They brought new people everyday to Patagonia, and store bought goods, which meant new stores were sprouting up all over town, and now there were even men who came sometimes to fish in the rivers all the way from Buenos Aires.

The bridge had taken three years for the engineers to build. They dredged and sank the massive pilings across the riverbed in the late summer when the water was at its lowest level, and attached some of the connecting beams across the top before the snows came. Then in that first winter, there was a massive flood coming down from the mountains that wiped the bridge out, and they had to start all over again.

The bridge was only wide enough for one automobile or truck to go across at a time. Which was exactly what caused all the excitement this morning. A flatbed truck hauling cases of peaches from Neuquen City was coming south across the bridge, and a rich landowner from San Martin was traveling north with his wife in their brand new Ford Fairlane, which had been ordered and shipped all the way from New York. It was the only one of its kind in Patagonia, and the owner was quite proud of it, frequently driving up and down the main street in the little town in the late afternoons so everyone could see it.

The two drivers both came across the bridge at the same time, and came to a stalemate in the middle. Horns were honked. Then yelling and cursing ensued, followed by peculiarly Italian looking hand gestures, which resulted in both men exiting their vehicles and beginning to fight in the middle of the bridge.

Pablito and Carlos were enthralled by the action, and tied their horses to a tree and sat in the shade by the river, watching. The yelling and cursing was more fun to watch than the fight, because they really just chest-poked and shoved each other around a little. Then the woman in the car started screaming and crying, which halted the battle. But when the fight on the bridge dulled to a sulking contest of wills, the two brothers started grappling themselves, having been worked up by watching the adults.

Carlos started it, pouncing on top of his big brother and pulling his hat off and throwing it down the hillside. Pablito countered by quickly manhandling him and pinning him to the ground, then sat on his chest and tickled his ribs until he couldn't breath and his face turned bright red like he was going to pass out. Then he stood and glared down at him and said, "Carleeetoooo" in the most baby-boy fashion he could muster, before walking down the hill to retrieve his boina.

These little scraps happened almost everyday, but

the two brothers couldn't have loved each other more. Pablito was almost a man, and Carlos worshiped him. He usually started the fights simply because he wanted Pablito's attention, and because he wanted him to think he was tough and brave. Almost every stupid thing he did, he did to impress his big brother.

Pablito came back up the hill and sat down in the grass and pulled his knife from the sheath, and started cutting loose threads from the bottom of his pant legs.

Carlos watched, and then asked, "When do you think Papi will give me a knife?"

"I don't know. Maybe when you are my age," he answered.

"The other boys are all learning how to fight with knives. Will he ever teach us?" he asked.

"I don't know that either."

JUAN CARLOS HAD BEEN RAISING the boys on his own for five years, and having to make the decisions about what to teach them or not teach them, by himself. It wasn't always easy to know what a young boy needs, and never having a father of his own to learn from left Juan Carlos to guess his way through it. The myth of Juan Carlos' skill with a blade hovered in whispers around the community, and Pablito had heard the stories many times from other people, but never from his own father. This year he finally asked him directly.

They were in the horse barn one afternoon, washing and brushing out a young gelding that was shedding his coarse winter coat.

"Papi, why haven't you taught me *escrima criollo* (gaucho knife fighting)?"

Juan Carlos hesitated, then kept brushing the horse without answering. It was a conversation he had hoped to never have with his son.

"All of the other boys my age started learning years ago, and everyone tells stories about how you are the best knife fighter anyone has ever seen. Why won't you teach me? Or do I have to learn on my own?"

Juan Carlos looked up at him, but still didn't answer.

It was a skill he hadn't asked for. One that was thrust upon him, and brutally so. He still had dozens of scars to prove it. It was a skill that sent him on a path to damnation. But as he considered it, maybe it wasn't the skill that put him on the path. It was Ramon.

Gisele had led him on a very different path, and when he was forced to use his fighting skills again he used them to save life, not take it. And whether he liked it or not, his sons were growing up in a world that was full of violence, and refusing to train them would only make them weak and helpless. A gaucho who could defend himself well, might only have to fight one time in his life. Then his reputation would shield him. But one who was weak would have to fight almost every day.

He couldn't ignore the realities of the world any longer, and he knew he wouldn't be there to protect his sons for the rest of their lives. The best way to protect them, was to prepare them to face danger on their own terms.

"We will start your training tomorrow morning, before your chores," he said as he went back to brushing.

PABLITO WAS UP EARLY the next morning, thinking he would make coffee and breakfast before his father got up, but Juan Carlos was already sitting at the table. He had been up for an hour, carving two long pieces of straight oak branches into a shape similar to a knife for training. Pablito looked disappointed when he saw them.

"I have had my own real knife since I was eleven, why can't I learn with it?" he asked.

"Do you want to really learn or not?" his father answered.

"Yes!"

"Then you will learn the same way I did. This isn't something you can learn in a day, like how to brush a horse. It will take years," he said. "This is where you start."

It was a challenge at first for Juan Carlos to keep

the boy's attention as he taught him the foundations of the craft. Learning to stand and step with balance, learning to move and flex his body and spin. It all seemed more like dancing; like girl-play.

As the months went by and he learned to hold and move the training knife, it became a little more interesting, but he still didn't understand why he couldn't train with a real knife. The things his father was teaching him were very strange movements compared with what other boys were learning from their fathers, and they got to train with real blades. After a full year of slow dancing with the sticks, the monotony overcame him.

"Papi, why can't I train with a knife, this is stupid. I am good enough now to use a real blade," he said in disgust.

"Let's find out," Juan Carlos said.

He took the two wooden training knives and rubbed the edges of them in a thick brown grease that they used on the wheels of the wagon, and handed one to Pablito. Carlos was sitting on a hay bale watching, as he did every morning.

"If you can leave a single grease mark on my body, I will let you start using a real blade."

Pablito's eyes perked up. There was no doubt in his mind he could win this match against his father and graduate to the next level. Carlos was cheering him on, "Grease him up, Pablito!"

They started about two steps away from each

other, Pablito in a low crouch with a menacing scowl on his face and his wooden knife held forward. Juan Carlos stood relaxed, with his knife held low at his waist. Pablito made the first move, a fast rush forward with all the speed he could muster.

Then, it was over.

Suddenly his father was standing on the other side of him. Carlos jumped off the hay bale and stared with his mouth open, but couldn't speak. He wasn't sure what he just saw.

"Wait. What happened? Why did you stop?" Pablito said.

"Because the fight is over."

Pablito looked down and saw brown grease marks slashed across his arms and his belly, then in a delayed reaction, he felt a tingling on his neck, and reached up and found grease smeared evenly across both sides of his throat.

"I will tell you when you are ready for a real blade. It will be soon, but you have got more work to do."

"Whoa!" Carlos said, still staring in amazement.

"Papi, how did you learn to move like that?" Pablito asked.

"The man who trained me wasn't gentle, like I am with you. But cruel," he said.

Pablito never complained about the training regimen again. He did precisely as his father instructed, and never questioned his methods. In time, he did get to transition to a real blade, dulled down to prevent injuries as the training became more serious. What he didn't have to live through, was the final process of painful instruction that Ramon inflicted on his father. He had seen the scars, and often wondered how they were made, but he was afraid to ask. Now he had some idea of where those scars came from.

"PAPI, the scars on your arms and your body; were those from your training, or from real fights?" he asked one day.

"Most were left on me when I was being trained."

"Will I have to do the same thing as you did?" he asked. "Will you burn me?"

Juan Carlos stopped what he was doing and looked up at Pablito. "No. Never," he said. "The man who taught me was a monster. These scars he left on me; he did this because he wanted me to be a monster too."

"Momma told me that you have saved lives. That you saved Guillaume years ago in a fight because you were so good," Pablito said.

"This thing that I am teaching you; I thought for a long time that it was a curse. That it was evil and it made me evil. But your mother showed me that it's not evil or good, it's whatever I decide to make it. You will have to decide how to use it yourself; but there are only a couple of reasons you should ever pull a blade against another man. One is to defend your life or someone you care about. That's a good use. Some people will tell you to use it for revenge; that's an evil use. But sometimes you meet men who are so evil that revenge is what they deserve."

COINS

The boys were eager to go to the Puestero. Pablito was going to enter the wild horse rodeo for the first time this year, and Carlos was going to show a young bull in the judging contest that he thought for certain would win first prize. Juan Carlos had plans to sell a pretty young mare at the horse auction, and use the money for some personal things. A new poncho for himself and new boots for him and both boys. The boys' feet were growing so fast he had to buy new boots almost every year. He also had in mind to look for something special for Pablito.

On the third day of the event, he sold his horse for a very handsome price and he found the vendors that he owed money to, having already picked up the other items and made bargains for the prices. Then he went looking for what he had in mind to buy for Pablito.

He was nineteen years old now, and he had been working very hard on the estancia alongside his father since he was eleven. He still carried the small field knife that Juan Carlos had given him, and he sharpened it and kept it clean, but it was time for him to have something more suitable for a life in the saddle. A more practical gaucho's knife.

And as well, he had been training with his father for three years now, and he was ready for a blade that would be useful if he ever had to defend himself or someone he loved. The older he got, the more likely that adult-size trouble might find him someday.

He visited the shops of two different knife makers in the town, but found nothing he liked. He wanted a long working knife, but one with very good steel and a little character, like his son. The third shop he walked into was owned by a tall Portuguese. Juan Carlos walked in and said hello, then looked around at some of the knives he had available for sale on the wooden table in front. As he turned, the Portuguese noticed his long facón, tucked into the wide waistband, and recognized it immediately. He was the one who forged it from the sword of Claude Ballofett.

"You are Juan Carlos, from Estancia Ballofett," he said.

"Yes. I am sorry, have I met you before?" Juan Carlos replied.

"No, but I know who you are. Everyone knows

who you are," he said. "I am the one who fashioned that facón that you are wearing."

"You are the one who made it? It's an honor to meet you!" Juan Carlos said, as he reached out his hand.

"No. The honor is mine," The Portuguese blade smith said. "Are you looking for something special?"

"Yes, a knife for my son. He needs a more practical knife for working on the estancia, but I want something a bit longer than normal, with a more flexible carbon steel blade, and balance. It must be balanced well, just past the hilt."

"A knife with two lives in mind. One in the field, and one for the fighter," he said. He nodded as if he knew exactly what he needed. "I have just what you are looking for, but it's not out front for sale." He turned and went through a hanging curtain doorway into the back of his shop, and returned a minute later carrying a knife in a hand-woven rawhide sheath, and laid it on the counter in front of Juan Carlos.

"You know, I came here from Portugal many years ago, and I was a knife maker for several blade masters in Portugal and Spain. I have had this piece of Spanish steel with me for many years, and it's of the variety that would normally be made into a fighting blade. It's light and flexible, and it holds a sharpened edge better than most.

I decided to make it into a classic *belduque* shape and style, because it works well in the campo and also for many other things. It's very unusual for this area, but it seemed right to make it this way at the time. I have had it in the backroom waiting for its owner to come find it for a very long time. The sheath is for normal wear in the field, and the handles are made from very well-aged oak wood, but they can be changed if you would like something more flashy."

Juan Carlos pulled the knife from the sheath, and looked at the blade along its edge and tested the sharpness against the grain of his thumbnail. Then he held the blade flat on the table and slightly lifted the handle to bend the long blade and test its flexibility. He lifted it and held it flat in his palm, then with a lightning fast reflex he spun the knife, and stopped it balancing on the upper edge of his index finger.

The blade smith smiled broadly. "You have skills that you didn't learn here. Where are you from?" he asked.

"It doesn't matter," Juan Carlos said. "This is very fine steel. The handles are perfect for a working knife, and the blade has a strong soul. It will be perfect. I also have a younger son who could use a knife, but something just for the campo if you have something."

"I have a nice blade that I forged from a leaf spring off an old Citroën truck! I reforged the steel in my own furnace and tempered it perfectly. It's not expensive, but it's a very good knife, and it has nice stag antler handles. It would be perfect for a young man in the campo. I'll give you a discount for buying them both."

THEY SPENT the final night of the Puestero camped along the shore of the Chimehuin River where it looped close to the town, under the cover of ancient maiten trees. None of the three had any interest in going to the big dance, as it was mostly for the young men and women who were looking for partners. Pablito was nearing the age now when he might consider it, but his life was too busy with work on the estancia and training with his father to make time for anything else. And perhaps, the sadness of losing Gisele was still weighing too heavy on all of them.

Juan Carlos would never again find the love that he had with Gisele, so he preferred to stay focused on the other aspects of living and raising his boys. He had had more good years than he thought he probably deserved, and he was grateful for that.

They sat by the fire in the late evening, listening to the crackling of wood and an occasional "pop" when a fat grub buried deep inside a log burst from the heat. The flickering flames made the trees dance with shadows over their heads, and they could see small clusters of stars through a hole in the canopy. When he thought the time was right, Juan Carlos pulled his canvas rucksack up into his lap and untied the strap and opened it.

"I have something for both of you," he said.

He could have made a more grand event of it, but that wasn't his way. The two boys sat up on the edge of the tree trunk they were resting on to get a better look into the rucksack. He reached in and pulled out first the long knife with the oak handles and laid it across his knees.

Both boys inched up closer, and their eyes were wide enough to see the flames reflecting. Then he pulled the second knife with ivory colored stag antler handles and laid it next to the first. The two boys came off the tree stump and were perched on their knees in front of him.

"This blade came all the way from Portugal, and has been waiting a long time for the right man. You are that man," he said, as he placed the knife into Pablito's hands.

"The steel in this blade came to Patagonia in another life, and was reforged to live again. It will serve you well," he said as he handed the second knife to Carlos.

The two boys stood, and one at a time they put their arm around their father's neck and thanked him. They sat back on the tree trunk and drew the blades from their sheaths, and admired them in the orange glow of the fire.

Receiving a knife is like a right of passage for a young gaucho. It's more than a tool, it's a crest of his lineage. It signifies him as a man who makes his living with horse and saddle, and ranging across the vast pampas and mountains of the Andean range. And they both understood that these were not gifts. A knife is never given as a gift in Patagonia. They had to be paid for with a "coin". Loyalty, honor, love and respect were all valid coins that can be given for a blade.

THE FAR HORIZON

The next few years passed in quiet sameness. The long, wet transition of autumn painted the mountain landscapes in gold and red and yellow, as the lenga trees responded to the sun's arc falling slightly more to the North with each passing day. As the nights grew colder, the evening rains left a layer of snow dust high on the mountaintops, like sugar sprinkled over odd shaped pastries. It would normally melt off by noon, until the day arrived that it didn't. Then winter was officially present.

Some years the snow was deep, and others it mostly rained, but the earth soaked up the wetness like a sponge and held it until the first days of spring. When spring came, the grasses and flowers showed their tips in a day, then burst from the moist ground the next.

Each spring that came, the two brothers also burst upward. Pablito was twenty-one years old now, a fully-grown man and an impressively natural gaucho on the open range. Carlos was still a teen but he was growing by leaps and bounds with the spring winds. He was taller than his big brother now, and completely opposite in his nature.

Where Pablito was born to be a part of the Andean range, Carlos had dreams of traveling the world. He liked working with his father and his brother on the estancia, but another life was calling to him. Don Claude shared a picture book with him one time, of other places like Buenos Aires, Paris, and Spain. Carlos marveled at the architectural wonders that waited to be seen, and often felt constricted by the routines of life on the estancia.

He and his brother would sometimes sit together on the high grassy ridge looking out over the Limay River valley, and yet be lost in totally different worlds. Pablito reading the changes in wind and bird song, and taking note of the rhythms of life in the water below. The endless cycles of birth and death that carried on each day around them. Insects hatching, fluttering in the breeze, laying eggs in the swaying willow branches, then ending their lives in the mighty river, to be instantly consumed by the waiting trout. He could see and feel the beautiful orchestration of this play, as nature carried on around them, and he knew he played a role in it all.

Carlos sat by his side and envisioned an alien world that he had never seen in person, but longed for. A world of towers and bridges; of elegantly carved stone marvels that he imagined only a human hand being guided by God could have made. Streets of brick and stone and concrete, and tall buildings with so much glass they shined in the morning sun like a beacon to the horizon. These were the things he knew existed someplace else, and craved to see.

ONE OF THE more mundane things, in Carlos' opinion, that also came with the spring, was the roundup of the beef cattle that free-ranged across the estancia. It would take several days to find them all and herd them to the main corral to select the breeding stock; choose the ones to be sold at auction; and brand the new calves to make sure they were properly identified with a big floral "B" scorched into their rumps. Juan Carlos decided to let his two sons handle the locating and herding of the stock, while he tended to repairing the corral fences and the chute where they narrowed the herd down to a single file.

Pablito and Carlos packed a bag with food and coffee and bedrolls for a two-night stay out in the mountains, then rode off together to find the scattered cows. They rode across the green pasture, glancing over at the little white house and thinking about their mother. At the same time, they both reached up and touched their fingertips to the forehead, then down to the chest, over to the left side and to the right to complete the sign of the cross. Then they brought their fingers to their lips and lightly offered a kiss to bless Gisele, wherever she was.

They didn't feel the same resentment as their father when they looked at the white house, but rather saw it like a little chapel. A place where they could remember her and think of her resting on a heavenly cloud.

They passed over two valleys and ridge lines, and as they came over the second they could hear a small band of cows mooing contentedly in the next meadow, grazing on fresh grass shoots and out of the wind. They rounded them up and pushed them slowly back to the West, and by late afternoon they had found three more small groups and two stragglers.

Last year's summer had been one of the best they could remember for grazing, and there was a bumper crop of fat young calves in the mix. Born in the late winter, some had never seen a horse and rider before, and they frolicked and snorted with curiosity when the two brothers came along.

The first night they pitched a camp with the herd on the lee-side of a hill so the Pacific winds would pass overhead without chilling their bones, and they had a grand view of the eastern horizon and the valley. They could see the roadway twisting back and forth down the mountain and along the river on the far side. They built a fire and made maté, and ate biscuits with round slices of hard salami they carved off one at a time.

Carlos loved coming to this spot, because he would often see a car or truck moving slowly along, then roaring up the winding mountain road, then cresting and disappearing over the top. He always wondered who they were and where they were going. How far they would be an hour from now, and what life was like where they would be in just a few days of driving. He could see the train tracks that now moved over the Collon Cura River to the East, and wondered about that too.

"Those trains move so slow when they cross the big black bridge, I bet I could just walk up to it and jump on. Then it would carry me all the way to Buenos Aires. Don Claude told me that Buenos Aires is just like Paris, France where he came from when he was a boy, and he showed me pictures of it. It looks wonderful," he said.

"Why would you want to go someplace where they don't have grass and horses, and you can't even see the sky because of all those huge buildings?" Pablito asked.

"I think it would be the greatest adventure in the world! Tall houses and buildings that are painted bright colors, and hard roads, and everyone drives an automobile. There must be thousands of people all in the same place like the biggest flock of sheep you have ever seen!"

"But you have all the colors you could ever see here!" Pablito said. "The green grass, and the blue skies that change to orange and red and gold in the afternoon. And the rivers and rocks have more colors than I have ever seen in any painting. You wouldn't see those things in a big city."

Carlos frowned, "It would just be different, that's all. And I am going to see it someday!"

The light was fading into darkness now and the stars were peeking through the blue-black cover. Carlos watched the headlights of a car bouncing and quivering up the mountain road, then disappearing into the stars where they joined the top of the mesa.

"I am going there someday."

Pablito turned and rolled himself up in a dark brown wool blanket, "Just go to sleep now, and you can go there some other day."

ON THE MORNING of the third day, Juan Carlos could see an enormous dust cloud rising above the eastern hills and swirling into the sky. The brothers had rounded up every last cow on the estancia and were herding them back to the corral, and would be there in just a few hours. He had asked two other gauchos from the neighboring estancia to come help with their spring selection and branding, and he knew there would probably be a few cows that belonged to them that wandered over and got mixed in with the herd.

As Pablito and Carlos moved the cows up, they narrowed them down into the chute and gave them a little nudge with a stick to keep them moving down the pipeline. Along the way, Juan Carlos put a small patch of white paint on the cows that would go to market, and a red patch on any that had the wrong brand on them. The calves were sent into a smaller corral to get their branding done.

Most of the estancias made a big festival out of the spring herding day, and had a grand asado and even music and dancing for the ranch hands after the work was done. But Don Claude hadn't made an asado in almost four years now. He barely came out to give a brief inspection of the cows, then went back to his study to be alone.

Juan Carlos didn't seem to mind much, as the big fiestas didn't suit him either, but the boys missed it. This year, the owner of the neighboring estancia who sent two gauchos to help, decided to come over and bring some wine, and make a small feast for all the men at the end of the day.

The last work of the afternoon was branding the new calves, and that required four men all working as a team. Two men on horses would work to cut a single calf away from the group, and one would lasso it by the head and hold it steady while the other rider lassoed the hind feet. Then a third man would come up and drop the calf to his side and lay across his neck while the fourth brought the burning red branding iron and did the mean work.

Pablito was remarkable on his grey horse and he could swing and throw a lasso more accurately than any man in the valley, so he was the calf catcher lassoing the head. One of the gauchos from the other estancia was pretty good too, so he was the other rider. He rode a big sorrel gelding that stood over sixteen hands high and was lightning fast, but it was always a little nervous around cattle and branding irons.

The two riders approached the group of calves from opposite sides, and the calves clustered and shifted back and forth and bawled for their mothers at the top of their pitiful little lungs. Pablito picked out one at the edge of the group and pulled out a big loop from his braided leather lasso, then made only two big swings before launching it forward and snapping it tight around the calf's neck. He tapped his big grey mare and made a loud clicking sound with his mouth, and she backed up smartly and held pressure on the lasso. Then in an instant, the other rider had the calf's back legs cinched together with his lasso and pulled back, sending the calf to the ground where the other gaucho promptly jumped on his neck to hold him steady.

This was Carlos' first year to do the branding, after having watched his brother do it for the last three years. Pablito had taught him how to hold the iron firmly and press it flat against a wide part of the flank, and hold it steady for three seconds. Anything less than three, and it might not fully sear the skin. Then you would have to do it all over again.

They had a small brick furnace with a bellows at the edge of the corral, with a raging fire and two matching branding irons that they rotated in and out to keep one glowing orange at all times. Carlos had thick leather gloves and chaps on, and he went to the furnace and pulled out one of the irons and turned around to walk back to the calf.

Just then, the neighboring estancia owner came flying up the road to the house in his brand new Peugeot sedan. As he crested the hill and came by the corral, he waved out the window then pushed down hard on the French car horn, which sounded like a submarine dive warning, "Ah-oooooh-gaa."

Pablito's big grey jerked her head and stamped her feet, but he calmed her fast, "Shhh. Easy girl."

The other gaucho's gelding launched straight up into the air and stood, pawing furiously with his front hooves. The gaucho pulled back hard on the reins and heeled him with a jab of his spurs, which sent the panicked horse into a frenzy. He threw his head down and arched his back up to buck off the painful spurs, then spun in a circle and started to buck again. This time he backed up directly into Carlos, who was standing frozen with the red-hot iron in his hands.

When the hot iron scalded the back of the gelding's leg, he squalled and instinctively drew up his hind leg and lashed back with his massive hoof, catching Carlos cleanly on the side of his head.

Juan Carlos watched helplessly from the outside of the corral as the moment unfolded. From all the years of training with Ramon, his eyes and his ability to see the slightest movement had been honed to an unnatural level. It was a talent that kept him alive in the midst of flashing blades. When something dangerous happened, his mind decelerated the sights and sounds around him into slow motion.

As if it happened one frame at a time, he could see the car coming up the gravel drive and the dust and tiny pebbles churning in slow, rotating spirals in the air. The driver's hand reaching outward and waiving side to side, then his face broadening into a wide smile, and the skin lines compressing at the edge of his eyes, as he pressed down on the horn. He saw the long flowing mane on Pablito's horse roll in a wave straight up into the air as it jerked its head, and the big sorrel gelding raising onto its hind legs and clawing at the sky.

If he had been closer, he might have been able to snatch Carlos out of the way of the hoof as it came thrusting back. But he wasn't close.

The sixteen hundred pound horse was fitted with

neatly shaped iron shoes, nailed securely to his hooves. The impact twisted Carlos' head grotesquely to the right, and propelled his body up into the air and ten feet backward, crashing into the brick furnace and plunging to the dirt. The horse was still screaming and spinning up a dust cloud inside the corral as Juan Carlos leaped over the rail fence and raced to his son.

Pablito threw his lasso loose in the air and jumped from the big grey and came running from the other side. They arrived at the same time. Carlos lay face down and limp in the powdery soil of the corral.

"Carlos!" Pablito yelled, as he grabbed him by his shoulders and started to roll him over.

Juan Carlos reached out and stopped him. He knew it was over.

Pablito looked up into his father's eyes, and saw the same painful stare that he had seen the moment his mother had died. A stare that acknowledged the presence of Death. A cold, calm that came over him when he instinctively knew someone had moved beyond the veil. The stare held like stone for only a moment, then a single tear welled from his eye and rolled a clean wet streak through the dust on his face.

"Leave him, Pablito. Don't move him," he said. "Just...let him be still for a moment."

Carlos' neck had been broken the instant the kick hit him. Juan Carlos had seen it and saw how he fell, and how his head lay sideways now on the ground.

But he didn't want to roll him over and look into his son's lifeless eyes. Not just yet.

CARLOS WAS BURIED on the grassy hillside next to Gisele. The young minister who baptized Pablito in the river, who was not so young anymore, came to lead the prayers. Many of the local gauchos and people from town came to pay their respects, including two young girls who had met Carlos at the Puestero last year, and dreamed that one day he might choose one of them to marry, and take her away to a foreign land. He had spent hours telling them stories of Buenos Aires and Paris, as if he had been there already; and made it known that one-day he would venture across the ocean.

Claude Ballofett was there as well. He stood back from the crowd, his shoulders and head hung forward, staring at the ground as the minister spoke. When the crowd had gone, he walked to the open grave before the shovelers started their task, and kneeled down and placed a book on top of the wooden box. A book of pictures from Paris that he would never look at again.

"Take this with you, young man," he said, as he placed it in the grave. Claude hugged Juan Carlos and Pablito a long time and sobbed, but never spoke another word. Then he climbed aboard the wagon and made his way back to the house where he lived alone.

Pablito took to his horse the moment the service was done. He threw his leg up and over the saddle and kicked the big grey into a gallop and flew down the mountainside. They turned east at the river and raced along the trail. The grey's hooves echoed through the valley like a thundering drum, pounding out a fast rhythm. Her mane stretched back into Pablito's face in the rushing wind, and mud and dirt flew in great clumps into the air behind them.

He pushed her harder, and harder until he could hear her breath coming in bursts like a steam engine. Then they neared the end of the trail. She felt him relax on her back, and she slowed to a cantor, then a walk and caught her breath. Pablito sat up and took a deep breath, then in front of him, he saw the big black wooden bridge across the Collon Cura River, and a freight train pulling sixteen cars slowly across to the East. So slow that he could have walked up and jumped on board, and ridden it all the way to Buenos Aires.

"Go Carlos. Catch your train," he said. "Vaya con Dios, mi hermano (Go with God, my brother)."

JUAN CARLOS STOOD and stared out across the river valley, again in the same general direction from where he and Gisele had come so many years ago. His mind was drawn back to the same torment. In his mind he saw the white dress stained in blood, and the faces of everyone who fell to his blade in La Paz. The fear swept over him. The only fear that ever really gripped him deeply; that he had lost his soul to the darkness, and doomed everyone around him to the same fate.

"Is this my fault? Have my sins brought a curse down on everyone I love?" he whispered to himself.

Then he heard her. Gisele's sweet voice finally coming to his ears.

"It has never been your fault, my love."

He looked around as if she might be standing there beside him, but he was utterly alone on the grassy hill. He strained to hear her again, but he could only hear the wind grazing over the tall grass. Then a warm spring breeze wrapped around him, like a woman's warm flesh; and he felt a peaceful wave washing through his body. He looked around the valley once again, and her words flowed through the center of his heart.

"Life is a very delicate dance, my love. A balance of pleasure and pain; miracles and tragedies; living and dying."

Juan Carlos smiled. Smiled from somewhere deep down inside.

"Every moment of happiness is a blessing. We were blessed over and over again," she whispered.

He didn't have the words to say what he felt in his heart at that moment, but he understood her message.

The number of years we might live means nothing. Life is tallied in single moments of joy. Life, however long, should be lived with passion, and courage, and purpose. And when the end comes, we should embrace it like the plum falling ripe from the branch, savoring each ray of sunlight, and committing our form back to the earth that nourished us.

WORLDS COLLIDE

The big grey shifted her weight from one side to the other, and snorted away the pesky *tabano* fly that was trying to suck moisture from her nostril. She shook her big head from side to side, then lashed her long black tail forward across Pablito's leg to get his attention. She was bored, and didn't quite understand why they had been perched high on this ridge for so long.

Pablito loved being here. Watching the mountains move in the shifting light on cloudy days, and the river below rushing and bubbling over the rocks and fallen trees. He felt a connection to this world. He understood it, and to him, it was like watching a grand play or an opera, performing just for his benefit.

But since the day Carlos died, now two years past, he started taking notice of other things in the landscape. Things he had never seen before, or just ignored because they weren't important to his vision of the world and his place in it. Things like roads, and trains, and cars and trucks. They were oddities, misplaced in this vast natural land. And they were slowly bringing change to his world, whether he liked it or not.

Ruta 40, the road that stretched all the way from northern Argentina and followed along the Andean cordillera, was nearly complete. It came across the flat mesa and twisted in a spiraling ribbon down the mountainside to the Limay, then followed the river for many miles before crossing the single lane bridge over the Rio Collon Cura at Rinconada.

Now people from all over could come and go to Patagonia as they pleased. Some of them were good people. Normal types who just wanted a vacation from the noise of the city. Pablito didn't mind them so much. They came with canvas tents and small gas stoves and store-bought fishing poles, and spent a week or so camped by the river. They caught trout and slept in the afternoon sun. Then built big fires with the winter-killed driftwood that lined the banks at night, and drank whiskey, and sang songs until they fell asleep under the stars. He would ride out at night sometimes, and count the fires along the river. Every year there were more, stretching all the way up to the volcano Lanin.

Some of the people weren't so good. Every day

now when he rode the property lines along the river's edge, he found their garbage scattered in the grass, and floating down the river. A few times he had to put out fires that were left burning before they caught in the brush and swept across the pampas. Then others who came were bad, evil people. The kind who steal, and poach, and murder. The roadways and railroad had made it easier for them to move about and find opportunities to carry out their mischief.

Pablito remembered his father's stories from the war years. Instead of spending his time tending to the sheep and cattle and fences, he spent most of it protecting them from intruders. Most of them were just people who were hungry, but a few had evil intentions. It seemed like those days were returning.

His life was slowly shifting from being a simple gaucho, to being a guardian. Juan Carlos had seen it coming, which is why he decided his son needed to be trained to fight. The Gendarmerie had outposts here in Patagonia, but their job was mostly cleaning up the mess and filing reports. They left the gauchos alone to handle their own affairs and administer the order of law and justice as they saw fit. If a man were caught poaching or stealing his fate would be decided in the moment, and rarely questioned afterward.

Today as he sat high on the ridge, Pablito saw something magical. A giant, silver bird streaking across the sky and making a thunderous racket. It was the first airplane he had ever seen, and it was flying low over the hills and going to the headwaters of the river. Don Claude had told him about airplanes, and how they carried people in their bellies through the air from one place to another at incredible speeds.

He always believed Don Claude, but to actually see one flying was a shock. How did it stay in the air without flapping its wings? Or maybe it flew on the rising thermals like the great condors, which almost never had to move their wings. He had no way of knowing that this magical bird carried two men in its belly who would change his world, and the future of all of Patagonia, forever.

THE MIGRATION of settlers to Patagonia began in earnest in the 1800s, as land became too valuable a commodity in Europe, and life under the rule of the monarchies became intolerable. The young Argentine government welcomed the settlers. Men, women and children travelled in great sailing ships from Europe to the port of Buenos Aires, then endured severe hardship to venture westward by horse and carts across the vast deserts and mesas until reaching the Andes Mountains in southern Argentina.

It couldn't have been a more perfect destination. Even though life on the frontier was incredibly difficult, the landscape was nearly identical to the Alps and the forests and mountains of central Europe. It was just like home to the people who came from Germany, France, Austria, Italy, and Switzerland, and they knew how to survive here. The only things they lacked were the animals, fish and birds that thrived in their home lands. Soon the ships that followed were carrying stocks of majestic red stags, wild boar, hares, and brown trout and rainbows that would soon fill the rivers. Argentina was destined to find its greatness in immigration and diversity, from both man and beast, blended with the natural inhabitants.

Within the next one hundred years after the seeds of animals and fish were sown, nearly every river, mountain stream and lake was overflowing with trout that reached proportions never seen before. They thrived in this magical land beyond the wildest imagination. The stags roamed the forests in vast numbers, and every summer the hills and valleys filled with the sounds of crashing antlers and roaring lions (as the red stags sound much like lions).

When the roads and railways were finished, and people from the cities went to visit Patagonia, a rare jewel was found. A paradise for the fly fisherman who ventured out with wispy bamboo rods and tiny hooks decorated with feathers and deer hair. They found trout leaping and grabbing with every cast they made into the crystal rivers, and fish so big they broke their flimsy rods into pieces. The men who came guarded the secret of this paradise like a treasure. They banded together like a Masonic lodge; brethren defending a gift from God that only they had access to. But secrets never stay secret, and inch-by-inch, the whispers traveled to the outside world.

Rumors circulated among the dedicated fly fishermen in the United States about the land at the end of the world with rivers and lakes bursting with trout of enormous size. So enormous it couldn't be real. So an expedition was hatched by two men, Curt Gowdy and Joe Brooks, and they came south with a small band of videographers in tow to document the truth of it. They came by ship and train, and airplanes all the way to Argentina, then persuaded locals to take them into the wilderness.

Their grainy black and white films stunned the fishing world. They pieced the films together to create a single broadcast for a Saturday afternoon television show in the early 1960s, and it changed the lives of fisherman around the world, forever. That one show gave birth to a new industry, with The American Sportsman television series.

PABLITO COULD STILL HEAR the droning prop for a while, echoing through the valleys after the airplane became a tiny speck and then disappeared. He wiped it from his mind and moved on down the trail to where the horses were grazing in the sun. It was almost time to move them to the high summer pasture again, and he needed to see the river up close. The wide vado had to be crossed after the heavy snowmelt, which made it treacherous with fast water, and tree trunks and debris washing down from the mountains. But as he came to the river, he saw that it was starting to clear. They would be able to move them across the river very soon.

THE SCARCITY OF CONDORS

They were harbingers of death: gigantic Andean condors with wings spread twice as wide as a man's outstretched arms. The grim reapers of the wild kingdom and the final stop on the food chain, a spiraling black cone descending from the clouds to rip flesh from bone; nature's disposal unit.

JUAN CARLOS SQUINTED into the late afternoon sky and tried to count the birds as they spun downward like a whirling tornado to the valley floor. He pulled the tightly braided leather cord that hung from his belt, a gaucho's abacas of sorts, and slid the silver beads forward with his thumbnail as he marked each of the scavengers gliding below the crest of a rocky peak. He pushed the beads forward and backward again, until he reached thirty, then he stopped counting. He had never seen this many condors come to the site of a kill. It must be something big. Or something they rarely held the favor to feast upon.

He shifted uneasily in his saddle to one side, and turned to catch Pablito's eye. He didn't need to speak. His thoughts, his worries, and his intentions were revealed in the expressive lines of his face and furrowed brow. It was too late in the day to ride across two river valleys and find the source of the condors' interest, but tomorrow they would have to find it. And they might find something gruesome.

Pablito had seen condors high in the wind, and sometimes finishing off the remains of an animal on the ground many times. This was Patagonia, and they were a regular part of his world, but he had overheard his father and a few of the other men speak of this spectacle in muted whispers a few times. It was a scarcity of condors; a great swarm that only gathers to sample another apex predator, man. The question that rolled through both their minds during the long ride back to the cabin was, whose corpse were they going to find tomorrow?

Juan Carlos held his arm fully extended to the mountain horizon and positioned the top of his index finger at the lower edge of the falling sun. It was one and a half fingers above the tallest mountain ridge, which meant they had only twenty-three minutes of daylight to ride down the ridge and cross the river. Once across, the trail was well know by the horses and they could navigate through the forest to the cabin by memory, if full darkness overtook them. They had spent the entire day, since before the sun rose, in the saddle; moving the herd of criollo horses, mostly mares and yearlings this time, up to the familiar high summer pasture.

The two men had just started back down the mountain and paused on the precipice to look down at the Limay river when Juan Carlos caught sight of the soaring scavengers over a valley to the West. The great river was coming to life again with the spring thaw, just like everything else in the Andean cordillera. And father and son were adjusting to living and working alone, just the two of them.

The muddy snowmelt had cleared and from above it was crystalline with deep pools of green and bubbling eddies around the granite boulders in the current. Pablito was mesmerized by the view from above. Not so much by the beauty of the river, but at the sight of untold numbers of trout circulating around the rocks and moving in and out of the deepest pools and riffles. Monstrous trout, rainbows and browns. As long and as thick as a man's leg. This is why the men in airplanes are coming here now, he thought to himself.

They reined their horses downhill and let them find their own way down the steep descent. When they arrived at the river, they turned along the high-water line and followed the sandy trail for half a mile before they came to the wide vado. As they waded in, the riders pulled their legs up and lay forward on the horses' necks with their legs stretched backward across their rumps to stay dry. The powerful stocky horses plowed their way through the fast water, and in the deepest channel they tapped the rocky bottom with their hooves and lunged forward to the opposite shore. They came out splashing and bounding up the bank, and paused for an instant to shake and quiver the freezing water from their coats.

The sun had just settled below the snowy peak of Lanin as they reached the southern shore, and the light was fading and muting the spring colors of the river valley. It took on a cast of grey and silver as they found the familiar trail up through the forest to home. As Juan Carlos and Pablito worked their way up the mountain trail through the forest, the moon was rising behind them to the East. The light filtered down through the swaying branches and the shadows danced around them and made the horses uneasy. A horse's eyes are keen to movement, like Juan Carlos', and the forest was alive with movement.

As they cleared the edge of the pines and came into the open pasture near the cabin they snorted and shook their heads in relief. The horses knew to return to the tying rails where their riders would dismount, then the saddles would come off and a fresh meal would be waiting for them in the paddock.

Juan Carlos took care of the horses, while Pablito

went into the dark cabin and lit an oil lamp, then started a fire in the stone fireplace to warm it. He gathered a simple meal together of dried and salted meats and some bread left over from the morning ride. Father and son each had their duties and they followed a ritual.

Juan Carlos came into the cabin after a time, and hung his boina on the rusty hook next to the front door, then sat at the small table by the window, and looked out into the dark night. Pablito came with a demijohn of Bonarda table wine, and poured a cup for his father, then sat across from him. The condor sighting had shifted the minds of both men to the thought of death, again. It reminded them that all life ends, but the world continues to move around the passing.

They were both thinking about the same person.

"Papi, tell me again about Momma. What was she like when she was very young?" Pablito said.

Juan Carlos sighed, but kept staring out the window as though he could see the hills and river valley below, but all he could see was his own haunting reflection staring back at him in the warped old glass. He took a sip of wine, then began to describe her, as he had many times before. Pablito remembered only bits and pieces of his mother, the things a child sees and feels. But he was a man now, and he wondered what she must have been like when she wasn't tending to motherly chores. She was etched deeply into Juan Carlos' mind, and he thought of her every single day.

"Gisele was light and soft. Not thick and hard like you and me. She was graceful and quiet. When she walked, she barely made a sound or left a mark in the grass as she passed through the fields. She was like a deer that glides through the wet pasture and never leaves a trace. And when she reached out with a gentle hand, even the wildest stallion would calm and shudder under her touch. She had a way with animals. You have that same way, just like her," he said.

It made Pablito happy to think he was like his mother, at least in some way.

"The horses loved her, didn't they?" Pablito asked, even though he had asked this same question about her before. He just liked hearing it from his father.

"Everyone loved her. I loved her from the first time I saw her," Juan Carlos said.

"In the garden by the fountain? Right?" Pablito said.

"Yes. It was late at night, and she stepped out into the moonlight. My heart stopped, and I could hardly speak. I had never felt the power of love before, and it terrified me."

Pablito giggled like a boy, "I can't imagine you being afraid of anything!"

"I was afraid of her. Well, I was afraid of how she made me feel. The first time she reached out and touched my arm, it was like a bolt of lightning jolting through me."

"But you knew. You knew right then that she was the one for you," Pablito said.

"I knew."

"Please, tell me about her eyes again," Pablito said.

With that thought, Juan Carlos smiled, and nodded his head. He almost never smiled anymore, except when he thought about Gisele's eyes. Pablito had seen it before, and whenever he wanted to see his father smile, he asked this same question.

"I have never seen the ocean, but people tell me it's so big that it makes you feel small and weak. That's the way I felt when I looked into your mother's eyes. They were so blue. I have never seen the same color anywhere else. I have been searching since the day she left us. Searching in the sky, the flowers in the fields, and in the deepest lakes in the Andes. But I have never seen the same blue again."

Pablito could remember his mother's eyes, but there were other things that stayed with him. He remembered her soft voice as she laughed at him when he was little, and the gentle touch of her hand across his forehead every night when she tucked him into bed. But the bad memories were the ones that are hardest to forget.

He remembered most vividly when she fell ill and suffered with a fever. He remembered how she moaned and flailed from side to side in the bed, and the sweat pouring from her face and soaking the cotton sheet as she clawed and pulled it into a wrinkled heap around her. The young *machi* witch came and sang and danced a vulgar dance. Then his mother went to sleep, and never woke up. And Pablito remembered seeing his father shed tears for the first time in his life; on the day that would have been her birthday, as he sat in the spring flowers by her side and softly spoke to her.

Juan Carlos changed the subject, "We might find something terrible tomorrow, Pablito. I think those condors have found a man's body, and we will be seeing what's left of it. I couldn't tell if the birds were going to our side of the property, or to the other side of the ridge on the next estancia, but we will get there by afternoon I think. You should pack a roll and a few camp things and some food, in case we need to stay out on the mountain overnight."

"OK, Papi."

That night, Juan Carlos had fitful, terrible dreams. Dreams of pounding thunder and flashing bolts of lightning. He heard horses screaming, and saw condors spinning in a giant tornado to the heavens. And as he started awake and lurched up in his bed in the hours before dawn, he felt the old familiar calm come over him. The blankness in his soul that recognized it is coming. Death.

THE STORY A DEAD MAN TELLS

Juan Carlos was up early and waiting when Pablito came into the kitchen.

"Have some coffee, but don't eat breakfast. We will eat before we ride out, but there is something else we need to do first, and it's better done on an empty stomach." Juan Carlos said.

"I packed up the food and blankets, and some grain for the horses last night. What else do we need to do?" Pablito asked.

"I want to train this morning."

"Train? With the knives? We haven't done that in a very long time," Pablito said.

"That's why I want to train now."

"But..."

Juan Carlos snapped at him, "Just do what I say and stop complaining!"

Pablito was startled. His father had almost never

raised his voice to him in his entire life. Why was he so angry? And why did he want to train with knives again after so much time? He tilted his head down, and acquiesced.

"Alright, Papi. I will train when you are ready."

THE GREY SKY to the East was just warming to a yellow glow when Juan Carlos walked out to the barn. Pablito was there waiting for him. He had two oil lamps hanging on the walls burning bright, and the enclosed barn was well lit. Juan Carlos came in and turned them down to a shadowy flicker.

"It's good to train sometimes in near darkness. Unless you start the fight, you can't always choose when and where it will happen," he said. "I want to use the wood training knives this time."

Pablito nodded his head. This was something new. He had never trained in very low light before. His father seemed anxious and troubled. He wasn't behaving like himself. He went to the box on the shelf and pulled out the carved wood training knives and the can of axle grease.

"Will we use grease today?" he asked.

"Yes."

Pablito smeared the two training blades with grease, then handed one to his father. He backed up two steps, and took his natural stance. His left foot pointed forward, his right slid lightly back and turned vaguely to the outside. He dug the back foot in slightly for traction, then flexed the knee and shifted his weight to the rear, so that his front foot was barely floating on the dirt floor. His parry hand waived softly out in front of him to gather his opponent's eye, and his knife hand was low, in front of his waist, serene and imperceptible.

Juan Carlos studied his pose. It was stable and quick. His grip on the handle was light, as it should be, but he had a unique way of hiding it behind his front hand. He thought it was clever. He stepped to his left, then quickly back to his right. Then he sprung forward with a faux lunge to draw Pabilto out of his stance, but he never moved. Juan Carlos stepped back into the shadows, and smiled to himself. Then he came at his son in a burst.

He slashed hard from right to left and back again, and his wooden blade was met with a "whack" as Pablito's countered and blocked. He thrust straight and low, and felt his forearm diverted with a parry from Pablito's open hand. Then he used a move he had never shown his son in training; one he had only ever used in real combat. He rolled in low and sprang straight up into him, slashing him with grease across the middle and up through his shoulder, and shoved him violently back into the barn wall. Pablito's back hit the wood slats with a crack, and he caught himself just before falling to the ground. This was serious.

His father didn't give him an instant to recover.

He came rushing at him again with a high strike, but Pablito vanished before his eyes, then came up behind him and shoved him hard, face first into the wall. Juan Carlos was startled. He spun around and his eyes flashed with anger for an instant, then he calmed himself. He leaned back against the wall and looked at his son.

"That was fast. I have never seen you move like that. Never seen anyone move like that. But you didn't block me when I came in, I mortally wounded you. You have to be better than that, Pablito!" he said. Then he pointed to the grease marks from his blade across Pablito's stomach and shoulder.

"You have never shown that move to me before! No one could block that move, it's impossible!" he yelled back at his father. "But I wouldn't have died alone."

Juan Carlos looked at him, confused for moment, then he felt the warm residual sting, and reached up to his throat. It was smeared with the grease from Pablito's blade from one side to the other. He never saw it coming, nor felt it in the heat of the moment. He took a deep breath and relaxed. He didn't know why he was so agitated and why he was pushing his son so hard. The nightmare had triggered it. It was like a small burning ember in the back of his brain, telling him that something bad was coming. But he wasn't afraid for himself. He was afraid for his son.

THEY LEFT after breakfast and spent a long day in the saddle. Winding back down the hillside through the forest and crossing the river, then working their way west along the shoreline. It was early afternoon before they reached the stream that would lead up to the ridge where they saw the condors the day before.

Juan Carlos chose his route up the steep valley carefully, avoiding the well-worn trails where the rocks would clatter against the horses' hooves and echo upward to the ridge. He had no idea what they might find on the other side, but just in case, he would rather come in without attracting attention.

As they neared the top, he eased back on the reins and pulled his big gelding to a stop, then motioned for Pablito to dismount here. They tied the horses to a short mesquite bush, then carefully walked to the edge to look over into the pasture. Juan Carlos lowered himself onto his belly and slid his hat back, and pushed his face gently through the tall desert grasses that grew on the border between the rocky edge and the green pasture. As his face slowly emerged from the barrier grass, he saw the obsidian-colored flock huddled closely on the ground, not fifty feet from his nose.

One of the giant birds was nearly close enough to touch, and he was standing with his back facing Juan Carlos. His enormous wings were spread twelve feet wide, drying off the early morning mist they collected on the flight down through the cliffs that were engulfed in a dense wet fog.

If you didn't have to look at the head, they were actually beautiful birds. Their bodies covered in silky black feathers that glistened with a damp coating. Around their necks was an elegant furry wrap as white as fresh snow. And the wings were nature's final mastery of the concept of flight. Broad and long, and shaped with a thick leading edge that tapered backwards to provide lift. And long slender feathers at the tip, like fingers that gently tap the air to tilt their flight path with the slightest touch, rather than flapping the entire wing.

They can soar for hundreds of miles in the upper currents with nothing more than a single great thrust of the wings to push them aloft into the wind, then ride the waves of air. Their eyes are keen, with binocular vision, and they can spot a carcass from a mile above the earth.

But the face, the face spoils any admiration. Their vicious heads are meant to be thrust into a bloody corpse, so they're completely devoid of any feathers... leathery, crusty, sunbaked skin covers their head and face. The beak is a jagged, flesh-tearing tool. It's not long and penetrating, like the hooked beak of an eagle that is designed to kill as cleanly as their talons. But short and sharp, like a surgeon's scalpel. Designed to carve away the skin and meat from the bones.

Nature made them in the most efficient way for their intended purpose, but not with any mind for reflecting on their beauty.

Juan Carlos looked carefully around before he stood up in the field. The condors turned and squawked and screeched, but didn't take flight. They had just arrived and weren't ready to leave yet. He waved his arms and lunged forward at the giants, and they hopped and bounced back away from the remains and leaped into the sky. The dust on the ground swirled into curling spirals as the massive wings all beat the air down against the ground at the same time, and in a few seconds they were all airborne and drifting overhead.

As the giant wings stirred the air from stillness, the scent enveloped him. The putrid, sweet smell of rotting flesh. It burns the back of your throat and reaches deep into your gullet and tugs at your last meal. Luckily Juan Carlos and Pablito had only drank water this morning before leaving camp. And even more lucky that the condors had already consumed the juiciest and most odorous parts of the body.

The grass was matted and stained, but there was little left of the body but scattered bones. The birds had done their job well. Were it not for the clothing, shredded and flung aside, you wouldn't have known it was a man. There was no way to identify the poor soul, but Juan Carlos recognized the boots, and a single silver spur. It was a gaucho who worked on the next estancia. He had seen him many times. Shared drinks with him, and played cards a few times. He knew his spurs, because the man had been a champion at the rodeos during the summer Puestero, and his spurs were very unique.

What he couldn't tell from the meager remains, was how he died. He started working his way out from the body, in larger and larger circles, looking for any evidence or signs. Fifty feet away, he found it. Boot tracks from another man, a heavy one. There was sign in the grass and dirt, of a rolling fight. Then a clear blood trail that dribbled back in the direction where the body lay. Dark blood, almost black. The gaucho had been stabbed in the liver.

He also found a clear trail where the fat man had fled. He had tried to take a group of horses with him, but it looked like only a couple went in his direction. The others ran down the mountainside in the direction of the river. He had come to steal the horses, and when the gaucho caught him he turned into a murderer.

Juan Carlos and Pablito went back to their horses, mounted up quickly and took up the trail. He wouldn't normally go after a thief on someone else's estancia, but this man had murdered. He felt a duty to hunt him. They followed the trail slowly and carefully; zigzagging back and forth to make sure they didn't miss anything.

It would disappear in places and they would have

to make large circles to pick it up again, but Juan Carlos didn't want to come up on a killer too suddenly. Especially with his son along. They stopped as they approached each ridge and peered over before going forward, and scanned the valleys from above before moving down the trails.

Once, they came to narrow canyon where the trail of horses clearly went through, but it would have been a *kill box* if the murderer had set an ambush for them, so Juan Carlos backed out, and went the long way around. By 9:00 p.m. darkness was closing in on them so they had to stop and make camp, but he could tell from the crisp edges of the tracks and the damp droppings of the horses that they were very close.

If the murderer didn't think he was being followed, they would catch him early in the morning. They made a cold camp that night; no fire or hot food or maté. A campfire in the mountains can be seen for miles, and he didn't want to be seen. Just cold bread and dried meat tonight. Juan Carlos slept first while Pablito stayed awake to guard, then they changed at midnight.

Before dawn, Juan Carlos gently nudged Pablito awake.

"Let's go. I know where he probably camped. The ridges are steep between here and the border of Chile, and there is only one meadow that is down out of the wind and has fresh water. If we leave now, we might catch him still sleeping in his bed."

Pablito nodded, and rubbed his eyes and rolled out from under his blanket. It was still dark, with a million stars sparkling overhead, and he could see his breath fogging in front of him as he yawned and stretched.

"I wish I could have some coffee," he said.

"Drink some water, you will be fine," Juan Carlos said.

They saddled the horses quietly in the starlight. Pablito pulled a piece of dry deer jerky from his saddlebag and chewed on it for a few minutes. Then he leaned over next to his saddle and tilted his face up to the night sky, and pulled the cork from his water bag that was hung on the saddle loop and let it drip into his mouth. Juan Carlos was watching his son, and his mind flashed back to the Franciscan mission in La Paz, and the drops of early morning drizzle coming down the drainpipe. The thought made a shiver run through him, and he pulled his poncho tighter around him.

THEY CAREFULLY LED the horses by the reins down the steep hill until they reached the soft dirt trail, then stepped up into the saddles and moved along quietly. Juan Carlos stopped periodically and looked up at the stars and took his bearings, then kept moving to the west. An hour farther and the horizon behind them was turning from black to grey, and Venus peeked over and shone like a spotlight until the orange glow of the sun overpowered it. They were at the base of a tall hill with a rock ledge on top, and Juan Carlos motioned for Pablito to dismount his horse and tie both horses to a poplar stump.

He spoke in a low voice, "The meadow I think he might have camped in is just on the other side of this hill. I am going to move around the hill, through the poplar trees, and come up on him quietly. I want you to climb up to the top of that ledge, real quiet; don't make any noise and don't be seen. Just get in a position where you can watch."

"OK, Papi."

Juan Carlos moved quietly away through the trees, and Pablito climbed up the hill. At the top, he found a cluster of large rocks on the ledge, a perfect place to hide and watch. He tucked himself among the rocks, and waited for the morning light to illuminate the meadow below.

CROSSING THE VEIL

Pablito was perched on the ridge, but stayed hidden in the rocks as his father told him. He was over six hundred yards above the scene as Juan Carlos crept in on the horse thief and murderer. His perspective of time slowed to crawling milliseconds as he witnessed what followed.

JUAN CARLOS SLIPPED OUT of the trees and moved stealthily through the prickly michay bushes, as if the thorns all slid cooperatively past him without a snag. When he emerged from the dense cover into the open pasture, it was still wet with morning dew, and Pablito could see the spiderwebs sparkle and glisten between the tall stalks of grass.

He was perfectly silent as he placed one boot in front of the other, heel first, then gently rolling his foot forward to the toe. As he crept up to the sleeping fat man, who was still wrapped tightly in his blanket, he withdrew the long deadly facón from the sheath tucked neatly in the small of his back, beneath his waist belt.

He kicked the sleeper hard in the bottom of his foot and barked an order, "Get to your feet!"

The man yelped as he was startled from sleep, and jerked his head up to see the gaucho standing over him with a long glinting blade pointed at his face. He froze, and his eyes filled with fear.

"Get to your feet I said!" Juan Carlos repeated. "And if I see a weapon, you will be dead in a second."

The groggy man threw the blanket off, then eased slowly to his feet with his empty hands held open to the sides to show he was unarmed. Juan Carlos kicked the blanket aside to look underneath for a hidden blade or a gun, and then he noticed it. Off to the right, under a small mesquite tree was another flattened depression in the grass. The fat man wasn't alone in the camp; there was someone else with him. He knew he had made a terrible mistake.

From above, Pablito could see his father capture the sleeping man without a fight, and he felt the pride a young man feels when he sees his father do something courageous and skillful. Then he saw his father turn his head and scan around the campsite, just before it happened.

Pablito's eyes caught the rolling ball of fire

billowing forward from the shotgun barrel, concealed in the thick brush behind Juan Carlos. He saw dust and fiber and a hint of morning mist explode from his father's back and his body lurched forward; his arms and head flailing limply backward. His boina hat came off and hung suspended in the air. For an instant, it hovered like it was weightless. Then the hat rocked faintly from one side to the other, like a buoyant feather, and fluttered down to where his feet had been. Then about two seconds later, the thundering report of the blast carried up the face of the cliff and echoed in his ears. An instant later, the signature of the impact reached Pablito. It sounded like the hollow "*whump*" of a house rug, hung over a branch and beaten with a hoop. His father landed face down in the wet green grass, and never moved again.

JUAN CARLOS OPENED his eyes for a moment in a sleepy dream state, just as he did when he was young and he fought the tall boy for the food in front of the Franciscan mission. There were only muted distant sounds. Nothing he could distinguish. There was no feeling in his body or his limbs; just a slight gurgling sensation in his throat, and the early morning light flickering shadows and shapes. Then his vision cleared and he could see the tall boy's face as plainly as if he was standing in front of him. He saw him bloodied and dying on his knees on the cobblestone streets of La Paz; but he smiled at Juan Carlos and tipped his head to signal his forgiveness, and welcome.

Then, he heard her voice. Gisele. She whispered lightly into his ear, and he saw her standing above him; reaching out her soft delicate hand to him. Her voice quavered and swirled in the wind around him, like the voice of a melancholy angel, beckoning him home. They had been together for but a few moments in the course of time; but she was like a stone cast into the river, and the ripples of her presence had changed the current of his life. He ventured far, and became the man he was, riding the waves she left behind her.

They were all there with him. Gisele and his son Carlos, his friend Rico, and everyone who had fallen before him in this life. There to greet him to the next.

Then he could see Pablito, as if he were watching him from afar through a telescopic lens. He sensed the horror and helplessness in his son, and he feared for him. He tried to call to him.

"Run!" he yelled. But his screams were only heard on the other side of the veil, not in the world where Pablito still lived.

Then, he was gone.

PABLITO WATCHED the scene unfold in muted silence.

His eyes were transfixed with horror. He was holding his breath without realizing it, until finally his lungs burst into a gasp for air, then his eyes started burning and blinking. He rubbed the sand and water away from his face, and looked back at his father lying still on the ground. It couldn't be real.

Then he saw the tall man with long black hair and a long beard come slinking from the brush with the shotgun held at his waist. He swaggered into the grassy opening and yelled something at his partner. The other man was flailing his arms and yelling back, but Pablito couldn't hear them from so far away. The man who had been sleeping ran back to his bed and grabbed his blankets, then ran for the horses they had tied beneath the willow tree. He crammed a few items into a canvas bag, then frantically worked to saddle his horse.

Then the tall man with the shotgun did something that finally snapped Pablito from his suspended condition. He bent down and wrenched the elegant black handled facón from Juan Carlos' stiffened grip, and inspected it carefully. He held it out at arms length to see it in the light, then slashed it through the air like he was fencing with a phantom. The blade glinted in the sunlight and brightly flashed like a signaling mirror into Pablito's eyes. Then he reached down and pulled the scabbard from Juan Carlos' body and sheathed it and tucked it into his own belt, and he laughed. He looked pleased with himself, before he turned and walked away from the body.

Pablito's cold shock was displaced by a wave of warm blood flowing into his face, and his shallow breathing turned to a deep, churning cycle of inhales and exhales. Then he shuddered and trembled. Trembled with the same rage that his father felt the night he killed Ramon, and Pancho and Santi.

THE MOMENT FOR REVENGE

Pablito watched as the two men threw their gear together and carelessly saddled the horses, then rode away; taking note of their direction. He eased himself back from the ridge, then bounded down the hill to the tree line where the horses were tied. He jumped up onto his grey and she bolted forward into the trees as if she knew exactly where they were going. He left his father's horse tied to the stump.

They weaved in and out of the poplars, leapt over the thorny michays and came into the meadow in a full gallop. Pablito leaned back into the reins, and the grey reared her head skyward and drove her rump to the ground, sliding forward with rear hooves skipping and gouging a muddy trench through the grass. Pablito flew from the saddle before they came to a full stop and hit the ground running, but then he pulled himself back just before reaching his father's body, and took the last two steps slowly.

He approached as though Juan Carlos might have just been peacefully napping in the early morning, and he didn't want to wake him. Juan Carlos was laying stomach down, his head turned slightly that his face looked to the rising sun; and his arms lay tucked neatly by his waist, palms up to the sky. His poncho concealed the destruction below, showing only a few torn threads of wool, and the faintest of dark stains where the buckshot penetrated.

He kneeled down, and touched his father's thickly calloused palm. It was still lightly warm, but the color of life was fading. He felt the weight of emptiness growing deep in his stomach and the tears starting to well in his eyes. Then, something his father said to him years before rang in his ears, "*Mourning the dead will take a lifetime. There will always be time to mourn. But you might have only a moment for revenge.*"

From his first breath, Pablito had been a gaucho. They live by the rhythm of the land, and by the gaucho way. To watch someone you love be murdered, and do nothing, wasn't the gaucho way. He pulled the corner of his poncho up and wiped the tears from his face, and felt the steely hardness washing over his heart. The cold, calm blankness that shielded men from fear, when death is at hand.

Pablito reached for the worn black boina hat on

the ground, and placed it tenderly over his father's face to shield it from the sun. He pulled his knife from the scabbard and hacked a few thorny michay branches, and placed them over his father to keep the keen eyes of the condors from finding it before he returned.

He carefully searched the surrounding grass and open ground for sign. He found the tracks of the two horses, both unshod with slick, worn hooves, so they had probably been stolen from the campo. Then he inspected the tamped down beds where the murderers had slept. The one Juan Carlos caught sleeping was shorter and heavy. The other, tall and light. Where he slept, the grass was churned and twisted. He must have been suffering in his sleep.

He followed the footsteps where the tall man came up from his bed in the early morning and walked a distance away from the camp to squat in the bushes and ease his cramping. It was during his time away from sleep that Juan Carlos came into the camp. Then he followed the tracks to the place the man crouched in the bushes like a coward, and shot his father in the back.

Pablito gathered his horse now, and picked up the trail and followed it due west. They were heading straight for the Chilean border, but the way they moved was strange, haphazard and confusing. After three hours of following their random route and odd spoor from their horses, he knew he had the advantage.

These men weren't from around here and they didn't know how to handle a horse very well. He could tell by the way they were choosing their trails, and forcing the horses into climbs and descents that they couldn't navigate without protective shoes to grip, and protect their hooves. They were trying to find the trail to the most dangerous vertical pass on the border; the pass around Lago Tromen.

It was a high mountain lake in the uppermost part of the Andean range, and the trail around it, into Chile, was barely wide enough for a sure-footed horse. It wound along a sheer cliff that fell over a thousand feet straight down into the dark blue water. The lake was actually crystal clear, but so deep that from above the water still looked as dark as the night sky. It was nearly a perfect circle two miles across, the remaining basin of an ancient volcano, filled over a millennia with ice and snow and now home to fish and deep dwelling creatures unseen by men.

PABLITO BROKE AWAY FROM THE MURDERERS' trail and took a different route to the pass. It was longer, but faster on a shod horse, and he knew he could be there waiting for them in the upper tree line. He would have the advantage of surprise, and courage fueled by revenge.

It was during the race to the top of the mountain that he was in the most danger. Danger of losing himself to the animus, the pain and hatred that welled in his guts. With every hour farther he rode, it curdled and clabbered inside him and clouded his mind. He tried to push it down and stay focused, but the hate grew more powerful. It took control of the images in his mind, replaying over and over the scene of Juan Carlos face down in the wet grass, and the murderer standing over him, laughing. So he hated, and the hate propelled him ever faster up the trail.

When the two men finally reached the top of the trail, it opened into a small clearing, with the top of the pine forest on the left, and the cliff over Lago Tromen to the right. To the east, from where they had fled the scene of the killing, stood the Volcan Lanin, glaring down over them. The single track trail around the cliff and over to Chile lay just ahead.

They stopped and tied the horses and decided to build a fire. It was cold at this altitude, even in the early summer, and the wind was wet and biting coming over the pass. The short heavy man wandered off into the forest to look for some dry kindling and firewood, and the tall man sprawled out on the rocky ground and pulled his hat over his eyes to sleep. They had no idea they were being hunted.

The short man walked carelessly through the

forest, cracking and crunching with each step. He stooped over here and there to pick up small branches and twigs, then he stood tall for a moment and arched his back to stretch out the stiff muscles from the rough trail ride. As he tilted his head back to loosen his neck, he suddenly felt the stinging, razor edge of a blade easing across his throat. Then it halted, and held with just enough pressure that the outer layer of skin flayed open and seeped a trickle of blood down into his bandana.

"If you make a sound, or move an inch; your head will fall to the ground before your body," Pablito whispered into his ear.

The short man clenched and quivered as he slowly exhaled. He swallowed hard, and his bulging Adam's apple pushed the sharp edge of the blade deeper into his flesh, and he whimpered.

"Down to your knees. Easy now, or you will cut your own throat."

Pablito took the man down and tied his hands behind him with a leather strap, then bound his legs and drew them up and cinched them to his arms like a calf about to be branded with a scalding iron. He cut the bandana from around his neck, and stuffed it deep into his mouth. He grabbed him by his hair, twisted his head around and stared into his eyes. A cold, blank stare. Then he shoved his face into the dirt, and vanished back into the forest.

The tall man lay stretched out in the clearing, and

he had no clue that his partner had been captured. Before Pablito moved out into the clearing, he scanned from the edge of the tree cover. He could see the short-barreled shotgun slung across the saddle loop of the tall man's horse, twenty feet away. The man was stretched out on the ground and he could see his chest raising and falling, but not in the rhythm of deep slumber. He was still lightly awake, but not fearful of being followed or he would have kept the shotgun with him.

As Pablito came up on him, he felt the rage building with every step. He pictured in his mind just plunging his knife into the man's chest, as he lay prone with his hat covering his eyes. But that wasn't his way. He wasn't a cowardly murderer.

"Wake up, murderer," he said, as he approached.

The tall man jerked upright and scrambled to his feet, startled and angry. He looked at young Pablito, standing with a knife in hand and at least a head shorter than him, and chuckled under his breath.

"Who are you, boy?" he sneered.

Pablito didn't respond. He just glared at him, then his eyes shifted down at his father's facón, tucked awkwardly into the man's front waistband.

"You like my knife, boy?" the man said. "You think you can take it from me?"

Again, Pablito stayed silent. He slowly slid his right foot back, and dug the boot heel into the sand for balance; then raised the Spanish steel blade forward, pointing at the man's nose. He had wrapped his poncho around his left arm to protect it, and he was ready.

He had never been in a real knife fight, but his father had prepared him for this moment for years. And perhaps Juan Carlos had known it would come to this when he pushed him to train again yesterday morning. Pablito was ready. He needed only to wait and let the moment unfold. Wait patiently. Blade masters from around the world, throughout history, have all known one crucial fact. The first man to move is usually the one who dies.

"I have already killed one gaucho today. I don't mind killing another!" the tall man yelled.

Then he pulled Juan Carlos' facón out from his belt and threw the scabbard away to the dirt. He waved the long blade up and down, and bounced impatiently on his toes.

"Come on boy! Come get it!" he bellowed.

But Pablito was settled now, almost calm in fact. His heart beat strong and steady. He was breathing slowly through his nose, and his back leg was building pressure for the next move.

The fight felt agonizingly slow and long in Pablito's mind, but it was over in a few seconds. The tall man lost his patience and came screaming at him and slashed down with the long facón. But Pablito came up with his poncho-wrapped arm and blocked the strike, and gracefully sliced through the inside of the man's elbow, severing the muscles and ligaments to his knife hand. The man winced and the knife faltered in his grip, but he grabbed it with his left hand and swung it wildly to back Pablito away. Pablito took three steps backward away from the swinging blade, and neared the edge of the drop off.

The tall man looked at his limp dangling right arm and grimaced, then he charged again. Pablito couldn't go back any farther, he was on the edge. As the tall man came rushing in, Pablito instinctively rolled forward. The facón sliced through the air just above his head. He came out of the roll directly under him, then drove his blade straight up into the man's groin and deep into his abdomen.

The man kept stumbling forward, releasing his grip on the facón and it dropped to the ground beside Pablito. Then he tumbled over the top of the small gaucho, and plummeted over the edge. He fell for six long, terrible seconds in near silence, hearing only the whistle of wind and the flapping of his clothes, before crashing into the dark water below.

Pablito was still hunched low on his knees listening after the tall man disappeared over the edge of the cliff. He heard a brief brush of air, then nothing. He looked down beside him and saw his father's facón laying in the gravel, and he reached down slowly and picked it up by the handle and brought it up onto his lap. Just then, he heard the muted cacophony, like the sound of breaking glass, echoing around the circular lake. He had no interest in looking down to see.

He held the long blade up and blew the dust away from the handle, then pulled it across his pant leg to wipe the dust from the blade. He found the scabbard on the ground and sheathed it, then slid it under his waist belt, where it rightfully belonged.

.

THE LONGEST RIDE

I t was afternoon when he started back down from the high mountain pass at Lago Tromen, with two horses ponying behind on a lead and the short heavy man perched and tied on the third horse. At dusk, they reached the meadow where Pablito's father waited for his return.

There were four gauchos gathered around his body when he came into the open meadow. They were all from the neighboring estancia, come looking for their missing compatriot, when they came up on Juan Carlos' horse tied to the stump. Then they followed the fresh tracks into the meadow and found his body. They recognized Pablito as he came into the open, and all four pulled their hats from their heads and held them in front of them.

Pablito rode up and sat wearily on his horse

looking down at them, then at his father's body on the ground.

The oldest man of the group broke the long silence, "Hola, Pablito...how...how did this happen?"

Pablito shifted in his saddle to relieve the ache in his back, and the leather squeaked under him. He wasn't in the mind to talk about it all, but he knew he had to give them an explanation. He tilted his head back to the gaged man on the horse behind, "This one, and another, killed my father this morning, here in the meadow."

The gauchos' eyes widened and they all turned their heads back and forth to look at each other, then all turned to stare at the man on the horse.

"Did you capture him by yourself? Did the other get away?" the old man asked.

"He didn't get away," Pablito answered. He hesitated before continuing on, "I caught up to them at the Tromen Pass, and captured this one first up in the trees. I tried to capture the other, but he tried to kill me, with my own father's facón. He was the one who shot my father in the back and took his blade."

The four gauchos shuffled their feet and murmured among themselves. They saw the long facón sticking out from under Pablito's belt.

"Isn't that Juan Carlos' blade there, in your belt!" he said with a look on his face that begged for more detail.

"That's right. I gutted him in the fight, and he fell over the cliff into the dark water," Pablito said.

"Oh!" the old man responded. The other gauchos gathered closely around him now. One was stroking his big grey horse on her neck, and the others were nodding their heads and reached up to lightly pat Pablito on his legs to acknowledge his courage.

Pablito swung his leg over and stepped down from his horse, and untied the lead to the two others. He handed it to the old man.

"I think these horses are yours. We saw the cloud of condors in the late afternoon, day before yesterday, and came to inspect. We found your friend's body. What was left of his body; up on the plateau, two arroyos east of here. We followed the tracks and found the murderers here early this morning."

The group of gauchos began to look at the fat man tied to the horse with anger in their eyes, and he squirmed in the saddle and croaked through the dirty red bandana that was still wedged in his mouth. Then Pablito told the men about his father's approach into the meadow and the cowardly ambush and murder by the tall man, and how he tracked them alone to the high pass. But it was more talking than he wanted to do right now. All he really wanted to do now was take his father back to the cabin in the tall trees.

"I am tired. I need to take my father home. Will you help me put him on his horse?" he asked the men.

The group scattered quickly, one going to retrieve the gelding from the base of the hill and the others tending to Juan Carlos' body. They rolled him over and one of the men damped his bandana and gently wiped the dust from his friend's face. Then another pulled a dark brown blanket from his saddle, and they wrapped him carefully in the blanket. When the other gaucho arrived with his horse, they lifted him all together like four pallbearers, and lowered him lightly over the tall sheepskin saddle, then secured him for the ride home.

"Two of us will come with you to help, Pablito," the old man said.

Pablito shook is head, "I will do this myself, señor. But I will need help tomorrow, if you could send word to Don Claude for me tonight."

"What should we do with this one?" the old man said, glancing back at the other man tied to the horse.

"Do whatever you want with him. My revenge is done."

Pablito pulled himself up into the saddle again, and started away, pulling his father's horse behind him. As he passed, the four gauchos made the sign of the cross on their chests and hung their heads down, then each man reached out with his hand and touched Juan Carlos' body as he came by, draped over the saddle.

The sun was falling below the mountaintop and the first stars were beginning to flicker on the eastern horizon as he started his journey. It would be at least eight hours more to reach the cabin, and he should have probably built a fire and rested, but all he could think about was getting his father home. He didn't want him to spend another night out here in the cold, so he continued on.

They reached the base of the arroyo where it met the Collon Cura around midnight and turned up the shoreline towards the confluence of the Limay. It was clear and cold tonight, but the moon was nearly full and he could see well enough to navigate the trail. The two horses' hooves clacking over the river stones seemed to be the only sound in the valley, as if the world was silent in respect for a fallen hero passing by.

Pablito looked up into the sky just as a falling star burst into view with a brilliant green tail, then arched across the sky in the direction of home. He smiled, and thought about his mother. Giselle had always loved watching the meteors that arrived in the early summer. Juan Carlos would build a low fire outside at night sometimes, and they would sit together wrapped in a blanket, watching and counting the stars as they fell from heaven.

He was exhausted, and couldn't keep his eyes open. So tired he was going to fall off his horse if he tried to stay upright in the saddle, but he refused to stop. Instead, he lay over forward across her big neck and draped his arms around her, and gave her the reins. "Take us home, girl," he whispered. His cheek was nestled over her coarse mane, and his head rose and fell slowly as she continued on the trail. Then, he was fast asleep.

THE UNCOMFORTABLE STILLNESS shook him awake. Like a sailor who has been on the rolling ocean for months, and suddenly comes ashore and is sick to his stomach as he tries to sleep in a bed on the firm ground. He lifted his head to look around. It was dark and enfolded with shadows and shapes. Where was he? He sat up in the saddle and rubbed the sleep from his eyes, and squinted to see. Then he realized, he was home.

The big grey had somehow found her way in the darkness up the shoreline, then courageously crossed the river at the wide vado without losing her rider, and pulling Juan Carlos' horse all the way across. Then she had taken the trail up through the trees all the way home. Standing patiently, but exhausted in front of the barn, she was waiting for Pablito to dismount and free her from the heavy saddle.

He reached down and patted her lightly on her neck, swept his leg over her rump and slid down from the saddle. He led his father's horse into the barn, loosened the straps that bound him, and lifted him onto his shoulder; then with his last ounce of strength he carried him to the long table and laid him down to rest for the night.

ALONE ON THE MOUNTAIN

A noise woke him. The sound of a horse snorting and shuffling, or was it people talking? Momma and Papi must be up in the kitchen, he thought. His eyelids were sticking together with the salty goop of dried tears, and he blinked and rubbed them open. What time is it, he thought? I must have slept late. The sun is up over the house. Then his memory came flooding back to him.

The cabin was still and silent. Completely noiseless save for his shallow, soft rhythm of breath. He was laying across the top of the quilted covers in his mud-caked clothes, just as he had fallen on the bed in the early hours of the morning. He had never awakened in this cabin surrounded by absolute silence. From the day he drew his first breath from his mother's womb in this cabin nearly twenty three years ago, until this moment, he had always woke to the sounds of his father sitting at the small table, lightly polishing the edge of his blade; and the aroma of coffee on the wood stove. Sometimes his brother would wake him with a rowdy shove to the head, as he climbed out of the wood-framed bed that lay next to his in the cramped little bedroom, but Carlos had been gone for two years now. Pablito was utterly alone for the first time in his life. One by one, they had all been taken from him. He was the last of his clan.

But something had awakened him. He held his breath for a moment and listened. There was something outside. Stirring. Rustling. Murmuring.

He sat up on the edge on his bed, then stood up slowly, but every bone in his body was sore and throbbing. He stood hunched for a moment, then pulled himself upright and he felt the nerves in his back screech with pain. He hobbled out into the main room of the cabin and was oddly aware of the hollow thud of his boots, as he was still wearing them, and the light creaking of the floorboards as he came into the vacant space. Sounds he had never paid attention to before. Then he heard the light noises from outside again, and he walked to the window and looked out. There was a huge crowd of people milling about in front of the cabin.

He opened the front door and stepped out, and the crowd went silent, everyone turning their eyes on him. Even the horses, twenty or thirty of them tied to the railing, and the stumps, and trees at the edge of the clearing, all paused and turned their heads and cocked their ears forward in his direction. He had never been the object of so much attention, and the intensely focused energy of pity and sorrow burned through him like a laser, until he couldn't stand it anymore. He turned and walked back into the cabin without saying a word.

Claude Ballofett followed him in, and closed the door behind them.

"Pablito, I know how hard this is," he said.

Pablito turned to looked at him, the man he had often thought of like his grandfather, "Why are all of these people here?"

"The story of what happened to your father, and what you did all alone on that mountain, is spreading across the valley. People from every estancia are coming. Many more are on the way here, from every corner of the province. Everyone wants to pay their respect to Juan Carlos."

Pablito's mind was hovering in that dark, numb place of disbelief. The place where your senses and feelings are switched off for self-preservation. He nodded his head, and Claude stepped forward and put his arms around him. "You should clean yourself up and put on some fresh clothes. Some of the women have brought food, and I suspect you need something to eat by now."

"Yes, I am hungry," he said.

"We will take care of Juan Carlos, and this

afternoon when you are ready, we will put him to rest next to Gisele and Carlos, on the grassy hill."

JUAN CARLOS, the orphan from La Paz who became a gaucho, and a legend across the pampas of Patagonia, was put to rest as the sun was setting. The sky above was so blue that it looked like a deep mountain pool. Hundreds of people came and gathered on the grassy hill that day to say farewell. Farewell to a man who might just as easily have perished in the streets as an unknown *casta*. But his life had been changed; no, not changed, liberated. He had been freed from the cloak of a world that masked who he really was. Freed by the love of a young blue-eyed girl, and a dream. And now they were dreaming together once again.

For three days, the people continued to arrive. The news of Juan Carlos' murder, along with the other gaucho from the neighboring estancia, fell hard on the community. Dying at the hands of villains was thought to be the worst ending for fine men, even though it was always a possibility for working gauchos. But Juan Carlos was a man thought to be nearly invincible. The people came as much to see Pablito as to say goodbye to his father, because Pablito gave them hope. Hope that good, in the form of a young kind man, could still triumph over evil.

The crowds disappeared on the fourth day, and

Claude sat with him at the breakfast table in the cabin, sharing a gourd of maté.

"I am leaving, Pablito," Claude said.

"Leaving? Where, for how long?" Pablito asked.

"I am going to live with my cousins in Buenos Aires. I am getting older now, and I have been alone in the big house for a long time. I am not happy here anymore."

"But, Don Claude, what will happen to the estancia?"

"I leave it in your hands, Pablito. Just as I left it once before in the care of your father. You are like family to me too; I was here when you were born and I have watched you grow up on this land. You belong here, for as long you want to be here," he said. "I will check in on you from time to time, and make sure you have everything you need, and I have hired an administrator to see to the financial matters and legal details, and manage the care of the house." Then he stood and moved to the door, "I am sorry, Pablito. I just can't be here anymore."

Pablito understood. There had been no joy here for Claude for many years, and the disappointment of his daughter not coming had been great. Juan Carlos' death had been the final wound for him.

THE DAYS, weeks, and months of summer drifted past

in quiet solitude. He lost any sense of time, because each day was much like the one before. He rose alone in the early morning, and put water to boil for coffee. Then sat at the small table to hone the edge of his knife; the Spanish killing blade that masqueraded as a working knife. He always pulled his father's facón from its sheath and checked the edge, giving it one light swipe across the wet stone, though it never needed the attention. It provided him with an instant to reflect on his father.

He saddled the big grey each morning and they rode the ridges and valleys to mind the sheep and cattle, and check the fence lines; and scouted along the river's edge to look for any signs of intruders. And he spent the early afternoons sitting up on the grassy hill with his family, watching the condors soaring over their high cliff rookery in the opposite valley. He hated looking at them at first, because the memories of that day came flooding back; and the memory of seeing them the day before his mother died. He hated them as his father had come to hate the little white house across the green pasture. He thought about climbing to the top of the rookery and killing them, killing them all. But then he remembered how much his mother had loved watching them. She spoke about them like they were magical beings, watching over the whole of the world from the clouds. "They are not evil, they are just messengers," he thought.

He made his way up the trail through the trees in

the afternoon, pausing in the pasture to look at the white house, then finished his daily chores by brushing down the big grey in the paddock and cleaning her hooves. They were closer now than before. Bonded to each other, and she loved the attention of being brushed. When they came home everyday and he walked her into the paddock, she would reach for the brush and take it in her mouth and fling it over to his feet, before he had even taken the saddle off her back.

He made a small meal for himself and sat alone, looking out into the darkness through the warped-glass window; and sometimes sitting in his father's chair by the stone fireplace. One night, near the end of summer when the temperatures started to fall, he built a fire and sat close, and sipped Bonarda wine from a wood cup. He looked around the room, and the kitchen, then to the two doors that led to the bedrooms. The one on the right, was his and Carlos', or, just his now. The other belonged to his parents. He hadn't entered the room in all these months, and the door had remained closed. He had no idea what might be inside.

He lay awake half the night thinking about it. What was in the room? What might he find that belonged to his father and his mother? Were their ghosts in there, waiting to escape?

The next morning he followed his normal ritual, all the way up until the sun was shining in all the windows. Then he steeled himself to open the door to the bedroom and go inside. After all, this was his cabin now, he needed to know. He went to the door and put his hand on the old iron handle, and gave it a twist. He could hear the latch click, but the door was swollen with age and humidity from the summer rains. He pressed harder and it popped and swung fully open. He stood for a moment in the threshold of the doorway looking in, as the bright sunlight filled the room.

It was sparse, as one might expect of a gaucho and his woman living a simple life. A bed in the center of the room, a small table on one end with an oil lamp, and a large cedar chest against the wall that held their clothes and any worldly possessions they might treasure. On the wall were several hooks, with a coat, a merino wool sweater and a few scarfs, and his father's special wide-brimmed hat, that he wore only to Puestero, hung by itself on another. His father had made the bed before leaving the last morning; the linen was stretched and blankets folded neatly at the foot.

He sat on the edge of the bed and lifted the lid of the cedar chest. It contained their other clothes and two additional winter blankets. There were no trinkets or treasures, or mysteries to be found. Only the things they used in daily life. But as Pablito sat on the bed with the warm sun shining in all around him, he found something he wasn't expecting. A sense of peace. He felt the love that Gisele and Juan Carlos had felt for each other, and for him and Carlos too, encasing him. Comforting him. He suddenly felt less alone.

HE MADE his way up to the high summer pasture that day to bring the horses down for the winter, and as he came over the rise he was greeted by all of the foals born in the spring, now fat and happy and racing each other around the green field. They were all safe and well fed, and everything was exactly the way it should be. He looked back over the river valley, at the rushing green water and the hills that were just starting to spot with orange and yellow leaves. He hesitated before looking to the west, to the sky where they had seen the condors soaring the last time they were here; but when he did, it was full of nothing but blue sky.

THE PUESTERO

Over a year had passed. A year of living and working alone, but he really didn't mind so much. The work in the field with the horses, and sheep and cattle, tending to the cabin and cooking, and splitting and stacking ten cords of wood for the winter kept him occupied. The extra workload had made him lean and hard, and his face had lost that soft, boyish look. He had a trace of the fine lines at the corner of his eyes, from squinting into the cold winter winds. And his cheeks were tautly drawn over his facial bones and his angular jaw. He was only a year older, but appeared much more.

He was riding into the lower pasture near the main house when he saw a rider coming up along the road. As he grew closer he recognized him as Alberto, a happy young man whom everyone called "Beto" for short. He lived on a neighboring estancia.

"Hola, Pablito!" he said as he came up waiving.

"Buen dia, Beto!"

The young man rode up close and reached out his hand to shake, and smiled broadly.

"Pablito, the Puestero begins in three days, and everyone wants to know if you are coming?" he asked.

"I don't know, Beto. I haven't even thought about it. I have so much work here to keep me busy."

"Pablito you must come!" he said.

"I said, I am busy. Can't you understand that?" Pablito snapped back at him.

Beto's smile dropped and he sat quiet for a second. "What is it, Pablito? We all want to see you, why won't you come?"

"Beto, I don't want to see all of those people. The ones who all came to the cabin, and to the grassy hill. They stared at me like I was a poor, pitiful animal. But I don't want their pity, Beto. I am doing the work of three men, and I run my own puesto!" he said.

"That's exactly why you have to come! Don't you see? You are a man now, and everyone in the province needs to see you for a man. They won't see you for what you really are if you hide away in the campo!"

Pablito looked at him, and realized he was right. He couldn't hide out on the estancia for the rest of his life. He needed to show the world what sort of man he had become. He nodded his head. "Alright, Beto. I will be there."

·   ·   ·

LAST YEAR, he had missed the Puestero in Junin de Los Andes for the first time since he was a small boy. It wasn't a year for celebration or social gathering. But it was time for Pablito to rejoin the world. He had a young appaloosa gelding that he wanted to sell anyway, and he needed a few provisions. And it was time he took his place among the men who ran their own puesto, as he now did. Very few men of his age had such responsibility.

He cleaned his bombacha pants meticulously and polished his boots. He put on his best blue long sleeve shirt and a black and red silk bandana around his neck with a stag antler clasp. He borrowed his father's special hat, the wide-brimmed felt beauty. And he took his father's long, elegant facón and slid it beneath the waist belt in the small of his back.

His poncho was worn and tattered, and he was a little embarrassed by it, but he folded it up as neatly as he could and draped it across his shoulder, front to back. Since his mother died so many years ago, there had been no new ponchos made, but perhaps he could buy one with some of the money from the appaloosa.

He left the cabin an hour before the sunrise, as the glow from the eastern horizon was just starting to light the valley. It was a half-day ride to Junin, and he took his time, stopping twice to rest his horses and sip a maté. As the trail from the estancia intersected the main road, only a few miles outside of town, he met the family coming in from the next estancia to the south. Two men, three women, and four children all on horses and dressed in their best Puestero clothes.

Normally, the families like to come into town one group at a time, so they can make a show of it, and all eyes will be on them for at least a few minutes before the next group comes along. The town people who live year round in Junin all gather along the walkways and streets, and cheer the men and women who live in the campo, and clap for the most beautiful horses. But this family knew that Pablito would be completely alone for this journey, and the headman invited him to ride in with them, directly behind himself and his eldest son.

"Buen dia, Pablito. It makes me happy to see that you are coming for Puestero," he said. "Would you like to ride into town with us?"

"Gracias, Señor Martinez," Pablito said. "But I must represent my estancia, and my family alone." Then he politely tipped his hat, and reined his horse in a backward step to allow the Martinez family to pass ahead.

Señor Martinez smiled and nodded his head in respect. "Very well, Señor Gonzalez," he said.

It was the first time a man had spoken his name with respect, and the loneliness that filled him was replaced ever so slightly with a sense of pride. He had earned his own puesto, and everyone would know it.

As the family heeled their horses past, the men

first, followed by the women and children, he caught the eye of the third woman in the group. A young woman, a girl really, in her late teens, with raven hair tied neatly back against the wind, and wearing a red boina hat slid to the back, gaucho style. She stared back into his eyes without the slightest hesitation. And after she passed, she turned back once more and smiled.

As THE LONE rider came into the main street of Junin, he pulled the big grey's head up and tapped her into an elegant trot. With her hooves rhythmically clattering on the brick street, he held his head high as he passed the crowds. The entire town was there to greet him. Lining the walkways, they cheered for the brave young man who had avenged his father, and then took the reins of a large puesto entirely in his own hands. Everyone knew the story of Pablito.

He sold his appaloosa gelding for a good price on the third day, not taking the first or second offer, but bargaining wisely. He didn't compete in the rodeos because he couldn't risk injuring his best horse, and he had no need to bolster his pride or reputation anymore than it already was. He had already proven himself to the world. On the fifth day, he walked along the town square where the families had arranged tables to display the crafts made during the winter.

There were handmade leather bridles and fittings for horses, with shining steel buttons and badges. Spurs and bits tooled by metal smiths. And knives, many knives of all shapes and sizes. There were skinning and field knives, short working knives, and a few long, beautiful facóns. But Pablito now carried the most famous facón in this territory, he had no need of another. What he did have need of was a new poncho.

As he approached the last table on the street, he saw her. The girl from the Martinez clan.

"I have been waiting for you all week," she said. "I thought maybe you were afraid of me." Then she laughed.

"I am not afraid of anyone!" he said. Then he turned his eyes away from her, to keep from revealing his fear of this beautiful, bold young girl.

"It was just a joke, Pablito. I know you aren't afraid. That's why I have been waiting for you," she said.

Her name was Juanita Benitez Martinez, and she was eighteen years old with the strength and character of a much older woman. She had been refusing the courtship of young suitors for the last three years, because she thought they were all "stupid young boys"; and a boy was not what she wanted for a husband. Her father was growing impatient, and their puesto was too small to keep all of his children at home forever.

"Why were you waiting for me?" Pablito asked.

"Because I have something you need," she said.

Then, from under the table she pulled a handsome new poncho. It was dark brown and trimmed in white and grey along the borders, with an emerald green stripe that waved down the center. Woven from the softest wool he had ever seen, and bound so tightly the rain would never pass.

"I made this for you. I heard about you living all alone up there through the last winter, and I was making two ponchos to sell. But this one I made special for you. The white borders are for the snow-capped peaks that surround the estancia where you live. And the green pattern down the center is for the Limay River that runs through the middle of your puesto. Don't you think it is beautiful?"

"Yes! It is very beautiful, but how much does it cost?" he asked.

"A dance," she said.

"A dance? I wasn't planning to go to the dance festival," Pablito said. (The dance festival on the last night of the Puestero every year, was often when young men and women of the appropriate age began their courtships.)

"A dance is a fair coin for this beautiful poncho. Don't you think my work is worth one dance?" she said, as she locked her gaze on him.

He stared back into her eyes and felt the hardened shell that had formed over the past year of living alone beginning to soften. She was lovely, and powerful at the same time. And she knew what she wanted, and wasn't afraid to go after it. He slid his hand under the poncho and lifted it to feel its weight, then brushed his fingertips lightly over the green stripe in the center. Then he leaned in closer, and stared deliberately back into her eyes to show that he had power too, and wasn't afraid to pursue what he wanted in his life.

"I will give you a thousand dances," he said.

TRADITIONAL GAUCHO DANCING isn't really that much different from other dancing around the world. When it comes down to it, how many different ways are there to dance? They dance in large groups where the young men and women weave and twirl around each other, everyone getting a chance to lightly touch, or at least see every other potential partner on the dance floor.

The men tapping their boots and not really moving much, and the women gathering most of the visual attention in brightly colored long dresses that open up like Chinese umbrellas as they spin in circles around the men. This kind of dancing doesn't really do much for the courting process, it is more of an opportunity for the girls to present themselves to all of the possible suitors in the crowd.

If you have already got your eye on a partner, you

might refrain from the group dancing. The festival always begins with the group dances, then continues with dances for couples.

The couples dancing will start with very ritualistic dance steps, with the couples a safe distance from each other. The young gaucho presenting his most macho style and footsteps and waving a bandana around in symbolic lasso fashion. The young lady acts coy, and moves in a way that suggests she is only mildly interested most of the time. As songs end and new songs begin, they will change partners several times if they haven't caught another's eye.

The final dances are reserved for couples who have made it through the elimination process, and know precisely who they want to be with. It's the beginning of the formal courting.

Pablito and Juanita both stood on the outside during the group dances. When the couples songs began, while most of the young men and girls traded partners and danced with a dozen others, Pablito and Juanita danced only with each other. They danced to one song after another, until the band rested, then they sat at a small table on the outside of the courtyard and shared a refreshing apple cider. When the band resumed, they danced again; and by the end of the night, Pablito knew he had found the woman he was meant to spend the rest of his life with.

Juanita was beautiful and bold, and strong and passionate, and she loved the life of the open pampas as much as he did. After so much hardship, he was convinced she was the blessing sent to him by the heavens.

The formal courtship of Pablito and Juanita began after the final dance. Pablito walked boldly to the table where the entire Martinez clan was seated for dinner and spoke directly to her father, but in front of the whole family. Juanita stood to the side of her mother to watch.

"Señor Martinez. I am Pablo Gonzalez, son of Juan Carlos and Giselle Gonzalez, and I have responsibility for 25,000 hectares of land in the Estancia Ballofett. I have a home, and three horses that belong to me. With your permission, I intend to court your daughter, Juanita, and to marry her."

The two Martinez men feigned disappointment, but they couldn't have been more pleased with the young man who would soon become kin to them. The women all covered their mouths with both hands, to keep their excitement from spewing forth in bursts of screaming joy. But the children jumped from their seats and ran to Pablito and wrapped their arms around his waist, completely unafraid to show their approval.

The women all turned to the father of the family, waiting silently for his next words. He stared at Pablito as if he were carefully inspecting a young horse, looking for a bad tooth, or a bum leg, or a sign of weakness. Pablito stared back like a statue carved from cold granite. Juanita looked on nervously, flashing glances back and forth from her father to Pablito, then to her mother, and back to her father.

"Papa!" slipped from her mouth. Then she pinched her lips tightly, and looked apologetically at her father as he cast a frown in her direction. She didn't want to spoil the game for him.

Her father stood up, and maintaining his serious face, he reached his hand forward, but didn't move; forcing Pablito to come to him to complete the agreement. All eyes were rapidly darting back and forth now. Pablito took a step, then another; and reached forward and grabbed her father's hand with a grip so firm his knuckles turned white. The handshake was the final test of worthiness.

Señor Martinez's mustache turned up ever so sightly at the corner with a smile, and his left eye began to twitch as he bore down with his clenching hand. Then at once, both let go and gasped for a breath as they shook the blood back into their hands and laughed. The Martinez women leapt to their feet and screamed.

Juanita ran over and threw her arms around her father's neck, "Gracias, Papa!"

"You waited a very long time to find a husband, but I think you found a good one!" hc said.

Then Juanita ran to her mother and was engulfed by the Martinez women.

It wasn't just Juanita who had found the perfect

mate that night. Juanita's beauty had drawn a great deal of interest from young men in the last few years, but her boldness, her ferocity, was more of a challenge than her father's crushing grip. She wasn't in any way like the typical young girl who acts like she needs to be cared for, when she really doesn't, or says the opposite of what she means in hope that a man will know the difference. Nor did she fold like a wilting flower when looked in the eye or faced with a challenge. Beneath her soft and warm flesh was a pillar of iron, and only a man with an equally strong core would do. She was exactly what Pablito needed in his life, an equal partner.

PABLITO AND JUANITA were married in the autumn, when the weather was cool and the leaves golden, and before the rains came. The small chapel on the edge of Junin de Los Andes was full and over-flowing, and a great feast was held in the provincial fairgrounds; and then the entire Martinez clan rode with them back to Estancia Ballofett and all the way to the little cabin. They cheered as Pablito swept Juanita up in his arms and carried her through the cabin door, then stayed for the night and half the next day outside, drinking and eating around a huge fire in the pit.

Pablito rose from his wedding bed in the middle of the night and walked into the living area of the cabin, and stood listening to the chattering and storytelling going on outside; and in a moment, Juanita came out with a blanket wrapped around her bare body and leaned against him.

"It has been a long time," he said.

"A long time?" she asked.

"Since I have heard laughter, and happiness around this house. A very long time," he said, as he looked down into her dark smiling eyes. "I hope it is like this forever."

"We can't expect life to always be happy, Pablito. But even when there is sadness, a house can still be full of love."

THE GREATEST GIFT

" **P**ablito. Are you awake?"

"What? Why?" he groaned as he pulled the covers over his head.

"It is time."

"Time for what? Did I sleep late?"

"No, it is time. Your son is coming, and he won't wait much longer," Juanita said as she gave him a firm shove this time.

"It is time!" he yelled as he came leaping out of the bed, and had one leg sliding into his bombacha pants before touching the floor.

"Please go wake my mother and my sister, and try not to scare them," she said calmly.

He was hopping up and down across the floor, trying to pull his pants up to the waist, and grabbed his shirt from the wall hook and ran barefoot to the door. Then he flung the door open so forcefully that it slammed against the wall with a loud "<u>bang</u>" and the tiny cabin shook and shivered like a tectonic plate had just shifted below the ground.

"Shit! I am sorry!" he yelled as he turned to look at Juanita, who was still in bed and beginning the processes of going into labor, and now giving him the vicious stink-eye.

Juanita's mother and sister had come to the cabin a week earlier, anticipating the birth at anytime, so they could help cook and take care of her and be ready to assist when the baby decided to come into the world. They were sleeping in the room next door in the two small beds where Pablito and Carlos used to sleep, and Pablito's hysterics and door slamming brought them abruptly awake and into a brief screaming panic. He was screaming, they were screaming, everyone but Juanita was screaming. The pregnant woman who was starting to experience pain akin to a gunshot in the abdomen, was the only one not screaming.

Pablito raced into the kitchen and lit a lamp, and then another in the living area. Then he built a fire in the fireplace, even though it wasn't particularly cold, he couldn't think of anything else useful to do, and he had to do something. Pablito was a man not easily rattled, like his father; but his wife going into labor incited a wave of insecurity and helplessness in him.

And like his father had done all those years ago, he began to pace. Pace desperately around the small room, with an occasional pause to glance into the bedroom and see if it was all over yet. Juanita's sister finally came over and closed the door in his face, "We will call for you when it is done!"

When his bare feet started to blister from the circling around on the pine floors, he finally sat down in the wooden armchair by the fireplace and gathered himself. He sat quietly and listened. With every moan and cry from Juanita he wanted to leap up and run to her, but he held himself down and waited. He took a deep breath and held it for as long as he could, to hear every sound from the room. Then, he heard it. A little gurgle and cough, and a cry.

He bolted for the bedroom door but stopped just short, waiting for permission. Then the door opened, and Juanita's sister, Maria, greeted him with a smile and invited him in. He tiptoed to the bedside and looked down at Juanita, who was cradling the baby across her chest. She was dripping with sweat and her hair was a long black bird nest of tangles, but she still beamed with strength. She was a rock that could never be broken.

"It seems I was wrong. We have a daughter instead of a son," she said.

"Did you count the fingers and toes? Everyone has told me that it is very important to count them!"

"Yes, Pablito, your daughter has all of her fingers and toes, but not too many."

He sighed, and took a deep breath like he had

been held underwater for the last hour. Then he smiled with a trace of relief across is face. He leaned over and kissed Juanita on her damp forehead, holding his lips firmly against her skin for a long moment.

"We didn't think of a name for a girl, what are we going to call her?" Pablito said.

"I thought maybe, Carolina. That was my grandmother's name, and I always loved it."

"Carolina. I like that. Can I touch her?" he asked, as if she were a puppy that belonged to a stranger.

"Here, take your daughter in your arms, Pablito," Juanita said.

He held his hands out, and she placed the bundle into them, and as he held her she wriggled her tiny arm from under the blanket and grasped the tip of his large rough thumb, and then, she smiled. Smiled as if she found a source of comfort in the darkness, because her eyes were still unaccustomed to the light and she held them tightly closed.

She had thick black hair like Juanita, plastered into a greasy swirl around her head, and fair soft skin that was coursing flashes of pink as the fresh air touched it for the first time. And just as Pablito was convinced he had been given the greatest gift in all the world, he received another. Little Carolina presented him with the best of all. She squinted and blinked, and opened her eyelids just a little bigger than slits, and beneath them lay the most beautiful blue eyes.

Eyes as blue as a deep mountain pool. Eyes the same color as his mother, Giselle.

Pablito, the fierce young gaucho, hardened man of the mountains and wrathful avenger, began to weep. He held his tiny daughter up and pressed his face into the soft wool blanket that was wrapped around her, and he wept with abandon. Then he lifted his head and looked again through gushing eyes at Carolina, who was now looking back at him with her eyes fully open.

"She has my mother's eyes, Juanita! The rarest eyes in all the world, she has them," he blubbered.

Juanita reached up and touched his arm, "The lost never leave us, Pablito. They are always here with us, and sometimes they send us a little gift."

THE FOG of sleep faded and Pablito slowly woke to the sound of music. A melodious song of the first spring birds. A male wren feeling the urge to sing, and beckoning for a companion. The sun was cresting the river platte earlier now, and it was easier to rise at 5:30 with the glowing light of dawn. He pulled himself gently from beneath the covers and eased out of bed to let Juanita sleep a few more moments, even though he knew she would be up in a minute and busily working to fix breakfast for the family and a snack for his ride out today.

He still thought of his father, his mother, and Carlito often. He felt sadness occasionally, when he was alone in the mountains, and usually when he watched the trains crossing slowly over the black bridge. His father and mother had lived full lives despite the number of years, but his brother's dreams had never been fulfilled. But Pablito knew it was better to embrace the living, rather than cling to the dead.

The girls kept them busy and filled the days with mischief and laughter. Especially the little one, Josefina, who came along two years after Carolina. She was feisty like her mother, and born without the burden of a filter, completely unfettered to speak her mind and do whatever felt right at the moment. Regardless of what the world around her thought about it.

Pablito and Juanita worried after her in the early years, because they frequently found her having conversations by herself. But then they realized she had been born with the same gift as her father, and perhaps more pronounced. The world spoke to her, and she openly spoke back. The trees, the birds, the wind, the flowers and fields, all had something marvelous to say and they spoke a language she clearly understood.

Pablito was among the most fortunate of men. He was born into a wealth that eludes most, even with a lifetime of effort to amass it. He was born unburdened by the veils of the world. The layers that men struggle to peel away in search of their true purpose. Their true self. He knew exactly who he was, and what he was meant to do in this world. And that knowledge brought him peace.

Pablito led his big grey horse from the corral and tied her to the post in the front courtyard, and gently brushed the dust and morning dew off her body. He pulled her hooves up, one by one, and checked them for stones or chips. Combed the burs from her long tail and mane, and clipped the matted hair at the tips. He held the horse's face in his hands and looked softly into her eyes, as he would a sweetheart, and the big grey murmured her affection and extended her quivering upper lip to touch Pablito's nose. They had a connection, these two. Different species bound by the natural world.

He laid the red wool blanket over the grey's back, and turned to pick the saddle up, and the horse turned her head back and grabbed the blanket by the corner and flung it to the ground. It was a grand game they played every morning. She only did it once, then snickered a little laugh to herself. Pablito smiled, but never scolded her. He finished with the saddle and cinched it, then went back to the cabin for a cup of coffee and a slice of homemade bread and marmalade before his ride out.

He sat at the small round table and Josefina came bounding into his lap. This was her first day to go to pre-school. Her sister had started last year at the schoolhouse that bordered the estancia, where children from several different ranches all gathered three times a week for lessons. Juanita would walk them down to the corner puesto, where a wagon passed by and picked them up, and then would bring them back in the early afternoon after a small lunch and a little siesta.

She begged her father to come with them this first day down to the corner, and impress the other kids in the wagon with his beautiful grey horse. So he saddled up the sorrel mare for Juanita, and they all made the ride down together as a family.

When the wagon arrived, the other children waved and the gaucho driving the team held up his hand and waved to Pablito and Juanita. He climbed down from the wagon and came over to lift the girls down from the backs of the horses and up into the wagon, then he motioned to Pablito to come aside for a chat.

"Hola Pablito, how are you? I am glad you came along today, I've got a message for you," he said.

"A message? From where?"

"The Gendarmerie came by the main house this morning, and said there has been a motorcar accident on the roadway. A family from the city traveling to San Martin de Los Andes. I don't know much about it, but it seems it was a terrible thing," the gaucho said.

"Where did it happen?" Pablito asked.

"On the far side of the Limay River, at the base of the great canyon. It's in the boundaries of your puesto, so we thought you would want to check it out."

"Gracias. I have to move the horses up to the summer pasture today, but I will ride out to the river tomorrow."

Pablito leaned down from his horse and they shook hands, then the gaucho climbed back into the wagon. He turned around to the children, and yelled, "Vamos!", and they all cheered the horses into a trot down the trail.

PABLITO RODE down through the pines and picked up the ranch horses that free-grazed in the forest through the winter months, fifteen in all, and the chatty little burro. Two of the mares looked like they were expecting, and he suspected they would drop their foals within the next month in the fresh green grass of the upper mesa.

As he drove the horses down to the Limay to cross at the vado, he looked to the east along the river where the roadway wound down from the high desert plain, straining to see any signs of the accident the gaucho had told him about, but saw nothing. Maybe he could see something from the upper pasture when they reached the top, he thought.

They splashed into the river and their hooves clacked on the clean river stones until the sound was a muted echo coming up through the water, and clacked again as they came out the other side. He lead them up the steep muddy bank through the willow trees that grew along the shore, then halted as they got close to the roadway. He listened for a few moments, to make sure no cars or trucks were barreling down the road, then drove the horses quickly across and up the trail on the far side. It was another two-hour ride up through the brushy canyons and steep hills to the summer pasture.

When they arrived, Pablito stepped lightly off the big grey, and pulled the woven sack from the saddle loop that held his biscuits and maté gourd, and a small kettle for heating water. Then he pulled the bit from his horse's mouth and let her graze freely in the grass with the others. He built a small fire with twigs and moss, and a few dried branches that he brought along on the back of the burro, and settled down on the edge of the field to eat and sip and relax in the spring sunshine.

When the water was hot, he poured it into the gourd that was stuffed with ground mate tea until it bubbled to the top, then he let it soak for a moment while he walked over close to the ledge.

Looking down from the ledge, he could see the

entire Limay River valley, from its headwater where it joined the Collon Cura River, and the Caleufu came twisting through his home puesto and joined the others in the rush eastward to the sea. He could see the roadway below, tracing along the river's path and breaking away, then tacking back and forth up the mountain and disappearing over the horizon to Buenos Aires. He had never been farther east from where he was born, than this very spot. And he felt no call to go any farther from his home, his wife, and his family. This was everything he needed in life.

THEN, he saw it. The scarcity of condors. They came from somewhere so high in the stratosphere that it looked like they just materialized from the ether above, one by one, joining the spiraling black cone that pointed straight down to the river bank. They were speaking to him. Telling him that death had come to call. There it is, he thought. That's where the accident is. He took a deep breath, and braced himself for the coming day.

WHAT DID YOU THINK?

Thank you for reading ***Andalusian Legacy***.

If you liked it, I have a favor to ask. Like all other authors these days, my success depends entirely on you. Your opinions and thoughts about the book are all that matter. People want to know what you think.

Please take a minute and share your thoughts in a review. As little or as much as you feel like writing would be great. You can help make this book a success.

Just sign in to your Amazon account, go to the sales page for ***Andalusian Legacy***, and follow the easy instructions to leave a review, near the bottom of the page.

Thank You!

William Jack Stephens

BONUS

Would you like to read the first chapter of the next book in this series for Free? Just sign up for my mailing list!

HERE'S a special link to get your free chapter of *Where The Green Star Falls*.

Also By William Jack Stephens

Where The Green Star Falls

*

Mallorca Vendetta

ABOUT THE AUTHOR

Novelist and adventure writer, Jack has lived and explored the world from the Arctic to the southern reaches of Patagonia.

In his former life, he served in executive roles with some of the largest companies in the world. Now he writes gripping and inspirational tales of adventure, and the occasional love story.

In South America he's known by his Spanish nickname, Memo, and when he's not writing, he can usually be found on a wilderness river with a fly rod in his hands.

www.williamjackstephens.com
jack@williamjackstephens.com

A Very Special Thanks to Eliseo Miciu for the extraordinary photography that graces the cover of Andalusian Legacy.

And to Tim Barber of Dissect Designs for the stunning cover art.

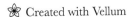 Created with Vellum

Made in the USA
Middletown, DE
08 September 2020